CECILIA

by

Vivian Connolly

FAWCETT COVENTRY • NEW YORK

CECILIA

Published by Fawcett Coventry Books, a unit of CBS Publications, the Consumer Publishing Division of CBS Inc.

Copyright © 1981 by Vivian Connolly

All Rights Reserved

ISBN: 0-449-50211-2

Printed in the United States of America

First Fawcett Coventry printing: September 1981

10 9 8 7 6 5 4 3 2 1

Chapter 1

"Kilwarden's here? But that's impossible, Bridie." The Dowager Lady Kilwarden set the delicate Wedgwood cup back in its saucer and stared wide-eyed at the breathless servant who had brought this surprising news along with the breakfast. "He'd surely have let us know. In that letter he wrote us last April, there wasn't the slightest hint of his coming to Ireland."

Bridie, sure of her facts, stood her ground staunchly. "His lordship's here, my lady. There's no doubt about it. My little niece, Peggy, was just here this minute telling me the story. He arrived at the Great House at midnight, and roused them all out of their beds. A rare carry-on that was, surely, with no bedding aired or fires laid, and just Peg and her mother and that useless old Thady to welcome the new young master."

"But what about Mr. Quinlan? Surely he must have known his lordship was coming?"

"The agent, is it? Not a bit of it, madam. He was asleep and snoring in Lord Corny's old bedroom. They roused him at once, of course. A rare sight it was, according to Peggy, to see him bowing and scraping to Lord Kilwarden. All those grand haughty airs of his went straight up the chimney."

"He really is here, then!" Lady Margaret's hand trembled a little as she picked up the silver teapot to refill an empty cup for her daughter Cecilia. "What on earth shall we do? He'll be calling on us any minute! If only he had let us know, so we could have prepared ourselves!"

Cecilia Annesley was startled to see that her mother's eyes, usually so serene, were now full of panic. "Surely he'll understand, Mama. He knows our circumstances. He seemed very kind in that letter he sent us when dear Papa died. He won't expect anything grand in the way of reception. We'll fill him full of tea, and Bridie's fine scones, and there's still a bottle or two of Papa's French brandy—"

"It's not food and drink that concerns me." Lady Margaret's voice had an unaccustomed harshness. "It's meeting an Annesley—and the head of the house, at that—after all these years. It's really so awkward, Cecilia. Surely you understand?" Cecilia's heart ached at the pleading look in her eyes. Despite all the pain and grief of the last few months, she'd never seen her mother looking so helpless.

But that's just the point, Mama! I don't understand. She bit back the words in chagrin. This was not the time to stir those particular muddy waters. "I've always known there was some sort of coolness between Papa and his family in England. I've never known what caused it. This English cousin of mine—the new Lord Kilwarden—is probably quite as much in the dark as I am." Cecilia beamed at her mother, pretending a confidence she was far from feeling. "All you need to do, Mama, is be as charming to him as you are to all the other young men in County Westmeath. You'll have him eating out of your hand, like all the rest."

Lady Margaret's face brightened a little. "Perhaps you're right, my dear. He seems a pleasant young man, to judge from his letter." She heaved a sigh, looking around the small, sunny dining room, with its bright flowered chintz curtains, gleaming rosewood sideboard and pillar-and-claw style mahogany table. "I wish now we'd accepted his generous offer and stayed in Kilwarden House. I'd feel so much more at ease in my own drawing room."

Cecilia summoned up a smile, firmly suppressing her own tiny pang of regret. "It's true the Great House was lovely, especially with all your improvements. But you know it was out of the question. With so little left of Papa's own personal estate, the unentailed part he was free to pass on to us, we couldn't have kept it up. The gate lodge is the right size for us, and comfortable, too. What do we want with grandeur?

What our sitting room lacks in space, it quite makes up for in elegance and charm." '

"*You* see it that way, my dear, and I bless you for it. But a young man who's come straight from London may find it a sorry come-down. When I think of my childhood home in Grosvenor Square..."

Cecilia sighed in practiced resignation. Mama was off again on one of her favorite scents, chasing those fugitive dreams of her youth in London. Through all those twenty years of devoted marriage, she had never managed to stir a foot out of Ireland. So far as Cecilia knew, she hadn't tried to. Papa, who loved to humor her slightest whim, would surely have supplied the means for a London visit.

And yet, after all this time, a tiny part of her remained thoroughly English—that part that made her eyes brighten as she spoke of the Park, Portman Square, Almack's assembly rooms, Drury Lane, the Mall, Ranelagh, the opera....

"I'm sorry, my dear." Cecilia came out of her reverie with a sudden start, to find her mother smiling ruefully at her, like a child with her hand in the jampot who knows she deserves a scolding. "I know how it bores you," Lady Margaret was saying, "all this prattling on about the pleasures of London. But it's so exciting to me to think of your having the chance to see it all for yourself—"

Cecilia gaped at her. "See it myself? What on earth do you mean? There's no chance in the world of my ever going to London. You know we've no money for such luxuries as travel."

Lady Margaret smiled at her archly. "Yesterday I would have agreed with you. But young Francis' sudden descent opens all sorts of new vistas. If you're right in thinking he intends to let bygones be bygones—"

Cecilia smiled back at her, shaking her head in indulgent good humor. "Dear Mama, you incorrigible dreamer! I see what's in your mind now—that we'll suddenly be enfolded in the collective bosom of Papa's haughty English connections."

Lady Margaret looked slightly aggrieved at Cecilia's tone. "I'm not quite that simple, my dear. The Annesleys have made it quite clear how they feel about *me*. But young Francis is only a few years older than you. Now that he's made a

7

point of seeking you out—he's quite an eligible bachelor, with those rich estates in England to balance the onerous burden of poor Kilwarden."

Cecilia tried vainly to suppress a peal of laughter. "Oh, Mama, how you love to matchmake! I'm sorry, but that hare won't start. After all, we *are* first cousins, Lord Francis and I."

Lady Margaret looked slightly miffed. "There are such things, my dear, as dispensations."

"So there are, indeed—and silly girls as well, who'd take advantage of them. But a horse breeder's daughter knows better than to run such risks."

"Really, Cecilia!" Lady Margaret looked genuinely shocked.

"Don't worry, Mama." Cecilia grinned impishly. "Just a bit of what Papa used to call his 'bluff Irish manner.' I promise I'll watch my tongue when we welcome young Francis. I've not the least wish in the world to go to England, but I'd be very happy indeed if his lordship could be persuaded to stay in Ireland."

"You will make an effort?" Lady Margaret's eyes grew bright with hope. "There's no one more charming than you, when you set your mind to it."

"I'll be charm personified, my darling Mama—at first, that is. But after his lordship's thawed by my girlish wiles, I have several serious remarks to make to him, mostly concerning that monstrous agent of his."

"No, no, Cecilia, you mustn't! You know men don't like women who meddle with business."

"But it's such a heaven-sent chance! You know yourself how vicious the man has been. Surely dear Papa would wish us to do anything we can to thwart Mr. Quinlan's disastrous tactics."

Lady Margaret rose to her feet, no longer the panicky suppliant seeking her daughter's support. "Your father is dead, Cecilia. You can't bring him back, no matter how hard you try to assume his burdens. I pray you'll soon learn your own frail shoulders are far too slight to carry Kilwarden. We've a new Lord Kilwarden now. You'll gain nothing at all for our tenants by angering him. Promise me now, you won't mention a single word about all those unladylike matters of 'hanging gales' and 'leases' and 'renewals.'"

Cecilia's lips formed a tight line of rebellion—but only for an instant. A moment later, her arms were around her mother, holding her close. "Of course, dear Mama. You're absolutely right. It would do no good at all to anger our new Lord Kilwarden. I'll be smooth as silk, I promise, and soft as a summer's day. Now, off with you to your bedroom and attend to your dressing, while I persuade Bridie to make one of her famous barm bracks. Kilwarden won't find the match to *that* in any fine London mansion."

Lord Kilwarden was agreeably surprised. He'd been dreading this duty call, expecting an uncomfortable half hour of tears and lugubrious glances. But the two ladies who rose to greet him as he entered the sitting room wore bright smiles of welcome. They also wore mourning, of course, but deucedly fashionable mourning, quite up to the standards he'd come to expect in London. The younger of the two—that would be his cousin Cecilia—wore lace-trimmed black muslin cut in the latest fashion, with Mameluke sleeves and wide-set lapels to the bodice, tapering down to a breathtakingly tiny waist. The gray-haired lady who must be his aunt Lady Margaret, wore black merino, more conservatively cut, its full sleeves tied in *à la Marie,* but allowed herself the tasteful sparkle of a handsome jet brooch and earrings.

He murmured some words of greeting and received a gracious answer from Lady Margaret which deepened his sense of agreeable surprise. He'd formed and discarded a hundred theories to explain the mysterious rift between the late Cornelius, Lord Kilwarden, and the rest of the Annesley family. The determination with which everyone avoided discussing his Irish aunt had pointed toward some kind of *mésalliance.* He'd pictured his unknown uncle, alone in the wilds of Ireland, succumbing to the charms of some peasant serving wench with brogue-thickened tongue, calloused feet, and kitchen manners. He realized now what a crackbrained notion that had been, as his long-lost aunt bid him welcome in the accents of purest Mayfair. His cousin Cecilia did have a touch of the brogue, but not the rough "dezes" and "dozes" he'd been hearing from the servants up at the hall, just a pleasant singsong lilt—most attractive, really. And that one charming dimple, that came and went with her smile...

"You had a good crossing, I hope? The Channel can be so rough at this time of year." Lady Margaret's voice sounded unnaturally loud in his ears. He realized he must have been staring rudely.

"Oh, yes, very nice." He struggled distractedly for some polite remark to keep conversation going. "What a charming room this is," he said, gazing appreciatively at the graceful Grecian sofa covered in green silk damask, the delicate lyre-back chairs, the splendid gilt-framed mirror above the mantel. "Not at all the sort of thing you'd expect to find in—that is to say, behind the severe exterior of this picturesque building."

"In a gatekeeper's house, do you mean?" Cecilia smiled at him sweetly. "Please, Lord Kilwarden, you need have no qualms of compunction. You made us a handsome offer, and we refused it. We *did* bring a few of our favorite pieces to furnish our new little home. But I do believe dear Mama could transform even a tenant's cottage into a thing of beauty. You've already seen what unerring taste she has; you've observed the way she furnished Kilwarden House."

"Indeed I have. Mr. Quinlan showed me over the house this morning. I was quite astonished to see how well it's done up. One hears such frightful tales in London of moldering old Irish houses, with curtains in tatters and furniture falling apart."

"With dogs in the drawing room and pigs in the kitchen?" A slightly malicious glint appeared in Cecilia's eye. "Don't apologize, your lordship; we're quite aware of our countrymen's reputation. To tell the truth, those legends are not *quite* without foundation. There are some of the neighboring houses—Count O'Hanrahan's, for example—but hush, I mustn't tell tales. You'll find all that out for yourself soon enough. That is, if you intend to stay a considerable time. You will be staying, I hope?"

Kilwarden was taken aback by the pleading note in that musical voice. "I'm afraid this is only a flying visit," he said uncomfortably. "A week perhaps; maybe two. I must be back in London for the start of the Season. To tell you the truth, this trip was the fruit of a sudden impulse. When I received my latest remittance from Mr. Quinlan, it struck me as rather strange that I'd never so much as laid eyes on one of my Irish tenants."

"Not really so strange," murmured Cecilia. "From what Papa used to say, most Irish landlords seldom set foot out of England. It was very different, I understand, before the Act of Union, when Irish landlords sat in our own parliament house in Dublin. I wasn't born then, of course, but Papa used to tell me some marvelous stories—"

She caught a warning glance from her mother's eye, and stopped abruptly. "Good lord, how I rattle on," she apologized. "What I meant to say is how very pleased we are that your lordship has decided to come here. The tenants will be delighted. They've all been longing to talk to you in person. Teigue Kavanagh, for instance—his lease ran out last month, and just because he couldn't scrape up the extra ten shillings—"

"Cecilia, my dear," Lady Margaret cut in smoothly, "we mustn't oppress Lord Kilwarden with such dreary matters. There are so many pleasant topics we might be discussing—for example, how delightful it is to make the acquaintance of your hitherto unknown cousin."

"You can't be half so delighted as I am, Aunt Margaret," Kilwarden bowed gallantly, then seated himself, in response to her gesture, on one of the lyre-back chairs. "I hope I may call you that, may I? And no more 'your lordships,' I beg you. Please call me Francis. I count myself fortunate to discover so enchanting an aunt. I never realized—you do come from England, don't you?"

"Yes, dear Francis. I was born in Surrey." The slightest of shadows dimmed Lady Margaret's smile for an instant. "I didn't set foot in Ireland until your Uncle Cornelius brought me here as a bride."

"I knew it!" exclaimed Kilwarden. "That explains the feeling I had in Kilwarden House, as though I'd been suddenly wafted back to my Aunt Lydia's house in Dover Street."

"Your Aunt Lydia? That would be Lady Annesley, Sir Edgar's wife? How is the dear creature? I hope she's enjoying the very best of health. She has a daughter, has she not, born just about the same time as my Cecilia?"

"You've met Lady Annesley?" Kilwarden tried to conceal his start of surprise.

"No, I've never had that pleasure, though I did have a note from her when Cecilia was born." She lifted her eyes and gave Kilwarden a calm, level look. "I'm sure you know, dear Francis, that my marriage to your Uncle Cornelius created a certain—coolness between him and his brothers. That's why I never had the good fortune of meeting your father, Sir Gerald. I heard, of course, of his gallant death in the War, and took the liberty of sending Lady Diana a note of consolation. But she, poor creature, must have already slipped away to join her husband in Heaven before it reached her. You were often in my thoughts in those days. How I regretted the unfortunate rift that prevented me from comforting my orphaned nephew."

"I've felt great regret myself over not having had the chance to meet you. I could never persuade anyone in the family to tell me what had caused the trouble."

"Of course not," said Lady Margaret, her soft, reminiscent tone turning to briskness. "And quite right, too. Children shouldn't be burdened with their parents' old nonsense. Enough of this gloomy talk. Tell me about yourself, my newfound nephew. What are you interests? How do you spend your time?" She smiled coquettishly. "I imagine you cut quite a swath in the rooms at Almack's."

"I wouldn't say that." Francis's tone was deprecating. It was true that he thought of himself as cutting a swath in London—but Almack's was not quite his style. He felt more at home among the fair Cyprians at the Argyll rooms. However, he wasn't about to confess as much to this elegant newfound aunt. "I go up to London every year for the Season, of course. But the rest of the time, I'm usually down in the country. I have an estate in Buckinghamshire—my mother's inheritance."

"I know." Lady Margaret beamed at him. "Quite a handsome estate, I believe."

"A thousand acres or so. It used to be mostly pasture, but now we have put a great part of the land into tillage."

"You're a serious farmer, then?" Cecilia's eyes brightened with interest. "You must have Mr. Quinlan show you the land Papa reclaimed from the bog. His drainage experiments were the talk of the county."

"I really don't know a great deal about that sort of thing," Kilwarden admitted. "I have an excellent steward. He keeps things humming, and tells me as much as I need to know, just as Mr. Quinlan does here at Kilwarden."

Surely you don't think Mr. Quinlan takes any interest in farming! The words trembled on Cecilia's lips. She bit them back just in time. Mama was right. This wasn't the time to challenge him openly. She cast about in her mind for a less controversial topic. "I've heard there's great hunting in that part of England. Perhaps you've had the good fortune to ride with the Old Berkeley?"

Kilwarden beamed at her warmly. "Now, dear Cousin Cecilia, you've hit on my ruling passion. I've a fine pack of hounds myself, and several excellent hunters."

"It must be a family trait." Cecilia's eyes were sparkling with excitement. "Papa was an ardent huntsman, and turned me into one, too. What a shame you're just too late for one of our meets. The Ballymacads are the terror and pride of this part of Ireland." Cecilia felt her pulse quicken as she went on to describe some of the more stirring incidents of the past hunting season. How splendid that he was a huntsman! It was evident he cared nothing for agriculture—and in any case, Kilwarden's difficult plight might be enough to daunt any man's interest in farming. But the hunting here was some of the best in Ireland. If she could somehow persuade him to come for next year's hunting season, she was sure he'd fall in love with Kilwarden, just as Papa had done when he first came over from England to claim his estate. He'd buy back the Kilwarden pack. Mr. Barlow would be glad to return them; he'd only agreed to their purchase as a neighborly gesture. He'd rehire Dick Murphy and Paidin King to staff the stables, and get back the full complement of maids and cooks. There'd be dinners and hunt balls up at the house, and all the lovely times they'd had in the old days...No, it wouldn't be quite like the old days. There would be a different face at the head of the table. Rather a nice face, though, with that fine straight nose and large deep-set gray eyes, with the tiny laugh-lines raying out at the corners.

She caught herself up with a start, hoping she hadn't been staring, and was glad to hear that her mother had taken up the thread of the conversation. What did it matter if his face was handsome or not? He could look like the devil himself, and still be welcome, so long as he bore the title of Kilwarden and the will to do his duty to Kilwarden's tenants.

"Ah, yes," Lady Margaret was saying, "you should see Cecilia dressed in her scarlet coat, taking the fences along with the Master himself." Something in his aunt's tone triggered a flicker of caution in Kilwarden's mind. He remembered other mothers, eagerly praising the talents of other daughters. He cast a wary glance at Cecilia. She was rattling on again about "sharp bursts" and "burning scents" and "swishing at raspers," as if she'd spent half her life glued to a saddle. He'd heard such talk before. He'd seen many eager young ladies decked out in their pretty pink coats. But taking the fences? That was hardly likely. Everyone knew why ladies came to the meet—for the chance to chatter and flirt 'til the hounds threw off, and then go home to prepare for the evening's festivities.

Still, the prospect she described really did sound tempting. "Are there really so many gentlemen who regularly ride to hounds here? I wouldn't have thought it. Mr. Quinlan tells me there are singularly few people of quality in the country surrounding Kilwarden."

"Mr. Quinlan is scarcely familiar with this part of the country." With considerable effort, Cecilia kept her voice free of sarcasm. "After all, he's a Dublin man. Actually, we're well supplied with acceptable neighbors. They'll all be calling on you, once they learn you've arrived. You'll probably be inundated with invitations."

Kilwarden felt a sudden lightening of spirits. "That's heartening news, Miss Annesley. I confess, up to now I've regarded this visit as a necessary but disagreeable burden. There's nothing I miss so much, when I'm out of England, as the pleasures of lively and civilized conversation."

Cecilia's smile was full of private amusement. "When it comes to conversation, Cousin Francis, I think you'll find

14

there's no place quite like Ireland. But you'll learn that for yourself, before many days go by."

"I'm quite sure I shall," agreed Francis. "If all my company here is half so agreeable as that which surrounds me this moment—" He finished out the phrase with a gallant gesture. Cecilia accepted the compliment with a fetching toss of her auburn curls and an impish smile. Then he saw her eyes grow bright with a new idea. "If you're feeling the need for amusement, wouldn't your very best course be to give a dinner yourself? That way, you're sure of meeting the pick of the crop."

Her high spirits were contagious. *A lively tableful of guests, instead of that prosy old Quinlan with his endless figures.* "That sounds like an excellent scheme," he said to Cecilia. "Won't you draw me up a list of prospective guests?"

"I'll give you their names this minute, with special emphasis on our ardent huntsmen." Cecilia sprang from her chair, clearly delighted, crossed to a small writing table in one corner, and quickly began to scribble a column of names. "Count O'Hanrahan—I know you'll find him amusing. Mr. Worsley, of course, and the Colonel; Lady Rosse and her daughter, the Barlows, Sir Jeffrey, Mr. Campbell . . ."

A second tremor of caution ruffled Kilwarden's thoughts. Wasn't there something almost too possessive in the way this young cousin of his was arranging his life? He glanced at Lady Margaret, and found her beaming complacently at Cecilia. A mite too complacently, as though dreaming of an endless series of dinner tables, with the charming Cecilia presiding as his hostess—but of course, that was out of the question. How could he make that clear?

Cecilia rose from the table, cheeks flushed and eyes aglow. "There's your official list. When shall you have the dinner? I fear your kitchen is sadly out of order. You must allow a few days, call back all our old servants, and especially our marvelous Sheila Reilly. She'll cook you up a truly Lucullan meal."

Kilwarden had a growing sense of things being taken out of his hands. He didn't much like the feeling—but all the same, he couldn't bear to dampen Cecilia's spirits. Poor girl, she'd had troubles enough these past few months. Why not provide her with just one happy occasion? "What do you say to this Saturday? Would that be time enough?"

"Saturday's perfect, Francis. I'll send out word right away, and gather in all the old staff—"

"No, no, Miss Annesley." Kilwarden felt he had to keep *some* control. "I'll see to that matter myself. With Mr. Quinlan's help, I'm sure I can manage. Don't give another thought to the preparation. With you and Aunt Margaret gracing my table, the dinner can't help but be a brilliant success."

Cecilia was sick with dismay at the thought of the agent having any part in the plans for the dinner. But she realized she mustn't voice her objections—not 'til she knew Francis better. Besides, she *had* promised Mama.

Kilwarden, meanwhile, was finding himself very anxious to make his departure. He quickly flicked his eyes down the list of names. "I don't see Sir Jonah Boothby's name on your list," he said in surprise. "From what Mr. Quinlan told me, he's the most substantial landlord in the district. He's already asked us to dine—Wednesday night, I believe—"

Cecilia's smile turned into a formal mask. "Mr. Quinlan is right. Sir Jonah is a very substantial landlord. However, he and my father could never see eye to eye. If you wish to include him, of course you must do as you please—"

"No, not at all." Kilwarden stumbled hastily to his feet, cursing himself for the clumsiness. "I wouldn't dream of inviting a guest who gave you any discomfort. I'm afraid I must leave you now. I can't begin to express how pleasant it's been to meet you."

"Come, come, dear Francis, you musn't rush off so quickly. Please stay and take tea with us." Lady Margaret's voice had an undertone of tension. "We've scarcely begun to talk. I've so many questions to ask you about the family."

Francis realized he was being unconscionably hasty. He seated himself again, Bridie brought in the tea, and Lady Margaret launched into a series of questions about the Annesley family, a subject on which she seemed surprisingly well-informed, considering the way she'd been cut off from them for a good twenty years. He rather enjoyed dispensing information about all sorts of elderly relatives. When it came to his own generation, however, her determined archness made him distinctly uneasy. "And Lady Annesley's daughter—the one who's Cecilia's age—what is her name? But you've already told me, of course; it's Constance. You must know her quite well, after all your visits to London. Is she an attractive young lady? I'm sure she is. The Annesley women are said to be famed for their beauty."

"I'm afraid my opinion on that is not very useful." Kilwarden's voice had become decidedly frosty. "As she's a first cousin"—he laid great stress on that *first*—"I suppose I judge her by quite different standards than I might some other young lady." He essayed a tight-lipped smile and turned to Cecilia. "Just as I'm sure that you, my newfound cousin, must judge *me* by different standards from those you might apply to an eligible suitor."

Cecilia flushed. Evidently she had caught his meaning. He was sorry he'd said it so baldly, but quite reassured all the same that he'd made his position clear. In truth, he was finding Cecilia *most* attractive. Which made it even more important that their growing acquaintance should not be complicated by any useless ambitions of hers—and her mother's.

Lady Margaret, he noticed, had raised a quizzical eyebrow. "I see that you and my daughter are quite in agreement when it comes to the rules concerning first cousins." She gave him a smile that was full of wry, knowing humor. Kilwarden felt more at ease. The woman was showing good sense, gracefully abandoning any fond hopes she might have had for her daughter.

"Of course we agree, Mama." The glint of amusement was back in Cecilia's eyes. "A horseman as experienced as Lord Kilwarden"—she caught her mother's eye, and made a quick change of course—"knows that fields furthest from home are the best for hunting. Is that not so, your lordship?"

Kilwarden flinched a bit when he heard that "your lordship." Back to formalities, were they? It seemed a pity. But he'd brought it on his own head, this hint of coolness. After a few moments more of light conversation, he rose to his feet, and made a determined farewell, which Lady Margaret accepted without further protest. He avowed himself afire with impatience 'til Saturday, and promised to call in before that, if the pressures of business permitted.

The moment the door closed behind him, Cecilia enveloped her mother in a breath-stopping hug. "Wasn't I good, Mama? No arguments, no pleading, not a word about poor Sadie Murphy or the O'Rourkes or the ruined plantation—"

"You showed great self-restraint, my dear. I hope you'll be quite as discreet at Saturday's dinner."

"But that's just the point, Mama! Once he's warm and replete with Sheila's cooking, I can say what I like without fear or favor. Especially with our friends and neighbors around us. I know they agree with me that Mr. Quinlan is ruining Kilwarden."

"I hope you're right, Cecilia. I know, whatever I say, there's no stopping you from riding straight at your fences." A veil of reminiscence clouded her eyes for an instant. "But dealing with Annesley men is something like walking on bogland— the straightest course is not always the safest way home."

Chapter 2

"He's brought Sheila *Ryan* to cook? But that's a disaster! The woman is scarcely fit to boil potatoes."

"That's just what me mam did be telling the agent, Miss Cecilia." Little Peggy's blue eyes were round with consternation. "Do you think he'd listen to her? Divil a bit of it! 'His lordship insists on a Sheila,' sez he; 'I've found him a Sheila.'"

"But surely I told his lordship Sheila *Reilly!* She'd cook him some splendid meals, as she used to for us. But Sheila Ryan!" Cecilia shook her head in commiseration. "Poor Lord Francis! I'm sure he's had terrible fare. Unless your mother has warded off some of the damage?"

"She tried her best to help, miss, but the agent wouldn't allow it. No one's allowed in the kitchen but himself and poor old Sheila. You can picture the food that comes out—burnt roasts, stews swimming with fat, dry praties without any butter."

"What in the world can Mr. Quinlan mean? You'd think he'd be trying to put his best foot forward. Kilwarden will be displeased enough when he sees how his agent has let the estate go downhill. A well-supplied table might keep him in better temper."

"There's nothing about the Great House that's well-supplied now." Peggy's small face was red with indignation. "It's a crying shame, Miss Cecilia! He won't let us make a decent fire, and forbids us to raise a finger to do up his bedroom."

Cecilia looked confused. "What's all this, Peggy? Lord Kilwarden refuses to let you see to his comfort?"

"No, no, miss, not Lord Kilwarden. He's a darling young man, so quiet and pleasant-spoken. But Mr. Quinlan's got him under his thumb. He sits shivering by the fireplace every evening, pretending he doesn't feel the lack of warmth."

"But that's terrible, Peggy!"

"Indeed it is, miss. It makes all our hearts sore—meself, me mam, and old Thady. To give such a meager welcome to his new lordship! But what can we do? When I tried to lay a few extra turfs on the fire, I nearly got skelped by that same Mr. Quinlan. 'You extravagant wench!' sez he; 'His lordship's an Englishman. He has none of the prodigal ways of we feckless Irish. He's death on all kind of waste—fuel or food or whatever.' 'But the poor man was shivering, sir,' I sez to him. 'No more of your lip,' sez he. 'His lordship's too gentle to scold you, but I'll see his wishes respected. And one thing more,' sez he. 'He won't have your dirty hands pawing his linens. He prefers to do for himself, rather than having you unwashed peasants near him!'"

"What a terrible thing to say." Cecilia was thoroughly shocked. "Mr. Quinlan knows very well how the household staff have been trained. And all this talk of Kilwarden's frugality! I'm sure he can't be as stingy as that. Why, he offered us back the house, even though it was his by law—surely that was a generous gesture."

"Indeed it was, Miss Cecilia. All of us wish you'd taken him up on that offer. It's been a sharp grief to us, all Lord Corny's tenants, to see Mr. Quinlan lording it over the Great House each time he comes down to Kilwarden to squeeze out his rents. There's no lack of blazing fires then!" Her gloomy face brightened. "At least there's one good thing in his lordship's coming. It's plucked Mr. Quinlan out of Lord Corny's bedroom. Even *he* was embarrassed to seem like he'd usurped it. He had all the linens changed and his lordship installed there the very first night he came."

Cecilia had a sudden vivid picture of her father's bedroom, with the high narrow windows that looked out over the well-tended garden. (Well-tended then; it was sadly gone to seed now.) She remembered the lovely smooth feel of the gleaming mahogany bedposts—and the rich jewel tones of the thick, bright Turkey carpet—and her father's ruddy face, his dark eyes gleaming with mischief...A wave of sadness began to swell in her heart. She pushed the disturbing thoughts away resolutely. "I'm glad Lord Francis has a comfortable bed at least. But the rest of it—" She shook her head in frustration. "I suppose there's nothing that any of us can do, except wait for Kilwarden to see how sadly his agent abuses the trust he has placed in him."

"May God speed that day, Miss Cecilia. But I fear 'twill be long in coming."

Little Peggy took her leave a few minutes later. Cecilia watched her trudge up the beech-lined avenue to the big stone house with a heart full of gloomy foreboding. The thought of Saturday's dinner, so pleasant before, now filled her with trepidation. Sheila Ryan to cook for all those discriminating palates? What a horrible prospect! They'd be polite, of course, and so would Kilwarden—but it would surely confirm all those English stories of the barbarous life led by the Irish gentry.

She must do something about it, and do it quickly. But what could she do? Confront the agent directly? Or make a quiet appeal to Cousin Francis, explain there'd been a mistake, have him summon Sheila Reilly to replace Sheila Ryan? But he might find that too presumptuous; he'd already made a point of asserting that he, not she, should make the dinner arrangements.

She turned to her constant refuge when faced with some thorny problem, a brisk ride over the moors on her black mare, Dido. For the hundredth time since her father's death, she breathed a sigh of thanksgiving that she'd had the good sense to accept *that* part of Lord Francis's offer. True, they could ill afford the modest few shillings that paid for the feeding and care of the two saddle horses they'd kept, and the pony that pulled the little phaeton. But what a solace it was, this wild dash through the countryside, with the wind rushing past her ears, lifting the veil that flowed from her pert high-crowned hat.

Turning back toward the road that led from Kilwarden House to the village, she saw a familiar figure, clothed in black, ambling along on a chestnut gelding. "Mr. Worsley," she called, and urged Dido to greater speed, then slowed her down to a walk as she took the road beside the Protestant curate.

"Good morning, Miss Annesley. Have you had a good ride?" The brown spaniel eyes Henry Worsley turned on Cecilia were, as usual, full of unspoken entreaty.

"Very pleasant indeed, Mr. Worsley." Cecilia kept her voice crisp, suppressing a spurt of annoyance. Why couldn't the man settle down and accept her refusal, become a good friend and companion, nothing more? "I hope you're keeping well. I suppose you've been to visit old Joseph Hogan. How is the poor man doing? Does he still have fever?"

"I saw him yesterday, and found him still very ill, I'm sorry to say. But he's suffering beautifully, so meekly resigned to his lot. It was really most touching, the way his face lit up when we prayed together. This morning, however, I'm on a more worldly mission. I went to pay my respects to the new Lord Kilwarden."

"So you've met my cousin. What did you think of him? I must say, I found him surprisingly pleasant. I had feared he might be one of those nose-in-the-air sort of people one so often finds among visitors from England."

"I really can't give an opinion, Miss Annesley, as I wasn't admitted into his august presence."

"He wasn't at home when you called? That's natural, I suppose. He was probably out inspecting his domain."

"No, he was there in the house. I'm sure of that. At home but not 'at home,' if you take my meaning. Old Thady's eloquent eyes convinced me of that. He's not used to telling those useful social lies."

"Oh, dear," said Cecilia, "that *was* inhospitable. I suppose it will take him some time to get used to our Irish ways."

"I'm not at all chagrined, I do assure you, so far as these lordly manners pertain to my humble self." Mr. Worsley's sulky look belied his meek words. "A curate quickly gets used to being snubbed. But to turn the count away in the same offhand fashion—"

"Count O'Hanrahan? He was turned away as well? I find that very surprising. A distinguished officer, a count of the

Holy Roman Empire—I can only suppose his lordship was absorbed in going over the books." Cecilia felt her heart sinking. "His visit here is only a very brief one."

"The count will be pleased to hear that. I met him on the road as he was coming away, and he shouted at me—you know his ebullient manner—'May the devil take his new lordship back to his own dominions, and never let him set foot in Lord Corny's house again!'"

"Oh, dear," said Cecilia. "That's most unfortunate. Won't you try to persuade the count to reconsider? You're so good at pouring oil on troubled waters. I've really been counting on him for next Saturday's dinner. I'm sure if he met Lord Kilwarden, they'd get along famously. And you could help things along, in your tactful way."

"Dinner?" Worsley's eyebrows shot skyward. "His lordship is giving a dinner?"

"It was my idea. Why do you look so surprised? Surely you must have received your invitation? We made our plans on Monday. I assumed the invitations would go out at once."

"I assure you I've received no such invitation."

"But you were the first on my list!" Cecilia was truly astonished. "After the count, of course. You, Colonel Harcourt, the Barlows, Sir Jeffrey—all the people whom dear Papa liked best."

Mr. Worsley blinked owlishly. "I fear your plan has miscarried. I spoke to Mrs. Barlow this morning after matins. She was bubbling with curiosity about the new heir, and asked my advice about calling at Kilwarden House. I'm glad I advised her against it. No doubt he'd have met her advances with similar coldness."

"Oh, dear!" said Cecilia again. The surge of disappointment that seemed to well up from her boot-tips precluded any more original formulation of her dismay. "I'm exceedingly glad to learn what has happened," she said in a formal tone. "I must go share this news with my mother. I'm sure there's been some mistake. Perhaps she'll have some advice that will straighten things out."

Mr. Worsley bid her farewell with a gloomy nod, and continued dejectedly back toward the vicarage. Cecilia, letting the mare take her home at an easy pace, was absorbed in her whirling thoughts. Why hadn't Kilwarden told her he had cancelled the dinner? And what was Mr. Quinlan's part in this sorry matter? Her intuition told her he was playing some devious game. But she couldn't for the life of her see how she could stop it.

Oh well, she told herself, *there's one ray of brightness in all this dismal gloom. The cream of the Westmeath gentry won't be forced to endure poor Sheila Ryan's cooking.*

"Here's to the candidate of the only true party, and may Mr. Peel and his spoilers go sup with the devil in hell!"

Kilwarden picked up his glass and obediently drained it, grateful that he'd had the foresight to switch back to claret on the previous round. He'd started the toasting with whiskey, yielding to Sir Jonah's urging, but had soon found its fumes too strong for his whirling brain.

The florid-faced man down at the foot of the table was raising his voice in a song. He seemed to have settled in for a solid evening of drinking. Kilwarden ventured a glance across the table at the drooping, basset-hound face of his principal agent. It was some small comfort to find Mr. Peter Quinlan looking as glum as himself. He realized now what Quinlan had meant by his warning before the dinner: "You'll find that the Irish gentry have different forms of politeness than those you've been used to."

Different forms indeed! To begin with, they seemed to take it for granted that a dinner "for gentlemen only" gave license for all sorts of low conversation. Kilwarden wasn't a prude, but he found that this endless talk of "plump, luscious wenches," interspersed with "glorious cockfights" and "grand carousals" did nothing for his digestion. Though after the fare at the Great House, even the greasy roast beef and soggy game pie had seemed a welcome change. And whatever Sir Jonah's taste lacked when it came to table companions, one had to admit that he served the very best claret.

He cast his eyes once more round the bare oak table, assessing the motley crew. Sir Jonah himself was quite acceptably dressed, in a handsome blue broadcloth coat piped with white satin. But the three other men who now had their heads together—no doubt concocting the next in this endless series of toasts—were dressed as though for the field instead of the table, with their thickly greased, knee-high boots, coats with long flapping tails, buckskin breeches clearly the worse for hard riding.

The florid-faced man appeared to be their ringleader. Kilwarden had only half caught his name—was it Linton or Hinton or Denton? He ended his song and launched himself into another rambling tale, chiefly concerned with what passed around here for "high life." "Do ye mind the time my brother-in-law, Charlie Harris, locked us all up in the huntsman's cottage with a hogshead of claret and a whole bloody cow we cut collops from for a week?"

The white-crested man at his side, leathery-faced and slight-bodied, leaned forward to click his bumper against his friends. "Do I mind? Will I ever forget it? There was two pipers there and a fiddler, but we filled them so full of wine that the three of them were stretched out on the floor before midnight."

"Isn't that the truth of it, now!" The stubble-chinned man on the opposite side of the table tilted back in his chair at a dangerous angle, steadying himself by cocking his boots on the table. "Ah, 'twas a grand old carousal, there's no doubting that."

Kilwarden suppressed a shudder. He'd found it distressing enough to see how his tenants lived, with their clothes in rags, huddled in tumbledown cabins along with their scanty livestock. But to find the gentlemen, too, living like pigs! He let his gaze sweep around the high-ceilinged room, noted the gaps in the ornately patterned plaster, the spots where the faded paper was hanging in strips, the bone-littered floor, the complete lack of table linen. Even Sir Jonah, the best of a sorry lot, had let his surroundings grow sadly dilapidated.

But that was too sweeping a judgment. They could scarcely all be like this, the Irish gentry. He remembered the Grand Saloon at Kilwarden House, as charming a room as any he'd seen in London. And despite the new cook's deplorable lack of skill, the cloth that covered the polished mahogany table was always first quality linen. And yet, and yet—the decay had set in there, too. Those shocking gashes made by some-

25

one's careless spurs in the wood of that fine old bedstead, the road dust ground into that once lovely bedroom carpet...

A voice at his elbow broke into his gloomy thoughts. Sir Jonah was beaming at him, his three greasy chins bobbing above his loosened cravat. "Now that you've come to Ireland, we hope you'll stay here, Kilwarden. Do you plan to make your home on your new estate?" He reached for the crystal decanter, now circling the board for the tenth or eleventh time, and topped off Kilwarden's glass—with claret, thank God, not whiskey.

"That won't be possible," said Kilwarden brusquely. "I did have some thought, when I first surveyed my land, of staying here a few months and trying to have things put into better shape. But from what Mr. Quinlan tells me, any such efforts of mine would be doomed to failure."

Sir Jonah's face turned grave. "Mr. Quinlan's right. He's done wonders since he's taken over, but the late Lord Corny had hopelessly spoiled his tenants. They're a lazy lot at best, our Irish peasants. Unless they're kept up to the mark, they won't lift a finger."

"I confess I don't understand them. One would think sheer hunger would drive them to overcome their inbred distaste for hard work."

Sir Jonah exchanged an understanding glance with the dour-faced agent seated across the table. "I see our clever beggars have been doing their tricks for his lordship. Ah, you needn't wince, Kilwarden; we've all been taken by those well-rehearsed lies. Paddy is such a shrewd fellow, it requires all a man's sharpness not to be taken in. But let me warn you, my friend, there's nothing worse for this country than soft-hearted landlords—as the late Lord Corny found to his doleful cost. He was always too soft with his people, granting all sorts of extensions on payment of rent, and frittering away a fortune with his so-called improvements."

"My Uncle Cornelius seems to have cared a great deal for his tenants' welfare. That row of well-built houses down in the village, for instance."

Mr. Quinlan laughed, a short sharp bark of a laugh. "What will these riffraff do with well-built houses? I've told you already, your lordship; a year from now you won't be able to

26

tell those expensive cabins from the usual sort of sty these people prefer. You really can't compare them to the tenants you know in England. Ours are a savage race, steeped in black superstition."

"A toast, a toast!" A shout from the foot of the table cut short the discussion. Tom Hinton—or Denton or Linton—was on his feet, swaying precariously as he raised his bumper. "Here's to the brave abductor, bold Dick Hennessey, who snatched himself a fortune last Saturday morning..."

"Dick Hennessey! Dick Hennessey!" The wiry, leather-faced man raised a shout to match his friend's. "And another to Miss Catherine Boyd, the choicest young heiress in County Westmeath!"

Kilwarden looked puzzled; Peter Quinlan looked disgusted; Sir Jonah distinctly embarrassed. "A local custom." He sounded apologetic. "Some impoverished young buck has carried off an heiress."

"Carried off?" exclaimed Kilwarden. "That seems a strange sort of courtship. You don't literally mean—"

Sir Jonah pursed his lips, then nodded abstractedly at the florid-faced man, and raised his glass in answer to the toast. "I'm afraid I do," he said. "Pray don't be too disconcerted. As you may have gathered, my other guests tonight are not really of my own circle. But just at the moment"—he paused, exchanging a glance with Mr. Quinlan—"it's important to me to stay in their good graces." He gave a meaning look toward Kilwarden's glass. Reluctantly, since he wasn't sure how proper a toast he was drinking, Kilwarden raised his glass and drained it of claret. "But—carried off?" he repeated once again.

Sir Jonah sighed. "Abducting an heiress was once a widespread custom. It's dying out now, but it still happens now and again. The young lady in question is usually quite nicely treated, though the need to secure her fortune sometimes leads to some excesses. Of course, it always winds up in a legal marriage."

"Good Lord!" exclaimed Kilwarden. "What a barbaric custom!" A sudden vision assailed him—a pair of amethyst eyes beneath pert auburn curls. "I had no idea that young ladies in this country were subject to such assaults. I should hate to think that such a thing might happen to my cousin, Miss Annesley."

"Miss Annesley?" Sir Jonah seemed vastly amused. "You need have no fear on that score. As I've said, the name of the game is abducting an *heiress*. Miss Annesley's poverty provides her with total safety so far as such pranks are concerned."

Kilwarden still hadn't grown used to the spasm of guilt he felt whenever he thought of Cecilia's misfortune. He stirred uneasily. "I was much impressed with the graceful way Miss Annesley has accepted her reduced circumstances. I trust that before very long some percipient gentleman will restore that attractive young lady to her proper station in life."

"That's scarcely likely to happen until the girl shows more sense," snorted Sir Jonah. "As things stand now, she seems to give little thought to safeguarding her future."

Kilwarden saw the glint of resentment that flashed in Sir Jonah's eyes. He felt an unpleasant sensation in the pit of his stomach. Could it be possible? A man three times her age, with not half her good taste and breeding?

The corpulent man answered his unspoken question. "You won't spread this about, I know. But since you're a relative, I might as well tell you. I made your cousin an offer, just after Lord Corny kicked off. Thought it the least I could do to help a neighbor. I'm quite comfortably off, as you see, and it's been a good few years since my second wife died."

Kilwarden's stomach was growing more and more queasy. *The young and vibrant Cecilia paired with this old tub of lard?* "She refused you, I take it?" He kept his face impassive.

"She did, the more fool she." Sir Jonah brought down his clenched fist, rattling the glasses. "And a proud stiff way she chose to go about it. If you'd seen the contemptuous look she turned on me! As if I can't have my pick of a score of penniless orphans."

"Quite so, quite so," murmured Francis. He found himself assailed by another vision—the delicate, pointed chin imperiously lifted, the wide, intelligent eyes flashing with fire.

"She'll be sorry, though." Sir Jonah was muttering, as though to himself. Kilwarden realized that the endless round of toasts had been making some dangerous inroads into the fat man's composure. "That little bitch will be sorry one of these days. She'll come crawling to me, she will; she'll come crawling on bended knees."

Kilwarden stared at him in distaste, as the wine-thickened tongue kept repeating its vengeful threats. He felt a wave of revulsion against this whole uncivilized country. If this was the best poor Ireland had to offer, it was surely high time to shake the dust from his heels and head back to civilization. *But Cecilia? What of poor Cecilia?* "Miss Annesley is my cousin," he said in a cold, formal tone. "I shall see that she never reaches such a nadir of destitution."

Sir Jonah, piqued by his tone, seemed to bristle an instant. Then a broad confidential smile spread over the triple-chinned face. "So that's what's afoot. You'll make an offer yourself? I suppose a rich man like you can well afford it."

"That's not possible." Francis's voice remained icy. "Miss Annesley, as you know, is my *first* cousin. But as head of the house, I shall see that she has her own free choice of a husband."

A husband fit for her. The scornful phrase was trembling on his lips. He knew he must take his leave, before the insidious claret turned him to a sorry beast like this vile Sir Jonah. He forced himself to his feet, taking care not to stumble. Through the swirling fog in his head, he saw that Mr. Quinlan was rising, too. Thank God for one man of good sense, among all these monsters. At least he was leaving Kilwarden in competent hands.

He made some perfunctory farewells, and left amid a chorus of genial protests. The moment the carriage moved off, he turned to the agent. "My mind is made up," he said. "There is nothing more I can do here. I won't stay 'til the end of the week, as I had planned. I will set off for London early tomorrow morning."

Peter Quinlan nodded. It was clear Kilwarden's decision came as no surprise. "I think that is wise, your lordship. What a fortunate stroke of luck, as things have turned out, that none of your neighbors accepted for Saturday night."

"Thank God for that." Kilwarden's assent was fervent.

"If the persons I met tonight were any example, I've been spared a most tedious ordeal."

Absorbed in his whirling thoughts, he was quite oblivious of the slow, complacent smile that spread over Quinlan's face. He sank back into the cushions, his mind full once again of that vision of Cecilia. Could such an enchanting girl face so dismal a future? No, it must not be! It would not be! The estate, he was now convinced, was beyond all rescue, but at least he would do his duty to Cousin Cecilia.

Chapter 3

Cecilia and Lady Margaret were still at the breakfast table when the traveling carriage stopped outside the gatehouse. Fighting off an insistent sense of impending disaster, Cecilia had Bridie usher Kilwarden into the dining room, and offered him the choice of coffee, tea or chocolate.

His lordship opted for coffee, and joined them at the table, his stiff demeanor proclaiming how uncomfortable he was finding this morning's visit. Cecilia, having exhausted her repertoirs of inquiries as to his health and comments about the weather, seized the bull by the horns and relieved him of the necessity of broaching the painful subject of his departure.

"You're traveling, I see." She gestured toward the carriage outside. "A brief excursion, I hope? You'll be back in plenty of time for Saturday's dinner?"

She saw the long, lean face turn pink with embarrassment, and abandoned her last fond illusion that the dinner she'd placed such hopes in might somehow be rescued. "I'm very sorry," he said, "but I'm afraid there will be no dinner. I won't have the pleasure of meeting those estimable persons you placed on your list of guests. I must leave for England at once—pressing matters of business—something quite unforeseen—"

His face, already quite flushed, was growing astonishingly red, as he floundered around in search of convincing phrases. "Pray don't apologize further, your lordship," said Cecilia coldly. "We quite understand your cancelling the dinner—my mother and I, that is. We shall do our best to explain to our old friends and neighbors—though I'm sure you're aware how withdrawing your invitation may ruffle their feelings."

"Withdrawing my invitation!" Kilwarden looked deeply shocked. "I had hoped you would credit me with better manners! I'm quite prepared to apologize for my hasty departure, but when it comes to a charge of bad manners, your neighbors must accept their proper share of the blame. Not one of those named on your list accepted my invitation, or even sent me a note explaining why they were too busy to come to a dinner where, as I expressly declared, you and your mother would be the guests of honor."

His face remained flushed, but his tone revealed that embarrassment had turned to righteous anger. Cecilia realized she had better tread lightly. "I must say I find that strange," she temporized. "Are you sure there's been no mistake? One or two of them might have had prior engagements, but that all of them should refuse, sending no explanation—"

"I was quite as astonished as you." Kilwarden's jaw jutted grimly "I appealed to Mr. Quinlan to supply a motive for this strange lack of courtesy. He was most reluctant to answer, but finally gave his opinion that since the recent decline in your worldly fortunes, the neighboring gentry wish to break off all connections with you and Lady Margaret."

Cecilia was stunned for a moment. Not by his accusation against her friends; she knew them too well for that. It was the hitherto unplumbed depths of the agent's duplicity that appalled her. She was already sure that Quinlan had not delivered his employer's invitations. But to cover up his neglect by making Lord Francis's new neighbors appear so devoid of generous hearts or civilized manners? The man was an utter monster, viler than even she had ever suspected.

Kilwarden mistook the reason for her silence. "I had hoped to spare your kind heart this bitter knowledge." His eyes were soft with pity. "I know from my own experience how shallow some friendships can be. Your sheltered existence has been a poor education for the callous world in which you now find yourself." He felt his embarrassment lift as he saw his way clear, at last, to broaching the fine new plan that had been on his mind from the moment of waking that morning.

"I hope you will let me help you find a new circle of friends, one where your lively affections will be truly reciprocated."

I have all the good friends I need, sir. They'd be your friends as well, if that odious agent of yours had obeyed your instructions. Cecilia forced herself to bite back the angry words. She knew he wouldn't believe her. It was Quinlan's word against hers, the experienced man of business against the sheltered maiden. She had hoped, given time, to expose to Kilwarden how little concern his agent had for his employer's welfare. But she hadn't been given time; a few minutes more, and Kilwarden's new master would no longer be within reach. She couldn't afford to waste those few minutes in quarrelling.

"You are very kind, Cousin Francis," she said demurely. "I appreciate your desire that I should be happy. But I hope you're not going to repeat your most generous offer that we return to the Great House. Surely you've seen on this visit that the two of us are much more comfortable here."

"As I've already told you, your new home is utterly charming. I, too, am much more comfortable here than up at the mansion. But you won't remain here forever. In due course, you'll find a husband and make your home elsewhere."

"Not necessarily, sir. Despite my sheltered life, I've seen enough of the world to convince me that I'd rather not marry at all than make a bad marriage."

"I quite agree on that point." Francis flashed her an eager smile. "That's why I propose to help you find a suitable husband."

"With all due respect, Cousin Francis, I prefer to make so important a choice for myself." Cecilia's quiet voice betrayed not the slightest sign of her rising resentment.

"Of course you must make the choice. But there must be a choice to make, a broader choice than this corner of Ireland provides. I hope you won't think me presumptuous; I'm merely pursuing my role as head of the family. If your father had lived, I am sure he'd have felt the same. You must have your chance to choose from the cream of the crop—which means you must be my guest for the coming London Season."

Lady Margaret gave a little gasp, and tried in vain to conceal her delighted smile. "What a generous offer. You're really too kind, dear Francis."

Cecilia was thunderstruck. She had never had any desire to go to London, and was genuinely unconcerned with the choice of a husband. If she chose to marry some day, she was perfectly sure she could find a good husband in Ireland. But all that seemed so far in the future, compared with her pressing worries about the Kilwarden estate.

Kilwarden quickly perceived the quarter in which he must make his next assault. "You do agree, then, Aunt Margaret, that you and Cecilia shall spend this Season in London? You shall be my guests in my house in Arlington Street, and of course you will let me take care of all your expenses. Aunt Lydia will be a great help to you. She's quite *au fait* with all the latest fashions."

Lady Margaret's eager smile faded abruptly. She looked subdued, almost fearful. A scarlet flush swept up from her neck to her forehead. "*I* can't go to London," she murmured. "That's completely out of the question. But that needn't stop you, Cecilia, from accepting this splendid offer." She turned toward Cecilia, her eyes full of supplication. "Miss Stowe will be glad to go with you as chaperone." She turned eagerly back to Kilwarden. "She's Mrs. Barlow's sister; she comes of very good family. Extremely fine taste in dress, as Cecilia knows."

"But, Mama!" exclaimed Cecilia. "You know that you've dreamed for years of seeing London again!"

"I've said I can't go." Lady Margaret's face was like stone. She evaded her daughter's eyes, nervously smoothing her skirts as though brushing off crumbs. "There are reasons for my refusal. I don't choose to speak of them now."

Cecilia was growing bewildered. Everyone seemed to be acting so strangely this morning. Kilwarden's abrupt departure—her mother's reluctance even to talk about London—her cousin's sudden concern to see her married. And hadn't her own reactions been somewhat strange? She realized with chagrin that she'd been about to accept Kilwarden's offer. Her only motive, of course, would have been to give her mother some rare, happy moments. But how would it have looked to her cousin? Would it not have made her seem a mere charitable object, grateful for any crumbs he might toss from his table?

She thanked her lucky star that the choice had been made for her. "If my mother does not choose to go," she told Kilwarden, "there is no point in further discussion. I'm afraid we must *both* refuse your very kind offer."

Kilwarden found himself in the grip of a highly surprising impulse: he wanted to reach out, grasp her by the shoulders, and shake her, shake some good sense into that unworldly head. He forced himself to keep his voice low and pleasant. "It is your decision, of course. But I earnestly hope you'll consider your answer further. I should hate to see you throw your whole future away on a moment's whim."

Cecilia's resentment could no longer be suppressed. "My future, sir," she burst out, "is here at Kilwarden. My father may have indulged me in other ways, but he taught me never to flinch from the call of duty. It is Kilwarden's tenants who have the first claim on my life—people like Maire O'Rourke, thrown out of her cabin while still deathly ill with the fever, like Teigue Maguire, deprived of his land for one day's delay in his rent, or Charles and Mairtin O'Grady, who broke their backs draining their tiny patch of bogland, and then had the rent jacked up beyond their reach. That is where my future lies—in doing what little I can to repair the disaster that befell Kilwarden when it lost its devoted landlord."

Kilwarden was taken aback by her vehemence. Then he realized what he was hearing: merely an echo. No doubt his Uncle Cornelius had filled her head full of impractical sentiments. He felt his heart flood with pity; did the poor girl not realize how that "devoted landlord" had wasted the private fortune that should have been willed to his daughter?

"Your kind heart does you credit, Miss Annesley. But I fear you've had little experience in matters of business. As Mr. Quinlan says, it's a fatal mistake for a landlord to be too soft-hearted."

"Mr. Quinlan! You still trust that odious man? That thieving knave, who's been robbing you right and left?"

Kilwarden looked at her coldly. "It is really not your place, even though we are cousins, to question my choice of an agent. But since you have cast this slur on him, I feel it my duty to say that I've found Mr. Quinlan supremely honest. The books

I've reviewed this week show that very clearly. He hasn't held back a single rent that was due me."

"The rents are the least of his income." Cecilia felt a desperate need to lay bare the truth. "What of the bribes he's extorted from every tenant each time the lease is renewed? What of the dues of corn and potatoes and pig-meat that the tenants must send to the agent up at the Great House before they can claim a single bite for themselves and their starving children? Did he pass on the price he received for the trees he razed to the ground, destroying our thriving plantations? Did he give you the auction price of the steeplechase champions he sold from my father's stables? Has he passed on the money the grand jury pays for the roads, roads which are never built, money that winds up in his well-lined pockets, while your faithful tenants starve for the lack of paid work?"

"Cecilia! You've said quite enough!" Lady Margaret's voice, unaccustomedly loud in her ears, brought the furious girl's tirade to a sudden halt. Her heart gave a lurch of dismay as she realized how far she'd outstripped the bounds of polite conversation. She looked fearfully up at Kilwarden, expecting to find him seething with unexpressed anger. He, at least, had full control over his feelings. He would never have let them burst out in this unseemly way.

She found him gazing at her in undisguised admiration. He'd been a bit piqued at first at her presumption—but his paramount feeling was one of surprise, as if his pet cocker spaniel had reared up on its furry hind legs and started preaching sedition. And she did look deucedly pretty, with the high color in her cheeks and those flashing eyes.

Cecilia felt a surge of relief. At least her hot words hadn't made him an enemy. She might still have a chance to convince him—but no; he was going away; all those high-flown plans of hers were an idle dream. "I'm sorry, your lordship. I'm afraid I was carried away. I hope you'll forget these few last unfortunate minutes and take with you only pleasant memories of Kilwarden."

"I assure you, Cousin Cecilia, I shall often think back on my stay here with the greatest pleasure. I'm sorry my visit has been such a short one." He set his cup on the table, rose from his chair, preparing to make his *adieux*.

"You *will* return soon?" Lady Margaret was on her feet, too, her voice once again full of eager excitement. "Now we've begun to restore the family connection, it would be a tremendous pity to have our acquaintance cut short."

Kilwarden was sorely tempted to give her the promise for which she was so obviously pleading. He turned his face away from her eloquent eyes, and hardened his heart. He'd seen for himself how little he could do for these tenants. There was really no other reason to return to this desert backwater, so devoid of comfort and charm, of everything that made life worth the living. "I feel sure we'll meet again." He hoped that his beaming smile would make amends for the evasiveness of his words.

Lady Margaret seemed reassured, but Cecilia failed to hide a look of disappointment. After a few more words of farewell, Kilwarden, with a sigh of relief, eased himself safely outside the door of the gatehouse. As his carriage rolled off, he cast one last lingering glance at his Irish estate, noting the broken fences, the untilled fields, the bony, shivering cattle. Superimposed on it all, he saw Cecilia's flushed face, heard her impassioned voice, convinced that a kindly landlord could somehow reverse all this ruin. Poor inexperienced girl, with her impetuous lack of judgment! She was sorely in need of a wise and prudent protector. And who else but Francis Annesley, Lord Kilwarden, would care enough for her welfare to take on that difficult role?

Chapter 4

Lady Lydia Annesley was having a difficult time maintaining her air of cordial politeness. Even at the best of times, she had no great fondness for her visitor, Lady Headfort. Today, with her mind full of questions about her nephew's impending visit, she found all this social chitchat especially tedious.

She was very fond of young Francis, despite the fact that she saw him so seldom. He had a good head on his shoulders, and seemed to realize, unlike the other young men one saw about town, that there were more serious matters in life than drinking, dancing and gambling. Not that she begrudged him his share of such pleasures; she knew the sort of pursuits that drew him periodically up to the city, and was not at all offended that he chose to spend most of his London hours in gayer company than that of his widowed aunt.

Yet here he was, straight from the Irish packet, making a beeline for her. What did they mean, those mysterious words in the note that announced his visit: "a family matter of vital importance"? A twinge of foreboding stirred at the back of her mind. Had there been some trouble in Ireland? Some hidden defect in the title? Some ruinous obligation assumed by poor Cornelius, only now coming to light? Or perhaps that unfortunate business about the marriage? No, it certainly couldn't be that. All that old gossip was long since dead and buried. A good thing, too; she'd never approved of the way the Annesleys had behaved in that painful matter.

"Do you really think periwinkle blue is a suitable shade for Constance?" Lady Headfort's voice, high-pitched and affected, cut into her ruminations. "It very much suits my Lucinda's fine, high color, but next to Constance's pale complexion...not that she isn't lovely, though somewhat on the delicate side..."

Why don't you say what you mean: that your daughter's a beauty and mine is distinctly plain? Lady Annesley suppressed the retort, and murmured that Constance might choose whatever color she liked in her gown for the Season's first ball.

"I daresay she'll look very pretty. I'm sure the young men will flock round her, whatever she wears. She has such an agreeable nature, as my Lucinda is never tired of proclaiming. She's so fond of Constance, you know; considers her by far her closest friend."

That will be news to Constance. Lady Anneseley wondered what strange attraction had drawn that accomplished flirt to her own pale and timid daughter. Lady Headfort's next sentence enlightened her on that score. "I trust that Lord Kilwarden will be back from Ireland in time to lead Constance out at Lady Carlisle's? It will be such a comfort to her, to have her handsome cousin dancing attendance."

I presume her self-styled "best friend" hopes to share that comfort. Lady Lydia reproved herself for the cynical thought. How could one blame a mother for doing her very best to smooth the way for her daughter's first Season? It was she who ought to feel guilty. She hadn't devoted much effort to helping Constance make an effective splash. But with the girl herself showing so little interest....

She winced as she heard Lady Headfort echo her rueful thought. "I must say, your Constance is taking it all very calmly. Most young girls would find it much more exciting, this trembling on the brink of their life's most important decision." The high-pitched voice turned coy and insinuating. "But perhaps your Constance has less cause to tremble than most? I've heard whispers here and there—one might almost guess the matter is already settled. So comfortable, I always think, to arrange these affairs within the family circle."

Lady Annesley, vastly annoyed by this clumsy probing, decided a flat-out answer would best meet the case. "If you're hinting about a match with Lord Kilwarden, that is quite out

40

of the question. He and Constance are clearly within the prohibited degrees of kinship."

"Oh, yes; we all know that. But others have found ways around that awkward situation."

"Others may. Kilwarden will not. He is very firm on such questions."

Lady Headfort leaned back in her chair, the complacent smile on her face reminding her hostess of a cat lapping cream. "Such a pity," she murmured. "It would have been a fine match." Lady Annesley saw in a flash why she was so pleased with this new piece of information. It meant that Kilwarden was still an eligible target. A qualm of dismay rippled through her, as she thought of Kilwarden, caught in the net of Lucinda's flirtatious charm. She brushed the vision aside. Francis had too much good sense. He'd perceive the empty head behind that beautiful face.

To her great relief, a footman came in at that moment and handed her Francis's card. "I hope you'll excuse me," she told her unwelcome guest. "My nephew has asked for a private conference on family matters. Pray don't disturb yourself," she added hastily, as Lady Headfort began to arrange her skirts in preparation for rising. "I'll have him shown into my study. I'm sure he won't keep me long."

"Oh, no; I must go. I wouldn't dream of intruding on *family matters*." Lady Headfort's inquisitive eyes begged for another tidbit of news. Lady Annesley, as much in the dark as she about Francis's mission, answered the unspoken question with a silent, mysterious smile, and made no further protest—a move which left the gossipy guest no further option. Mustering her most gracious smile, she gathered her skirts around her and made a quick exit.

Lady Annesley breathed a sigh of relief and rang for a fresh pot of tea. A few minutes later, Francis entered the room, wearing the latest in foulard cravats—and a puzzled frown. "Good afternoon, Aunt Lydia," he said in an abstracted tone. "Who was that lady who greeted me on the stairway? She appeared to know me quite well, but I can't for the life of me remember her name."

"I'm sure you'll know it quite well by the time the Season

is over. You are on Lady Headfort's list of prospective sons-in-law."

"So that's it." Francis looked nettled. "Another one of those mothers. I hope you will tell her politely that I'm not in the market."

Lady Annesley smiled at him fondly, and said in a teasing tone, "Still so adamant, Francis? I really can't scold you too harshly; you have plenty of years ahead before you need to think about settling down. Still, your note about *family matters* did cause me a quiver of hope. I thought you might want to tell me that you'd brought back an Irish bride."

She was startled by the sudden flush with which he responded to her feeble attempt at a joke. "You know me better than that," said her nephew stiffly. "As a matter of fact, the topic on which I wish to consult you has to do with marriage. Not mine in this instance, however, but my cousin Cecilia's."

"Cecilia is going to be married? What marvelous news! The perfect solution for that poor fatherless girl. But why do you need to consult me? Surely, as head of the family, your consent is all she needs."

"Not so fast, dear Aunt Lydia. You're rushing your fences again." Kilwarden's smile was indulgent. "I fully agree with you that marriage would, for Cecilia, be the perfect solution. She has not, however, found a suitable husband—and from what I saw of her neighbors, she never *will* find one in Ireland. That's why I'm appealing to you to take her under your wing and invite her here as your guest for the coming Season."

Lady Annesley tried not to appear as overwhelmed by the request as she secretly felt. The girl must be Constance's age, already past eighteen. If she hadn't yet had a suitable offer, it was either for lack of beauty or lack of a fortune. Either way, she seemed likely to prove a considerable burden to a mother already faced with her own child's questionable prospects.

Kilwarden mistook the cause of her hesitation. "I shall pay all expenses, of course. No, no; I insist. I know Uncle Edgar left you comfortably off, but presenting a daughter to London must make quite a dent in the richest mother's pocket."

"It's not the expense, my dear Francis. It's the shock of

suddenly finding myself with *two* daughters to marry off. Remember how little I know about your cousin Cecilia. She's spent all her life in that rustic corner of Ireland. Will her manners be up to the mark? Does she have any sense of style? The London *ton* can be very cruel; does the girl herself know the obstacles she will be facing?"

Francis shrugged impatiently. "She's a lovely girl, and her manners are very charming. There's a touch of the rustic, perhaps, but that may be an advantage. Men like an intelligent listener when they talk about horses."

Lydia's heart sank a few notches further. Kilwarden's stern sense of family duty would clearly provide him with answers for all her objections. The girl was, no doubt, in need of a great deal of polish, but she hadn't the heart to deny his urgent request. "Of course I'll invite her, Francis. It will give me great pleasure to be able to do you this service. I'll write Lady Margaret today—" She paused in mid-sentence, abruptly aware of a new set of complications.

"That's splendid of you, Aunt Lydia." Kilwarden was beaming at her, his face alive with eager gratitude. "Lady Margaret seemed strangely reluctant to make the trip when I suggested that they might stay at my town house. No doubt she felt somewhat embarrassed at the thought of an all-male household. But if *you* will appeal to her, woman to woman, I'm sure she will change her mind."

Lady Annesley suppressed a sigh of relief. So much for *those* complications; the woman was evidently showing a great deal of sense. "If Lady Margaret chooses not to come, I'm sure she has her own reasons. I won't presume to urge her against her best judgment."

"Aunt Lydia!" Kilwarden's voice was heavy with pained surprise. "Surely you're not resurrecting that old family quarrel? I can't believe you still cherish bitter feelings against that unfortunate lady."

"There has never been any bad feeling between Lady Margaret and me." Lady Annesley chose her words carefully, unwilling to give any hint of the long-buried secret. "It is only my concern for her welfare, and that of her daughter, which leads me to accede to her wishes. She has no objection, I take it, to Cecilia's coming without her?"

"Not at all; she seemed quite delighted, and proposed a quite suitable lady as chaperone. Cecilia herself was less than enthusiastic—but I'm sure it was her mother's refusal that led her to turn down my offer. If *you* would appeal to her—offer a kinswoman's care, argue the ties of family—I'm certain she'd change her mind and agree to come."

Kilwarden's persuasive smile melted away the last vestiges of doubt in Lydia's mind. "I'll do my best to convince her, I promise you that. I'll write today. The sooner she gets here, the better. Mlle. Doricourt is almost finished with Constance's gowns. We'll put her to work at once on this new project. Perhaps you will let her wear your mother's diamonds? From what I've heard of your Uncle Cornelius, I doubt if he left her well-provided with jewels."

"Of course, dear Aunt Lydia. I'll buy her some new jewels myself, if you think she needs 'em. You'll see her quite splendidly dressed, I'm sure of that. As I've said, you must draw on me for all the expense."

"Dear Francis, you have no idea what you're getting into. I won't let you offer her such unlimited bounty; five hundred pounds should take care of her basic needs. No use encouraging her in expensive tastes; unless she's lucky enough to find a very rich husband, it will do her no harm to learn how to count the pennies."

Francis couldn't help smiling as he thought how extremely modest his aunt would find Cecilia's current surroundings. "I'm sure she already knows *that*. But I bow to your judgment, in this as in all other things. Five hundred pounds it is. Rest assured that if you need more assistance, my purse is at your command."

A sudden idea struck Lady Annesley. She smiled roguishly up at her handsome nephew. "I *will* need some further assistance, and you're just the man to provide it. In fact, I intend to make it a condition of sealing our bargain."

"I've already said my purse is at your command."

"I don't mean money, Kilwarden. The assistance I speak of requires a far greater sacrifice. I shall require you to be in attendance at every ball during the coming Season, to lead out both of your cousins, and keep them supplied with partners."

Kilwarden vainly tried to hide his look of dismay. "Oh, come now, Aunt Lydia! That's not quite my dish of tea."

"I'm well aware of that. But I've just granted you a quite considerable favor. Don't I deserve one in return?"

"I assure you, my cousin Cecilia will have no trouble in finding partners. Wait 'til you make her acquaintance; she'll set all your qualms at rest."

"You find that quite easy to say, but you may have a prejudiced eye. In any case, my first duty is to Constance. You must admit that *she* won't find herself hotly besieged. Well, do you accept or not my *quid pro quo:* I sponsor your Cecilia; you do your best for my Constance."

"Confound it, Aunt Lydia; this all seems so cold-blooded. Can't matters take their own course, without all these contrived arrangements?"

"You know as well as I, Francis, that when it comes to the market for husbands, contrivance is very important. No more of your quibbling, now; be a good boy and give me your promise."

Kilwarden sighed resignedly. "Very well; you force me to it. I promise to act as procurer—"

"Francis! Your choice of words!" Lady Annesley pulled a face of mock-sternness.

"Provider of partners, then?" Francis raised an impish eyebrow.

"You might simply promise to do your *cousinly* duty."

"Done!" Francis cried, seizing her hand and shaking it warmly. "We've struck our bargain, then. Five hundred pounds and my cousinly duty. I'll leave you now, my dear aunt, before you dream up any further atrocious extortions."

"The more quickly you're gone the better, you miserable scapegrace." Lady Annesley gazed at him fondly. He gave her a companionable peck on her proffered cheek, and headed out toward the stairway. Lady Annesley watched him go, lost in thought for a minute. Then she seated herself at her little Chinese lacquer writing table, and began to compose the promised letter to Ireland.

Lady Margaret, hearing the front door open, sprang up from her writing table, eager to share with Cecilia the news from that morning's post. Her daughter's woebegone look sent a pang of dismay to her heart. "What's the matter, Cecilia? Don't tell me poor Maggie Leary has taken a turn for the worse? She seemed to be doing so well when I visited her yesterday."

"She's still doing well." Cecilia slumped into a chair, too dispirited to think of removing her damp pelisse. "She took most of the soup I made her, and she's finished the calf's-foot jelly you brought yesterday."

"What is it, then, that's making you look so upset? Not Joseph Hogan I hope. Was he spitting up blood again?"

"Joseph is doing fine." Cecilia's voice was listless and weary. "I met Dr. Tierney coming out of his cabin. That's when he told me the news I've been dreading these last two months."

Lady Margaret looked alarmed. "Dr. Tierney is really leaving Kilwarden? The dispensary will be closed? Our poor sick tenants will have no doctor to tend them?"

Cecilia nodded glumly. "He's hung on as long as he could. But without Papa's subscription to make up the half of his yearly salary, he simply can't make ends meet."

"That's awful, Cecilia." Lady Margaret looked horrified. "We can't blame the poor man, of course. He has to support his family. It's Mr. Quinlan who's really to blame. For the sake of a mere thirty pounds, he deprives our sick people of the skilled help they need! It's criminal, Cecilia; it's really monstrous."

The tired ghost of a smile tugged at Cecilia's mouth. "That sounds like one of my usual tirades, Mama. So at last you're beginning to see what Mr. Quinlan is doing?"

Lady Margaret blinked at Cecilia, a little chagrined. "I admit I did think you were somewhat uncharitable to him. But each day brings me closer to your way of thinking. If only I'd understood more about our financial affairs! But so long as your Papa was with us, we seemed to be doing so well."

"Of course we were doing well. Papa charged reasonable rents, and provided paid work as well to help his tenants afford them. Without all these dues and exactions, the people had enough food, and were fit to farm their land. We had

46

sufficient ourselves, and money besides to plow back into improvements. But now, with these streams of gold draining off to Dublin and London, the heart has gone out of our people. The best farmers have already left, hoping for better terms elsewhere. Like Mairtin O'Grady, for instance, who spent those two backbreaking years draining his bit of bogland. Now Quinlan calls it 'prime land' and raises his rent by ten shillings; then he has the gall to call him a lazy drifter when he says he can't pay the increase. Mairtin still has some spirit; he's gone off to seek out a better landlord—and that hard-won two acres will quickly sink back into wasteland. And that's only one example of Mr. Quinlan's methods. Repeat it by two hundred cases, and you see why the whole estate is crumbling away into ruin."

"But surely Kilwarden must know what is happening? He has some experience in running his English estate."

"Has he really?" Cecilia looked scornful. "I hardly think that experience amounts to much. You heard him say it himself; he leaves everything to his steward, and gives no thought to his tenants except to be sure he receives his monthly accounting."

"You don't really know that, Cecilia." Lady Margaret ventured a cautious defense of her nephew. "He seems a generous man where we are concerned. For all you know, he might be a model landlord to his English tenants."

"I don't care a fig how he treats his English tenants. It's our tenants I care about, the people we see every day, growing weaker and weaker while their heedless absentee landlord cavorts in the ballrooms of London."

"Cavorts! What a word, Cecilia. He's a quiet, well-mannered young man."

"I found him positively rude. To descend for a flying visit, patronize us up to the hilt with his condescension, and then dash back to the fleshpots in that precipitous manner."

Lady Margaret privately doubted that her daughter knew much about fleshpots. But she didn't reprove her again for her questionable verbiage; if she hoped to succeed in the highly important matter contained in Lady Annesley's letter, she would first need to soothe her daughter's self-righteous anger. "Perhaps it was not *all* his fault that he left in such haste. From what little Peggy told us, Mr. Quinlan made his life quite uncomfortable here."

"You don't know the half of it, Mama. It was Mr. Quinlan who did us out of our festive dinner. Not only that; he alienated Kilwarden from all his neighbors by turning them away when they came to call. I suspected that at the time, but I couldn't fathom his motives. Now I see what he was up to: he wanted Kilwarden to think that Sir Jonah Boothby's barbarous company was the only alternative to a lonely, badly-cooked dinner up in the freezing Great House."

"A devious scheme indeed, which succeeded admirably—from his point of view. But doesn't that prove my point? If Kilwarden were really a callous, unfeeling landlord, Mr. Quinlan wouldn't have had to hurry him off. It was only because he showed signs of becoming concerned that the agent felt this great need to speed his departure."

Cecilia's slumped posture gave way to a new alertness, as she weighed in her mind her mother's interpretation. Maybe Mama was right; there might still be some hope of appealing to Cousin Francis's nobler motives. "Perhaps we might write him a letter," she said in a tentative voice. "Give him the stark details of glaring injustice; explain in pounds and pence how much Mr. Quinlan is extorting."

"Cecilia, my dear, I'm sure you know better than that. Kilwarden's a man, after all. He won't take kindly to what he will see as you meddling. Remember his quick reaction when you started arranging his dinner. That young man is superbly wary of apronstrings. And then, when you lost your temper, and blurted out all those startling accusations—"

"Yes, that was a bad mistake." Cecilia's tone was rueful. "I'm sure you're quite right, Mama. Gentle persuasion's the only tactic for him. But I can't do much gentle persuading with two hundred miles of land and sea lying between us."

"They don't have to lie between you, unless *you* decide that they should."

"What in the world do you mean?" Cecilia sat bolt upright, her eyes fixed with rapt attention on her mother's face. "You're not still thinking about that absurd invitation? That I should go to London and leave you here at Kilwarden?"

"Is it really so absurd?"

"You know it is, Mama. He only made it to salve an uneasy conscience. Since I don't need his lordship's help to marry me off, why should I waste his money in so futile a project?" She shot a suspicious glance at the pile of correspondence on the table in front of her mother. "But what is this all about? Don't tell me he's written you repeating his offer? After I told him so plainly I wouldn't go?"

Lady Margaret's smile held the barest hint of mischief. "I *have* had a letter from London. It came this morning while you were making your rounds. However, it's not from Kilwarden. It's from his aunt—your aunt as well—Lady Annesley."

Cecilia's eyes widened in pleased surprise. "Aunt Lydia has written you, after all these years of silence? That's wonderful, Mama. I shall credit Kilwarden with one good deed at least; it must be his urging that moved her to heal the strange breach in the Annesley family."

"I think it's wonderful too, but not for myself alone. Your aunt wants to know *you*, Cecilia. She invites you to come for a visit as soon as you can."

The glint of suspicion returned to Cecilia's eyes. "In other words, she wants me to come for the Season? Kilwarden's proposal exactly, but he's using her as his mouthpiece. Now he's enlisted my aunt in his scheme to marry me off."

Lady Margaret gave a sigh of exasperation. "Really, my dear, aren't you being a little too touchy? Helping to find a husband is a perfectly natural goal for your relatives to pursue. I can understand that you might not care for the way Kilwarden so blithely assumed your father's prerogative—but surely you won't reject your Aunt Lydia's interest?"

An indecisive look crept into Cecilia's eyes. Her mother, encouraged, switched to the kind of appeal she rarely made to her daughter. "It would mean so much to me to see you well-established in your aunt's good graces. Won't you accept for my sake, if not for your own?"

Cecilia knelt by her mother's side and clasped her around the waist, laying her head in her lap. "If you really want me to, of course I'll accept. But I do hate to leave Kilwarden when our people are in such dire straits."

Lady Margaret stroked her hair affectionately. "I know

how you long to help them. I feel the same anguish myself. But what can we really do, with our slender resources? Only give them a few trifling comforts—a few ounces of tea or tobacco, a bowl of soup when they're sick, a shilling here and there that we save by scrimping on clothing. But now you've the chance to do so very much more. If you could convince your cousin to run the estate by your father's methods—"

Cecilia pulled away a little, smiling ruefully at her mother. "You incurable optimist! So you still think I might succeed where I made such a dismal failure?"

Lady Margaret grasped her daughter's chin and looked intently down into her eyes. "I know you can do it, Cecilia. You could charm the birds from the trees, once you set your mind to it. Just think of the marvelous chances you'll have in London—the gentle hints you can drop while you waltz with your cousin at Almack's, your casual suggestions as you drive through Hyde Park in his carriage, a whispered word or two between the acts of the opera, a lingering conversation as you walk *à deux* after dinner in your aunt's Dover Street garden."

"Perhaps he *might* really listen if I went about it that way." Lady Margaret saw her daughter's eyes brighten as she imagined herself a part of those London scenes. "And how *you* will love seeing your favorite places. I can hear it in your voice when you speak of them."

"I cannot go with you, my dear. But Miss Stowe will love it, I'm sure, just as much as I would."

Cecilia pulled away again, looking reproachfully up at her mother. "But surely Aunt Lydia's letter has changed your mind? I can see why you wouldn't go when your only relatives there were still estranged. But now Lady Annesley asks you—" She broke off abruptly, her eyes growing dark with suspicion. "Or perhaps she hasn't asked you? Is that what the trouble is, Mama? That the past isn't buried, so far as you are concerned?"

"No, no," protested Lady Margaret. "Lady Annesley has been very gracious."

"I don't believe it. Let me see that letter." Cecilia snatched the letter from the writing table and scanned it quickly. "'Lord Kilwarden tells me that you do not wish to come here.

I can understand some of your reasons for that decision, and so will not press you further. Be assured that if you ever should change your mind, you will always find a warm welcome awaiting you here.'" She handed her mother the letter, a little ashamed of her impetuous gesture.

"So you see, my dear, she could scarcely have been more gracious."

Cecilia longed to know more about those mysterious *reasons,* but the guarded look in her mother's eyes made her shy away from any further questions. She realized Mama was right; the letter was all one could ask in the way of a friendly gesture. She already regretted the way her own stiff-necked pride had made her lash out at her cousin. Surely she had a duty to help heal the family breach? What possible harm could come from this visit to England? She was sure no power on earth could lure her away from her duty toward Kilwarden's tenants. So why not do what everyone seemed to want, spend these few weeks in London, go through the social ritual? At the very least, she could strengthen the family tie, disrupted so long. And she might do more than that, far more than that, if she could learn to keep some check on her tongue.

"Very well, Mama. I'll do it." The words sounded faint and breathless. She cleared her throat and found a more confident tone. "Let's go visit Miss Stowe on the instant, and tell her the news: she's about to become my chaperone in London."

Chapter 5

Miss Stowe, when apprised of the plans for the visit to London, accepted the chaperone's role with enthusiasm. The gray-haired, retiring spinster of indeterminate age surprised both Cecilia and her mother with a vivid recital of some of her own experiences as an eager young girl making her bow to fashionable London.

She immediately arranged with her brother-in-law, Mr. Barlow, that she and Cecilia should travel to Dublin in his well-sprung traveling carriage, thus avoiding the inconvenience of the public stagecoach. Once out of the shadow of her ebullient married sister, Miss Stowe proved to be a most entertaining companion. By the time the two ladies boarded the London coach at Holyhead, Cecilia was fully convinced that, outside of Lady Margaret, she could not have found a more suitable person to shepherd her through the rigors of the coming Season.

It was only when they had settled themselves in the post chaise which was to carry them from the Islington coachyard to Lady Annesley's house in Dover Street that Cecilia began to feel some trepidation about what lay ahead of her. After her country existence, the sheer size of London threatened to overwhelm her. Back in County Westmeath everyone knew who she was—Lord Corny's daughter. Now she found herself in this vast urban hive, teeming with strangers, on her way to meet an aunt who was in some ways more formidable than any stranger.

A host of doubts rose up to assail her. What was she like,

this unknown aunt of hers? How did she really feel about her niece's visit? True, she'd assured Cecilia in her letter that she regarded her as a "second daughter"—but those gracious words might well have disguised a grudging acceptance of duty. Above all, there still remained that mysterious family secret, a secret so painful that her mother refused to discuss it. Would Lady Annesley finally reveal it to her? Did she herself really want to have it revealed? Whether revealed or kept hidden, was it not bound to cast its shadow, making the next few weeks strained and uncomfortable?

Meanwhile Lady Annesley, taking tea with her daughter Constance as she awaited her niece's arrival, was having her own share of doubts. The least of these had to do with the family secret; she had already determined how to handle that ticklish matter. The question that most concerned her was Cecilia's appearance. Would she be a plain little thing, gawky and awkward, or would she have at least the rudiments of beauty? Much could be done by skillful dressing and coiffing, and Lydia Annesley fully intended to do her best along those lines for her unknown niece. But what if the child turned out to be really hopeless? Perhaps Kilwarden was being more cruel than kind in exposing her to the scrutiny of fashionable London.

All her anxious fear dissolved completely the moment the graceful girl stepped across the threshold. Why hadn't Kilwarden said that she was an absolute beauty? Those lovely violet eyes, that glorious hair, setting off that translucent complexion. How charmingly the mourning dress displayed her excellent figure! It showed some signs of wear, but it couldn't be faulted for style. Copied by Mlle. Doricourt in yellow organza or peacock silk, it would hold its own in any Portman Square mansion.

She advanced toward her niece with a beaming smile. "Welcome to London, my dearest Cecilia. I hope I may call you that, not stand on formalities? It gives me the keenest pleasure to welcome you into my house. You will call me Aunt Lydia, I hope. And here is your cousin Constance, who welcomes you just as warmly."

Cecilia looked around in surprise as the fair-haired girl with the long pale face and huge deep-set topaz eyes rose from her chair by the fireplace and advanced to meet her. She had scarcely noticed her cousin, absorbed as she had been with the regal figure of Lady Annesley, whose crimson silk brocade gown, with its bodice cut *à la circassienne*, made such a striking contrast to her daughter's high-necked white cambric day-dress.

Constance echoed her mother's welcome, but in so cold a manner that Cecilia's fears, momentarily lulled to rest, were reawakened. She realized with dismay that this stiff, rather haughty girl would be her constant companion in the social ordeal ahead. Though the family breach was evidently forgotten so far as her aunt was concerned, her newfound cousin seemed not quite so willing to let bygones be bygones.

Resolutely dismissing her qualms, she presented Miss Stowe, and was relieved to see Constance's manner thaw a trifle. The two travelers were quickly installed in comfortable bedrooms, each with a personal maid assigned to her service, and left alone to repair the ravages of the journey.

Dinner that evening was a pleasant occasion, with Miss Stowe and Lady Annesley gaily recalling incidents and acquaintances of thirty years past. Cecilia kept the talk going with eager questions, and even the silent Constance showed some animation. But her air of distant reserve weighed on Cecilia's spirits. She felt quite relieved, after dinner was over, when her aunt summoned her to her study for a private conference.

Lady Annesley wasted no words in polite formalities, but came to the point at once. "As you're well aware, this has been a divided family for far too long. How much have your parents told you of that regrettable business?"

Cecilia was pleased with this direct approach. Here was a woman to whom she felt free to speak frankly. "They've told me nothing at all, but I couldn't help forming my own impressions. It seems that the Annesleys didn't approve of my father's marriage?"

"Your impression is right, my dear. I myself was new to the family then, and had no influence on their decisions. I was quite appalled that they treated your mother so harshly. While Sir Edgar lived, I was obliged to obey his wishes, but one of the widow's privileges is the right to think for one's self. I assure you that I'm genuinely delighted to have you here, and to do my small part in repairing some of the damage."

But what was the cause of that damage? Don't I have the right to know? The words seemed to flutter deep in Cecilia's throat, but she was strangely reluctant to ask the crucial question. Lady Annesley, sensing her hesitation, came to her rescue. "Since your mother has chosen not to speak of those ancient matters, it is certainly not my place to resurrect them. But I want you to be assured that I am wholly sincere in regarding you as a second daughter, and doing whatever I can to help you find a suitable husband."

"My dear Aunt Lydia, may I be as frank with you as you have with me? I'm delighted to make your acquaintance after all these years. I feel some of a daughter's regard for you already. That was my primary purpose in coming to London—to heal the breach in our family. To be honest with you, I'm not really interested in finding a husband."

Lady Annesley looked startled. "That's a rather astonishing statement from a girl about to enter her first London Season. Kilwarden appeared to think you were quite unattached. Perhaps there are private arrangements he wasn't aware of?"

"No, nothing like that." Cecilia could feel herself blushing. "I *have* had a few offers, but none I'd choose to accept."

"From what my nephew says, you have very few suitable gentlemen to choose from in Ireland. I'm sure you'll find things quite different here. With your charming appearance and manner, your lack of a fortune won't be a serious drawback."

Cecilia smiled, accepting the compliment in the spirit it was intended. "I'm glad you don't find me an embarrassment to our family. But an English husband would be quite out of the question. Our family owes a duty to my father's tenants; while that duty remains unfulfilled, my mother and I must live near our people and do the best we can with our slender resources."

Lady Annesley's expression conveyed a mixture of concern and wry amusement. "So you'd rather do good works than find a good husband? That sounds painfully familiar. But what's all this about your duty to Cornelius's tenants? Surely my nephew inherited that duty along with the title?"

Cecilia hesitated. She had no wish to disparage her cousin Francis, but she had to make her point clear. Lady Annesley had proved herself an eminently sensible woman. She might be a useful ally in Cecilia's campaign. "I'm sure Lord Kilwarden's *heart* is in the right place," she said tentatively, "but so long as his *body* remains in England, he can scarcely oversee his estate in the proper manner."

Lady Annesley's eyebrows shot skyward. "You're not suggesting that he should go live in Ireland? My dear Cecilia, no one does *that* anymore."

"My father did." Cecilia's jaw was set firmly.

"Your cousin belongs to a younger generation." Lady Annesley's voice held a touch of asperity. "You can scarcely expect him to exile himself so far from London."

"I'm not asking him to become an exile. I'm asking him to spend a few months of each year as a resident landlord. Then he can see for himself how his agent is robbing him and oppressing his tenants."

"Really, my dear! That's rather strong language to hear from the lips of a lady."

"In this case, my dear Aunt Lydia, I must be my father's daughter first, and a lady second."

Lady Annesley gave her a shrewd, appraising look. "You have the true Annesley spirit, I see, just like your cousin Constance. I'm sure an attempt to change your mind would be quite futile. But tell me frankly, Cecilia, what success have you had in your efforts to persuade Kilwarden?"

"None at all," admitted Cecilia. "There hasn't been time to even *begin* to persuade him. That's why I've come to London. I hope to see something of him during the Season. Perhaps in this atmosphere of gaiety and pleasure—"

"You might find him more amenable to persuasion than you did in the rough surroundings of his estate?" Lady Annesley's tone was crisp, but not unfriendly. She seemed to be more curious than disapproving.

Cecilia threw caution to the winds. Now her aunt knew this much of her plan, why not make a wholehearted bid for her assistance? "I'm sure you agree it would do no good at all to speak to Kilwarden as frankly as I have to you. He'd think me a meddling woman and refuse to listen. But a hint or two here and there, a few remarks dropped in the midst of some pleasant conversation—"

"When music and wine and dancing have begun to soothe that stubborn Annesley spirit?" Lady Annesley's eyes glittered shrewdly. "Well, at least you're likely to find *your* good works more amusing than Constance does hers. No, child, don't ask what I mean; you'd do better to hear it from Constance. We've spoken enough for tonight. You must give me time to digest this intention of yours. I thought when you came to England I had gained a daughter; now it seems you intend to rob me of a nephew."

Cecilia had sudden attack of compunction. "Perhaps I have acted badly in coming to London under these false pretenses. I know I'm causing you great expense and trouble."

"Not a word more, my dear." Lady Annesley rose from her chair, putting a definite end to the conversation. "It will give me great pleasure to present so charming a niece to London. And even greater pleasure to observe the results of that charm on my hitherto impervious nephew. Come along, now; you must get your beauty sleep. You've had a long, tiring day." She took Cecilia's hand and patted it fondly as she led the way back to the drawing room. Though she found Cecilia's motives distinctly surprising, she wasn't deeply disturbed in her plans for the girl. Once a few eligible suitors appeared, she was sure all this high-minded nonsense would fade away quickly. She heaved a sigh of concern. If only she could feel as secure about Constance...

Cecilia was already in bed when she heard the light tap on the door. Flinging a cashmere shawl over her linen chemise, she hurried to open it. Constance stood on the threshold, a resolute smile on her face. "I'm sorry to disturb you, Cousin Cecilia, but I just couldn't sleep. I was so pleased and excited to find a kindred spirit."

"A kindred spirit?" Cecilia stared at her blankly. What could have happened to turn this cold fish so cordial? Then she remembered her manners, quickly invited her cousin into her bedroom, and settled her in a comfortable armchair.

"Please don't feel you've caused me any disturbance," she told Constance warmly. "I'm delighted to have the chance of knowing you better. To tell you the truth, I had the impression you did not quite approve of me."

Constance looked keenly distressed. "Did I make my feelings so plain? A thousand apologies, my dear, dear cousin. I confess that on first acquaintance, I felt a sharp pang of resentment. I thought that your beauty and charm would make my evident plainness even more striking. But the conversation between yourself and my mother quite banished such unworthy thoughts."

Cecilia's eyebrows rose. "You heard our conversation? The one that was meant to be private?"

Constance's face turned crimson. "I know it's a terrible habit, this listening at keyholes. I've struggled to break myself of it, but tonight the temptation was just too strong to resist."

Her voice began to tremble. Cecilia, seeing that the girl was about to burst into tears, made haste to reassure her. "Please don't distress yourself. I've done the same thing myself on a few occasions. Besides, we said nothing I wouldn't have wished you to hear. Now I'm quite agog with curiosity. What was it I said that caused such a change in your feelings?"

"Surely that's evident? The fact that you've dedicated your life to serving the poor, just as I have."

Cecilia blinked. "I didn't quite say *that*, did I?"

"You said you placed your duty to Kilwarden's tenants far above that of finding a husband. Surely you know that's heresy in these precincts? My mother must have been horribly taken aback."

The bitter edge to her voice alerted Cecilia. There was some sort of family quarrel here. She'd better tread cautiously. "She did seem somewhat surprised, but I felt she accepted my words very graciously." A sudden thought struck her. "Now I remember, she did drop a few little hints about some rift between you. The way she mentioned 'good works' was a trifle sarcastic."

Constance breathed a deep sigh. "My mother, I'm afraid, has devoted the whole of her life to idle pleasures. One really can't blame her, of course. Her whole generation was steeped in frivolity. They thought material comfort the chief end in life."

"You evidently don't think so," ventured Cecilia.

Constance's face was suffused with pious rapture. "Thanks to the goodness of God, I've been saved from that folly. That saint, Mr. Wilberforce, has opened my eyes to the true end of man's existence."

"Mr. Wilberforce," exclaimed Cecilia. "I've heard a little about him. Isn't he the man who doesn't like dancing on Sunday?"

"My dearest Cecilia!" Constance almost shrieked with alarm. "Don't tell me your salvation is still so incomplete! Surely you understand that dancing is far too worldly an occupation for those of us who have chosen a serious life?"

"You don't approve of dancing? But surely this famous Season we're about to experience consists almost solely of balls?"

"It does. That's the reason I hate it. Balls and playing at cards and scandalous conversation. I'm not at all reconciled to my part in the vain charade. My mother and I have argued about it fiercely. I only gave in to her when she quoted the Fifth Commandment, and demanded my obedience to her parental wishes."

Cecilia was aghast. "But Lady Annesley seems such a sympathetic person. I can't believe she would force you to act against your conscience."

"You mustn't blame Mother too harshly." Cecilia was pleased to see how Constance, despite her opinions, rushed to her mother's defense. "I know she believes she's acting in my best interest. She wants me to find a husband, and this round of frivolities called the London Season is the only way she knows to accomplish that."

"But what about you, dear Constance? Do *you* want to find a husband?"

"Of course I do. It's the only way to accomplish my sacred mission."

"I'm really confused," said Cecilia. "First you praise me for my supposed dedication; then you tell me your sole ambition is a husband and children."

"I didn't say that at all." The large topaz eyes flashed with unaccustomed fire. "My mission concerns a far wider sphere than my own private family. I intend to spend my life ministering to the poor, elevating their souls, helping them find salvation. In order to accomplish that mission, I must first have a husband."

"I really don't see why you must." Cecilia was thoroughly puzzled. "Hannah More never had a husband. Her work with the Sunday Schools sounds just like what you have in mind."

"Miss More didn't start on that noble work of hers until after her clever pen had conquered London. How could I follow her footsteps? I have no special talents, and only a modest fortune. No, I *must* find a husband. If I'm lucky, I'll find some elderly gentleman with a large estate, who won't object to my ministering to his tenants."

"Good Lord!" exclaimed Cecilia.

Constance gave her a reproving glance, but made no verbal comment on what she obviously considered a blasphemous choice of language. "Good gracious!" amended Cecilia. "You'd really accept some elderly gentleman? I could only accept a man I truly loved."

"Love doesn't come into the matter. Even my frivolous mother admits to that. One chooses a husband of suitable family and fortune. Love, if it comes at all, enters the picture much later."

Cecilia was deeply shocked, but tried not to show it. Her ideas of marriage were based on her mother and father's obvious devotion to each other. Still, she realized Constance was voicing a widely-held opinion. But even discounting love, there remained some practical pitfalls. "This hypothetical elderly husband of yours—he might be out of the picture before that could happen."

"So much the better," said Constance implacably. "That would give me a freer hand to pursue my mission."

Cecilia, schooled in experience, was quick to pounce. "Not necessarily. What if a younger man inherited? Someone who didn't agree with your attitude toward your tenants?"

"I would simply have to convert him." Constance's eyes were once more full of her vision. "I would point out his sacred duty to his tenants, the fact that Providence, in making him their landlord, intended him to promote their spiritual welfare."

Cecilia was appalled by her cousin's naïveté. Did she really think one could *argue* a man into virtue? "That's all very well in the abstract," she said in a guarded tone, "but I can't imagine it happening in real life. Take a man like your cousin, Lord Kilwarden, for instance. How do you think he'd react to your moralizing approach?"

"Cousin Francis? He'd never listen; I grant you that. That's why my heart bled for you when I heard you and Mother discussing your hopeless mission."

"Do you really think it's so hopeless? Did you hear the way I plan to go about it?"

Constance gave her a patronizing smile. "Oh, yes, I heard all that. You'll fall in with his favorite pursuits—drinking and dancing. He'll agree with that part of your plan, I'm sure of that. But it's scarcely the way to appeal to a man's higher motives."

Cecilia breathed a sigh of resignation. "My dear newfound cousin, I fear we'll never agree when it comes to tactics. But we're fighting the same battle, aren't we? We're struggling to accomplish the duty we owe the poor."

Constance's smile was no longer patronizing. "There's much that separates us, my dear Cecilia. But I think we've begun to understand each other. I'd better slip back to bed now, and let you sleep. You've a gruelling day tomorrow, with the seamstress coming. What a pity we're forced into such worldly ostentation. I know you'll hate every minute, just as I did."

Before Cecilia could answer, Constance had slipped out the door, leaving her cousin feeling distinctly guilty. If the truth were told, she had been looking forward with pleasure to the day when she'd exchange her well-worn black for a new, much gayer wardrobe.

She crossed to the looking glass and gazed meditatively at her reflected image, seeing herself in a series of gowns modelled on those she'd admired in the pages of *La Belle Assemblée*. She could almost hear her cousin's reproving voice, chiding her for her worldly vanity. She exchanged a rueful smile with the girl in the mirror. Poor, sweet, earnest

Constance! What a priggish companion with whom to enter the lists of fashion. How shocked she would be if she knew how Cecilia's heart was dancing at the very thought of all the balls ahead. Though obviously, nothing in London could be quite so pleasant as the hunt balls back at Kilwarden House...

Her mirrored image gave way to a sudden vision: her father, wearing his pink hunting jacket above his dress breeches and hose, his round face perspiring and merry, exhorting the dancers on to a faster pace as he whisked her down the middle to the tune of "The Rakes of Mallow." "View halloo and away!" The familiar voice rang in her ears. "The fox is traveling fast, but we'll catch him, won't we, Cecilia?"

She felt a warm glow of elation. What would that genial carouser think of her current campaign? She was sure he'd adore it. When it came to saving Kilwarden, he'd agree with her against Constance: Music and dancing worked better than fasting and prayer.

Chapter 6

Lucinda Headfort looked up from the dressing table as Cecilia entered the ladies' retiring room at Almack's. "Yes, do rest yourself, Miss Annesley. I vow, you've been danced off your feet. I've seldom heard so many waltzes played here at Almack's."

"I am quite worn out," admitted Cecilia. "All the same, I do adore waltzing. One feels so light and free, being whirled around the room in one's partner's arms."

"You've had some very good partners here tonight. But of course, as one of the reigning belles of the Season, you're quite accustomed to that fortunate condition."

"A reigning belle? I fear you're being too kind." Cecilia gave a deprecatory laugh. She didn't trust compliments from Lucinda Headfort.

"Oh, but you are!" insisted the petite, dark-haired girl. "It's quite remarkable, you must admit, for someone without any fortune to attract such a string of devoted followers. That handsome Sir Rodney Bellington, the Marquess of Garwood, who's usually so aloof—and now it appears that you've added Sir George to your list."

"Sir George Damien is a very good dancer, but I certainly wouldn't call him my 'follower.' Nor any of the others you mention, if it comes to that." Cecilia's voice had an edge of embarrassment. "As a matter of fact, I have made it plain to them all that I didn't come to London to find a husband."

"A clever stratagem, I must admit, though scarcely original. Mama, who's a veteran of many Seasons, has often remarked that there's always at least one young lady who attempts to distinguish herself by pretended indifference."

"With all due respect to Lady Headfort, in my case it's no pretense. I'm enjoying the Season immensely, I won't deny. But when I return to Ireland three weeks from now, I'll still be quite as unattached as when I arrived here."

Lucinda smiled, a pinched, malicious smile. "Perhaps the attachment may occur after you return there? As you followed Kilwarden here, perhaps he may be inclined to follow you back?"

Cecilia was startled. How had Lucinda guessed at her secret hope? She could scarcely have made her campaign so obvious. She hadn't yet had much chance to proceed with her plan of persuasion. The lively pace of Kilwarden's waltzing didn't often allow for gentle hints about farm improvements. And her one attempt to discuss the question of leases had been met with a determined volley of comments about that evening's performance of *Semiramide*.

Then she saw the sly glint in the dark-haired girl's eyes, and realized what she'd been insinuating. She gave a little gasp of consternation. "Surely you can't think that! Lord Kilwarden has been very kind, but he *is* my first cousin. There's no possible chance of the sort of attachment you hint at."

Lucinda raised a skeptical eyebrow. "So Mama was given to understand by Lady Annesley. She and I were inclined to believe it, before the start of the Season, but to judge from his recent behavior he may have changed his adamant views on the subject of dispensations."

"His recent behavior? What on earth do you mean? Surely you can't accuse him of any improper action?"

Lucinda shrugged expressively. "Improper? One couldn't say that. But I must admit I've noticed some telltale signs. The look in his eyes while he's dancing with you, for instance. Or the even more eloquent look while he watches you dance with Sir Rodney or the Marquess. The number of times in an evening he chooses to lead you out—"

"That's easily explained," broke in Cecilia. "He's only doing his duty in seeing that I don't lack a partner. Any gentleman would do as much for any cousin."

"Would he indeed?" Lucinda's rosebud lips tightened into

an ugly, stiff line. "Then what of his cousin Constance, who is clearly in far more danger of lacking a partner than you are?"

"This is ridiculous. You can't have been watching Constance tonight, or you'd know how often he's led her out to the floor."

"You're wrong; I have been watching. That's why I know he's danced twice as often with you."

Cecilia quickly cast her mind back over the evening. Could Lucinda's startling statement really be true? With a pang of dismay, she realized that she *had* spent much of the night dancing with Francis. And rather than waiting 'til he saw if she needed a partner, he had several times engaged her in advance. She'd already promised, for instance, that he should partner her in the next quadrille.

What a mindless chit she had been to allow this to happen! Surely she knew by now how much a show of attention could be blown up by the gossips into a serious attachment? Had she let her own personal pleasure in having him near her blind her to the impression she was making on others?

No; she couldn't fault herself there. She liked Francis well enough—much better, indeed than someone like Sir George Damien, whose hand, clasping her waist in the waltz, was inclined to wander a little too close to the bounds of propriety. But the reason she welcomed his invitations so warmly was the chance they provided for advancing his tenants' welfare. This next quadrille, for example—she had her speech all prepared, a casual mention of this morning's letter from Ireland, with its news of a score of evictions ordered by Mr. Quinlan.

She thanked her stars for Lucinda's malicious words. They had opened her eyes just in time. What she had noticed, others would notice, too; these rumors of a match with Kilwarden might already be spreading like wildfire. What if they came to *his* ears? Would he not leap to the natural conclusion— that despite his explicit warning, she still nourished hopes of enticing him into marriage?

She suppressed a small gasp of dismay as she realized what that would mean: an end to all hope of her campaign succeeding. Once that monstrous suspicion had gripped him, h̲ was bound to regard any comment about his estate as proof of her hidden intention to rule there as Lady Kilwarden.

She realized Lucinda was regarding her strangely. Had her silence confirmed the girl's jealous speculation? She made haste to thank her profusely for her timely warning, assuring her once more that her feelings toward Kilwarden were merely those of a cousin. Then she made her way back to Miss Stowe, intending to seek her support in extricating herself from her promised dance with Francis.

Kilwarden was waiting for her beside Miss Stowe's chair, with an eager look that made his long, lean face look positively boyish. Just as she reached him, the music struck up again in the gallery above them—no dashing waltz this time, but a stately quadrille.

Kilwarden advanced to greet her, but before she had the chance to stammer out her refusal, a stocky figure appeared at Miss Stowe's other elbow, his salmon-and-crimson striped waistcoat presenting an elegant contrast to his austerely cut bottle-green coat. "I hope you'll grant me the pleasure, Miss Annesley." Sir George's tone implied that he took her eager acceptance for granted.

"Your pardon, Sir George. My cousin's already engaged for this quadrille." Kilwarden's voice, too, was brimming with confidence.

Sir George's eyebrows lifted. "Your zeal for your cousin's welfare does you credit, Kilwarden. But since you apparently stand *in loco parentis,* don't you agree with me that a suitor might well take precedence over a blood relation?"

Kilwarden's frown showed how displeased he was with this turn of events. Before he could find an answer, Cecilia, steeling herself, stepped into the breach. "It was very kind of you to ask for this dance, Cousin Francis. But perhaps our cousin Constance has a greater claim on your kindness. I'm afraid she's already spent far too much time on the sidelines."

Kilwarden looked startled. He was sure Cecilia must know that Constance, as usual, had chosen to stay on the sidelines as much as she decently could. But Cecilia's appealing smile left no room for protest. With a curt, little nod, he turned away to look for his other cousin.

Sir George's arrogant smile was oozing with triumph. As

he led her out to the floor, Cecilia was astonished at her own sense of disappointment. Her distaste for Sir George swelled into outright detestation. What a callous swaggerer, full of overweening self-love! Her choosing him over Kilwarden had inflated his pride even further; he clearly believed that no woman could resist him.

If only he knew how she really regarded him: a convenient puppet to use for her own secret purpose. There was only one way to scotch those dangerous rumors—Kilwarden's cousin must appear to have formed an attachment to someone else. She wished now she'd managed to choose someone more congenial. But she'd had to make do with what Fate had placed ready to hand. Sir George, whatever his faults, possessed one decided advantage: knowing how poor she was, he would never conceive any serious thought of marriage.

Sir George, leaning over toward her, was whispering into her ear. She couldn't quite catch the words, but nevertheless she gave him an ardent smile. She hoped Kilwarden was watching her performance, and that he, like the rest of the *ton,* would quickly become convinced that she couldn't be setting her cap for her handsome cousin.

Kilwarden leaned on the stone balustrade of Lady Annesley's terrace and gazed meditatively out across her neat, formal garden, puffing a series of smoke rings into the soft May twilight. He'd already praised his aunt for the excellence of the cigars which had topped off her dinner. She had gracefully passed the compliment on to Cecilia, saying she was the one who had actually made the choice, having ordered the make that had been her father's favorite.

The dinner itself—the prelude to his aunt's ball in honor of Cecilia and Constance—had been unexpectedly pleasant. He didn't usually care for these Frenchified dishes, but that blanquette of veal had really been most delicious. Cecilia's touch again; she had instructed the cook in its preparation. She had, she explained, learned the French style of cooking from her mother, who had spent her schoolgirl days in a Viennese convent.

It amazed him now to remember how he'd dreaded this evening. Much as he liked his aunt, he usually found her dinners leaden and boring. He knew that, as head of the family, he could make no excuse to avoid this one, and had steeled himself to endure it as a matter of duty. His spirits had sunk even lower when he met Lady Annesley's guests before going to dinner. She seemed to have purposely chosen the stodgiest people in London.

To his great surprise, the table conversation had been delightful. Cecilia's touch once again, he realized now. She had a charming way of raising provocative subjects, then keeping the talk going with an occasional witty comment, accompanied by her infectious smile.

Miss Stowe had helped things along, with those priceless anecdotes, especially the one about the foxhounds getting drunk on champagne. The amusing way she mimicked the Irish country accent—imagine an English lady of similar years allowing herself to play the buffoon with such zest! Indeed, both she and Cecilia were generally much less stiff and starchy than their counterparts among the ladies of fashionable London.

Which was why, he supposed, he had found his cousin's company so agreeable, in contrast to that of the other young ladies he'd danced with this Season. He was always so much at ease when he talked to Cecilia. She had none of that anxious stiffness, that fervent desire to please, that calculated flirtatiousness which marred his other encounters. Of course he knew what underlay such behavior. Most English girls were intent on a single object: finding a husband.

Cecilia, too, was intent on a single object. He'd quickly seen through all those casual allusions and gentle hints. She was still obsessed with defending her father's methods. He already knew, after talking with Mr. Quinlan, how impractical those methods had proved to be. But one couldn't expect a woman to understand that—especially one with so tender a heart as Cecilia's.

How vividly she'd described that one tenant family—the thin, exhausted mother, sacrificing her own share of food to her hungry children; the desperate father, walking the roads in search of a day's paid labor. Mr. Quinlan had made it clear how clever the Irish were at fabricating such stories to cover up their shiftless lazy habits. Sweet, unworldly Cecilia evidently believed all they told her. Remembering her flushed, troubled face, the film of tears clouding her amethyst eyes, he felt a surge of protective tenderness.

A burst of music startled him out of his musing. With a little qualm of guilt, he realized that the ball must have started without him. He quickly stubbed out his cigar and tossed it away. If he hurried into the ballroom, he might still be in time to lead Cecilia out in the first quadrille.

But when he stepped through the tall French doors into the elegant room, brilliantly lit with wax lights in its three crystal chandeliers, he found the dancing already in full swing. He searched the room for Cecilia, and finally saw her, forming one half of a couple in the long line of dancers. The other half of the couple was Sir George Damien.

He found her choice of a partner distinctly distasteful. This wasn't the first time he'd noticed that Cecilia seemed to encourage Sir George's attentions. Others had noticed it, too; he'd walked into a group at Brooks's the day before and heard them mention "Miss Annesley's latest catch." They had all frozen up when they saw him, and changed the subject, but he knew the sort of talk Sir George's amorous exploits were wont to evoke. The man had a most unsavory reputation. Why hadn't his shrewd Aunt Lydia warned Cecilia against him? He must find a chance to speak to his aunt tonight, and try to determine how serious the attachment had become. He felt a pang of remorse; he had clearly been neglecting his cousinly duty.

The thought of "cousinly duty" reminded him that he had another cousin. He scanned the room again and located Constance, seated between her mother and Miss Stowe. What a thoughtless fool he was! He should have sought her out the moment he entered the ballroom.

He made his way over to the three ladies, and persuaded Constance to let him lead her out. Despite her disdain for the "frivolous pastime," she had learned to dance very well; her graceful movements would have made his "cousinly duty" most delightful were it not for her dreary subjects of conversation. Tonight she insisted on dredging up one of Hannah More's fables, repeating it practically word by pious word, droning on about how "honest poverty" and "barefoot children" and "leaking thatches." How could he be expected to interest himself in such boring drivel?

You didn't find it boring when Cecilia spoke of such things. Remember how attractive she seemed to you then? The thought of the amethyst eyes and the flushed, rosy face impelled him to scan the line of dancers ahead for Cecilia's graceful figure, clothed tonight in a cloud of white tulle over myrtle green gros-de-Naples.

The music came to a stop just as he saw her. She and Sir George were standing near the French doors that led out to the terrace. His first impulse was to lead Constance toward them and suggest an exchange of partners, but he quickly realized that was out of the question. He could scarcely fulfil his duty to Cecilia by exposing his cousin Constance to Damien's dubious attentions.

Uncertain what to do, he kept his eyes fixed on the girl in the myrtle green gown. She was smiling up at Sir George in a highly flirtatious manner, tilting her chin and using her fan in an artificial way he had never observed before. His acute disquiet swelled to distinct alarm as he saw her nod, accept Sir George's arm, and step out into the darkness of the terrace.

He found himself waiting tensely, hoping that she had merely gone out for a breath of air. Surely she couldn't be so indiscreet as to walk with a notorious rake alone in the garden! Especially tonight, at the ball designed for her official presentation, with the eyes of fashionable London focused upon her.

The moments passed in a leaden procession, while Constance droned on at his side about "hard-earned bread" and "hearts grown weary with toil." He had clearly delayed too long in his duty to warn Cecilia, but he might repair some of the damage by changing that indiscreet twosome into a foursome.

"Dear Cousin Constance," he said abruptly. "I know you've no taste for dancing. Shall we escape to the garden before they strike up again?" Constance's eyes grew wide with unspoken questions. It was not like Kilwarden to cater so graciously to what he called her "puritan notions." But the chance of escaping more dancing was too good a one to resist; she quickly assented and moved with him toward the terrace.

The light was fading fast, but the sky was still bright enough to illumine two figures, silhouetted against a dark stand of cypress. Kilwarden was just about to call to them from the terrace, when he saw a sight that filled him with consternation. Sir George's hand was grasping Cecilia's chin, gently tilting her face up to his own. She was making no move to resist him. Her eyes were trustingly closed, her lips softly parted, as Sir George's lips came down, obviously about to bestow the kiss she so clearly expected.

Shocked to the core, Kilwarden moved quickly to block Constance's view of the garden, then pulled her back into the ballroom, hoping to spare her the sight of her cousin's indiscretion. He escorted her back to the corner where Miss Stowe and her mother were sitting, and abuptly demanded a moment of Lady Annesley's time. The thundercloud look on his face persuaded the lady that the matter he wished to confer on was extremely serious. Confiding her daughter to the care of the watchful Miss Stowe, she retired to her little study with her seething nephew.

"What a filthy, underhand trick!" Cecilia struggled free of Sir George's grasp. A stinging slap on his cheek made a sharp burst of sound in the quiet garden. He quickly stepped back out of range, smiling down at her in amusement. "My dear Miss Annesley, why all this indignation? When I see a girl turn her face up to me as you did, I assume she expects to be kissed."

"You know very well that's not so. I turned up my face to let you remove a smut you informed me you saw on my cheek. It never occurred to me that a *gentleman* would abuse my trust in this despicable fashion."

"Just a minute, my dear. You're not such an innocent as you pretend. You can hardly deny that you've been leading me on most outrageously. All those inviting smiles and languishing looks, those artful maneuvers to place yourself where I can't help but ask you to dance—they've convinced half of London you're madly in love with me. Can I be blamed if I've cherished the same impression?"

His self-assured tone forced Cecilia to reconsider her angry retort. It *was* true she'd led him on. She'd been so intent on disarming Kilwarden's suspicions that she hadn't considered the effect of her ardent playacting on this amorous rake. And now what a pretty pickle she found herself in! There was only one thing to do: dispel Sir George's illusions without further delay.

"There's some justice in what you say, sir. I suppose I did lead you on. But my motive in doing so had nothing to do with love. Those sighs and looks were a calculated show. By pretending an interest in you, I hoped to be spared the attention of other suitors."

Sir George looked slightly puzzled and a little deflated. "You're saying you pretended a counterfeit attachment to avoid a real one? My dear Miss Annesley, even you must be able to see that doesn't make sense."

Cecilia sighed with frustration. "Let me put it quite bluntly. My principal desire at the moment is *not* to be married. Therefore I decided to counterfeit an attachment to a man I was sure would never propose to me."

Sir George arched a quizzical eyebrow. "What makes you so surè I wouldn't make you an offer? A pretty, accomplished girl like yourself might make quite a suitable Lady Damien."

"Oh, come now, Sir George, be honest. You'd never consider a girl without a fortune."

A glint of cunning appeared in Sir George's eyes. "I admit such a marriage would be the height of folly. But the thought of further delights such as I've just tasted might very well make me swerve from the path of wisdom."

Cecilia's face flamed. "You're insufferable, sir. I see I must break off all communication between us." She hurried away from him onto the terrace. Sir George stayed in the garden, following her with his gaze until she disappeared into the lighted ballroom.

An original minx, this pretty Miss Annesley. He wasn't at all misled by her show of temper. The wench was still leading him on; she'd merely switched to a cleverer way of going about it. How well she'd assessed his nature; the role of the hunter was much more exciting to him than that of the quarry. And what a clever ploy, to be so forthright about her lack of a fortune. She was quite right, of course; he couldn't afford to marry anyone but an heiress. No doubt she was hoping these tricks of hers would inflame him to such a pitch that he'd toss away all discretion.

Very well; he'd nourish those hopes. What man knew better than he how to bait the hook without being caught himself? This provoking girl would learn, like a score of others, that in the amusing game of playing with fire, George Damien was the player who always emerged unsinged.

"I quite agree with you, Francis. I shall have to speak to Cecilia." Lady Annesley absentmindedly fingered the little china pastille burner that served for a paperweight on her writing desk. "But I don't understand why you've turned so livid with horror. Aren't you blowing this whole affair up quite out of proportion?"

"You wouldn't say that if you saw what I saw, Aunt Lydia. She was clearly leading him on in the most shocking way."

"You're very quick to accuse her of improper conduct. Does it not occur to you that she might have a perfectly innocent explanation?"

"To encourage that notorious rake to embrace her? What possible excuse could she give for that?"

Lady Annesley's face relaxed in a knowing smile. "Rakes have been known to reform under the influence of a sufficiently charming woman. Perhaps our Cecilia had just received an honorable offer?"

Kilwarden gaped at her, transfixed by shock. It was true such an explanation hadn't occurred to him. He was aware he should have been feeling some sense of relief at his aunt's suggestion, and was surprised to find he felt more disturbed than ever. "I can't believe Sir George would ever do that. He knows of Cecilia's penniless situation."

"You men are all the same—always believing the worst. You won't believe that a man like Sir George could reform, but you're quite prepared to believe your cousin has lapsed from virtue."

"I wasn't condemning Cecilia," protested Francis. "I was merely concerned to rescue her from a dangerous situation. So you really profess to believe he has made an offer? Surely you've been apprised of his unsavory reputation?"

Lady Annesley gave her nephew a shrewd, level look. "Are

you so insensible to Cecilia's charms that you can't imagine a man falling in love with her?"

"Of course not." Francis rushed to defend himself against her charge. "She's a most attractive young lady. I might fall in love with her myself, if she weren't my cousin."

A flicker of quiet amusement stirred in Lady Annesley's eyes. "I'm glad you admit it, Kilwarden. Then surely you'll grant Cecilia the benefit of the doubt? After all, wasn't that your main motive in bringing Cecilia to London—to help her find herself a suitable husband?"

"I don't consider Sir George a suitable husband for a pure and innocent girl like my cousin Cecilia." The words burst out with a startling vehemence, but Lady Annesley's composure remained unruffled.

"My, my, what a truly paternal depth of feeling. But I'm sure you'll agree that the choice must be up to Cecilia?"

A trace of steel had crept into her voice. Kilwarden had a galling sense of having been subtly forced into a false position. "Of course the choice must be hers. But we must be sure she's really been offered a choice. I shall call on Sir George tomorrow and demand to know his intentions."

Lady Annesley raised a commanding hand in protest. "I forbid you to do that, Francis. Such a precipitous act might very well put an end to Cecilia's chances. Believe me, I know much more of these matters than you do. There's a stage in every courtship where the two young people involved have arrived at an understanding, but have not yet reached the point of a definite offer."

"But my duty to Cecilia—"

"Does not excuse such clumsy interference. No, not another word." Lady Annesley rose from her desk and smoothed out her skirts, clearly intending to make her way back to the ballroom. "Leave Cecilia to me. If she's really blundered into a dangerous situation, I'm sure I can trust her to listen to my advice. And now, my dear Francis, please wipe that scowl off your face before we return to the dancers. After all, it's Cecilia's great night. I won't allow even my dearly loved nephew to spoil it for her."

"You wanted to see me, Aunt Lydia?" Cecilia paused at the door of the morning room, wondering at the cause of this unprecedented summons.

Lady Annesley laid down her needle and pushed the embroidery frame to the side of her chair. "Yes, child. How are you this morning? I forbade the servants to wake you at the usual hour. I knew you'd need your sleep, after last night's excitement."

Cecilia slipped into the room and seated herself on a footstool beside her aunt. "To tell you the truth, I didn't sleep very well. I was plagued with a host of very confusing dreams."

Lady Annesley nodded sagely. "That's not surprising, after all that champagne. Or was there, perhaps, a certain young man who made a special claim on your thoughts last night?"

Cecilia averted her face to hide her confusion. Could Aunt Lydia have guessed that most of those dreams had been of Francis? Or that the hours of wakefulness that followed the dreams had been spent fretting about his early departure and the cold, almost hostile tone in which he had bid her good night?

She managed to stammer out a few words of denial. They merely confirmed Lady Annesley's conviction that a serious talk with the girl was long overdue. "My dear Cecilia, I don't like to pry into your affairs. But when things come to the point of a serious proposal, I have a mother's responsibility to advise you."

"A serious proposal? Oh, no Aunt Lydia. I assure you there's no question of that."

Lady Annesley sighed. This interview was going to be difficult. She'd better stop skirting the edges and come to the heart of the matter. "A certain person whom I have reason to trust told me he saw you kissing George Damien in the garden."

Cecilia's face flushed. "That odious man! How was I to know it was all a trick? He told me there was a smut on my cheek. When I turned up my face so he could remove it, he had the insufferable gall to kiss me."

Lady Annesley was greatly relieved. Despite her pretense of calm, Francis's report last night had caused her some perturbation. It was not that she had any doubts about Cecilia's discretion; she trusted the girl to take care of herself. But she'd begun to form certain plans for Francis's future which would be seriously undermined if Cecilia's affections were to veer in another direction.

She decided to test the ground a little further. "It was very naughty of him, the way you describe it. But young men must sometimes resort to these stratagems. Don't fear to shock me, Cecilia. Quite apart from the propriety of the thing, didn't you rather enjoy it?"

"Enjoy it? Being kissed by that awful man? I absolutely detest him. I told him that in so many words. I shan't even speak to him from this day forward."

Lady Annesley smiled at her fondly. "Thank you, my dear, for confiding in me so frankly. My mind is at ease on the matter. And I'm sure your cousin Francis will be quite relieved to receive this explanation."

"Cousin Francis!" Cecilia was horror-stricken. "He was the person who saw us? But surely he must have seen me slap Sir George's face?"

"Apparently he didn't linger that long. I gather he thought you rather invited the kiss."

Cecilia buried her crimson face in her hands. "How can I face him again! I shall die of embarrassment. My dear Aunt Lydia, you will explain it all, won't you? Or do you think I should speak for myself? I don't know how I could endure that, but if I have to, I'll do it. No matter what it costs me, I must erase this dreadful misconception."

"Oh, no, you needn't do that." It didn't suit Lady Annesley's book to have Kilwarden's mind set *too* much at ease. "That might blow the thing up out of all proportion. I would strongly advise you to let time take its course. I shall explain to Francis all that he needs to know. Now, my dear, I need *your* advice. What's the best shade of thread for this other pansy? The heliotrope, do you think, or do you suppose we ought to try the magenta?"

Chapter 7

The puffy white clouds sailed past in a brilliant June sky. Miss Stowe and Cecilia strolled slowly across the clipped, green lawns of Lady deRoos's grand estate by the river. "My dear Cecilia, admit it; you've never seen anything back in Ireland to match that pavilion. What a magnificent gesture— to build a whole oriental palace just for one evening of dancing. And that sumptuous tent where we'll be dining—it's easily large enough for five hundred people."

"Yes, Miss Stowe, it's all quite splendid." Cecilia was making an effort to match her companion's rapture, but her heart wasn't in it. They had certainly spared no expense, the five noble gentlemen who had planned this open-air fête. But she couldn't help calculating how much those hundreds of pounds might have done to relieve her tenants' distress back at Kilwarden.

Perhaps she should have joined Constance in her firm refusal to attend an occasion of such "ostentatious display." But Miss Stowe had been growing so melancholic at the thought of leaving London that Cecilia had not had the heart to deprive her of this last crowning touch to the Season.

Miss Stowe, oblivious of Cecilia's halfhearted response, was rattling on about the plans for the evening. "You see those gondolas, moored by the steps of the dancing pavilion? The great Caradori will be singing barcaroles as he drifts about on the river. There's talk that Madame Vestris herself will be one of the entertainers. Can't you see it now? All these charming groves lit up with their colored lanterns, the cream

79

of London in all their handsome apparel, the King himself lending his august presence—"

"I'm sure it will be quite nice," said Cecilia impatiently. "But just at the moment, it looks like a stage set without any actors."

Miss Stowe looked a trifle crestfallen. "That was my mistake, I'm afraid. Lady Annesley warned me that very few people would come at the opening hour of two o'clock. But I didn't realize we'd appear so conspicuous. What a shame we dismissed the carriage. We might have bided our time there discreetly until the festivities were really under way."

"And wouldn't that have been a miserable way to spend this fine afternoon?" Cecilia was touched with remorse at the blight her comment had cast on Miss Stowe's enjoyment. She cast about for a way to repair the damage. The sight of a groom leading a thoroughbred Arab seemed like an answer from Heaven. "I have it," she cried. "Let's ask to visit the stables. Lady deRoos, I hear, is quite proud of her taste in horseflesh. I recall dear Papa mentioning her quite often. It was she, if I'm not mistaken, who took the last of the colts sired by dear old Principio. Shall we go try to pick him out, and see how he's thriving here in his English stable?"

Miss Stowe, a keen horsewoman too, strongly approved the plan. Arrangements were quickly made, and soon Cecilia and she, accompanied by one of the grooms, were eagerly oohing and ah-ing, as they pointed out to each other the particular beauties of Boyle Farm's equine population.

"Look at that chestnut gelding," trilled Miss Stowe. "Isn't he a real beauty? A little thick in fat about the crest, but his legs are clean as a whistle."

"He's a very nice horse," agreed Cecilia, "but isn't there a splint on his right hind leg?"

"May I congratulate you on your keen eye, Miss Annesley," said a familiar voice behind her. Cecilia, startled, turned to find Lord Kilwarden smiling at her in approval. "I noted the blemish myself, but very few of my friends would have been expert enough to spot it."

Cecilia forced a smile, feeling extremely awkward. She'd been avoiding Kilwarden, ever since that unhappy night in Aunt Lydia's garden. Even the thought of helping Kilwarden's tenants had not been inducement enough to dispel her embarrassment. She was sure her aunt had made some suitable explanation; otherwise he wouldn't have been beaming at her in so friendly a fashion. He must have noticed, too, how very distantly she'd treated Sir George ever since that evening. But try as she might to comfort herself with such thoughts, the memory of the humiliating scene still rankled, forming a shadowy barrier between herself and her cousin.

Once more, as she'd done a score of times, she chided herself for being foolish, and did her best to respond to him in a frank and natural manner. "What do you think of this sorrel mare?" she heard him ask, moving down to the neighboring stall.

"A little wall-eyed, isn't she, but that doesn't hurt a coach horse. She has the shoulders to make a very good leader."

"An excellent guess," said Kilwarden admiringly. "I noticed her yesterday in the Park, drawing Lady deRoos's fine new barouche."

As they moved from stall to stall, Cecilia grew more at ease. Kilwarden chattered on in an eager fashion, revealing a deep and expert knowledge of horseflesh. She found her own share in the conversation reduced to smiling assents and admiring murmurs. She felt a momentary disquiet when she saw Miss Stowe draw the groom away, ostensibly to discuss the merits of a spotted barb in the next line of stalls. Had she given her chaperone the impression that she had some intimate matter to discuss with Francis? She felt her cheeks flush and turned her head away, hiding her perturbation by laying her cheek against a handsome gray gelding's silky forehead.

Kilwarden, observing the gesture, found it extremely charming. Cecilia's love for horses was obviously genuine, quite unlike the forced enthusiasm of certain other young ladies, Lucinda Headfort among them. What a lucky chance, meeting her here in the stables, where their common interest in livestock had helped to restore the easy companionship he'd found so very pleasant up to that unfortunate moment in Aunt Lydia's garden.

He wished now he'd forced his aunt to be more candid about that situation. It wasn't quite good enough merely to be assured that Cecilia was not in danger of being disgraced. He should have found out more clearly if the courtship were on or off. Cecilia's obvious coolness in Damien's presence had almost persuaded him there was nothing between them. But if that was the case, why did he still seem so ardent? Cecilia, he realized, was not quite the artless creature he'd thought her at first. Could it be this assumed disdain was merely a way of retaining Sir George's interest?

Whatever the facts of that matter, the awkwardness between himself and his pretty Irish cousin had cast a decided cloud over the past few weeks. If only he could stretch out this happy encounter through the whole afternoon! He cast an inquiring glance along the long line of stalls, seeking a topic to keep conversation alive. "I say," he exclaimed in delight, "look down there under the hayloft. That handsome black stallion is Roman Oak. A marvelous racer; he's said to be a sure thing for this year's St. Leger."

That attractive dimpled smile. How pleasant to see it again. "We've already made his acquaintance, Miss Stowe and I. Would you be surprised to learn that he, like myself, is a native of Kilwarden? His sire and dam were two of my father's best horses."

Kilwarden was clearly astonished. "Your father sold him to Lady deRoos? I had no idea he kept such expensive stock. That horse must be worth a good two thousand. But of course, as a colt he might have been had quite cheaply; it's the schooling that makes him such a valuable animal."

The schooling won't go far without good bloodlines. Cecilia bit back the words with an effort. What would it do to become antagonistic? Mr. Quinlan must have deceived him about the value of Papa's horses, no doubt as part of some scheme to fill his own pockets. But she knew by now what would happen if she ventured any remark against his agent. Kilwarden would feel his prerogatives being threatened, and this pleasant warmth between them would congeal to an awkward coolness.

"He's obviously benefited from his schooling," she murmured submissively. "As you say, his price now must be twenty times what he fetched as a colt." A sudden analogy popped into her mind. Without taking time to consider, she

82

heard herself saying, in a voice that was rather too pert, "Just as Mairtin O'Grady's two acres, now that he's drained them, fetch ten times as much for his landlord as when they were bogland."

She stopped abruptly, already regretting her impulsive comment. What was the point of reviving that futile campaign? Didn't she already know how useless it was? Now Kilwarden's face would close up in sudden aloofness, and he'd find some quick, polite way of ending the conversation.

She glanced warily up at her cousin, braced for his icy reserve, and was surprised to find a thoughtful look in his eyes. He seemed to be giving her comment his serious consideration. Emboldened by a sudden upsurge of hope, she adopted a jesting tone and pushed the analogy further. "What a pity my dear Papa couldn't have leased the colt to Lady deRoos instead of selling him outright. Then as Roman Oak improved, Papa could have raised his rent, so that he'd have an income reflecting the colt's improved value."

"A most amusing notion." Kilwarden's wry smile let her know he was quite aware of the jest's serious purpose. "But surely that state of affairs would be quite unjust. He'd be taking advantage of Lady deRoos's labor."

She gave him an eloquent look in lieu of an answer. With a surge of elation, she saw the flush rise to his cheeks, and a look of perturbation appear in his eyes. "I see what you mean, Cecilia. You've caught me out fairly. It may be *I'm* reaping a profit from other men's labor when I charge an increased rent once the land is improved. Perhaps I should have raised the point with Mr. Quinlan. I must write him today and ask for an explanation."

Cecilia found herself wracked with two conflicting emotions: joy that she'd finally reached him with her point of view; despair at the thought of Mr. Quinlan's answer. She had no doubt at all that the wily agent would provide his employer with some glib explanation, dispelling the nagging doubts she'd manage to raise in his mind.

Kilwarden, observing her silence, made a good guess at its cause. "I know you don't think much of Mr. Quinlan's advice. I assure you I won't swallow it blindly. When his answer comes, I'll bring it to you at once, and give you a chance for rebuttal."

He smiled fondly down at his cousin, obscurely pleased at the thought that he might be justified in agreeing with her on this point. The look was lost on Cecilia, who saw her miniature victory turning to ashes.

"A generous offer, Francis, but I won't be here to debate Mr. Quinlan's answer. Have you forgotten that tonight marks the close of the Season?"

"But surely you'll stay in London a few more weeks?" Kilwarden was surprised to find how strongly he objected to Cecilia's leaving. "Now that the Season is over, why not spend some time at your leisure with the family to whom you've finally been restored? I'm sure Aunt Lydia is eager to have you stay on. And your cousin Constance, who calls you her only true friend—"

Cecilia's eyes clouded with sadness. "You've all been so kind to me. But I can't impose any further on my London family. If only my mother and I were in a position to show my dear aunt the same hospitality. How I wish that she and Constance could visit us at Kilwarden. But I fear that is out of the question, as things stand now."

"Out of the question? Why is it out of the question? I think it's a fine idea." Kilwarden's imagination, aroused by Cecilia's words, was taking the bit in its teeth and plunging ahead at a rapid pace. "You'd have to move up to the Great House, of course, and let me help with expenses."

Cecilia was startled and pleased with his sudden enthusiasm. That generous offer again! Why not accept it? She could continue her acquaintance with her aunt and Constance, Lady Margaret would take her place in the family circle. And perhaps—who could tell—the experience would be so pleasant that Kilwarden himself would be lured to join the party.

At the thought that Francis might join them, a bright new vista suddenly opened before her. Perhaps the campaign was not lost! Perhaps it had just begun. Kilwarden wouldn't go to Ireland for the love of his tenants—but the love of his aunt and cousin might be a successful inducement. And once she had him in Ireland, where Kilwarden's tenants were living, breathing flesh, instead of a series of figures in the monthly accounting...

Careful, Cecilia. You mustn't appear too eager. "The more I consider it, the more possible it seems." She flashed him a grateful smile. "You're sure you don't mind our using Kilwarden House?"

But Francis, too, had been doing some rapid thinking. "Kilwarden House is yours to use as you please, so long as I hold the title. But thinking back on my visit, I begin to have serious doubts. Do you think my cousin and aunt should be asked to endure its rigors? The shortage of fuel, the unfortunate lack of trained servants—such drawbacks, I fear, would severely limit their comfort."

"A shortage of fuel at Kilwarden? I find that most surprising." She wasn't really surprised, but she knew this wasn't the moment to raise any awkward questions about Mr. Quinlan. "There were always magnificent fires there when Papa was alive."

"I'm afraid that's not the case now. Mr. Quinlan says the people have grown too lazy to cut enough turf for the winter. The supply was so nearly exhausted that we had to make do with the merest wisp of a fire."

Cecilia flushed with resentment at the agent's slur on her hardworking tenants. The turf shed stacked full to the roof, and he said the supply was exhausted! But she mustn't dispute the point now; what could she say that would reassure her cousin without placing any blame on Mr. Quinlan? "Now that I think of it, the turf did tend to run low at the end of the winter." She excused herself for the lie with the thought of the good cause it served. "With time enough in advance to get the summer's turf well in hand, I'm sure we can keep the house comfortable for Aunt Lydia's visit. Now, as to the lack of trained servants, we'd have to add to the staff. Nora and Peggy are splendid workers, but old Thady's growing quite feeble."

Kilwarden cocked a quizzical eyebrow. "Nora and little Peggy seemed very eager to please, but their primitive background has scarcely prepared them to serve in a civilized house. They've never managed to learn how to make up a bed or to clean a room."

Mr. Quinlan's lies again! Cecilia was seething now. But she managed to swallow her temper and say with a gentle smile, "I'm sure there must have been some sort of misunderstanding. You must take my word for it, Francis: those servants were trained by my mother, and could serve quite creditably in any great house in London. There are twenty more just as good whom we were forced to dismiss when we left the Great House. It's merely a matter of making the proper selection. Mr. Quinlan can't be expected to know who's suitable. One can easily understand the mistake he made during your visit in hiring Sheila Ryan instead of Sheila Reilly."

A look of relief spread over Kilwarden's face. "That wasn't the cook you mentioned? I admit I found her cooking quite execrable."

"I'm sure it was revolting," agreed Cecilia. "Sheila Reilly, let me assure you, is an excellent cook. My mother declares she surpasses the chef who taught her in Vienna."

For a brief, mouth-watering instant, Francis remembered the excellent blanquette of veal. "You've set my mind at ease. With you and your charming mother supervising the kitchen, I'm sure my aunt and my cousin will dine superbly." Kilwarden's first enthusiasm flared up again. That beautifully furnished house, with Lady Margaret and Cecilia acting as hostesses! "It begins to sound tremendously appealing. Would you think me too presumptuous if I asked you to add my name to your list of guests?"

Cecilia felt her heart begin to beat wildly. Could this really be happening? Did he seriously mean to pay Ireland another visit? Would she have her second chance to convince Kilwarden? She concealed her breathless delight under a formal smile. "My mother and I will be pleased to be *your* guests, Lord Kilwarden. I hope that our presence under your hospitable roof will help make this visit more comfortable than your last one. And when shall it be, our family house party? Don't you think we should set a date before I leave London?"

"We'll set it this minute," said Francis. It suddenly seemed extremely important that Cecilia should not have a chance to disappear before some definite arrangement was made for their future meeting. "The sooner the better, so far as I am

86

concerned. Perhaps we should make it the middle of August? If I came for a month or so then, that would give me plenty of time to get back to Buckinghamshire for the harvest season."

Cecilia thought swiftly. The idea of so quick a reunion seemed very pleasant—but was August a suitable time to pursue her secret campaign? Wouldn't Kilwarden in summer provide a sorry contrast to its landlord's well-tended English estates? But Kilwarden in fall, with the hounds in full cry, and a field of Irish hunters soaring in effortless leaps over four-foot stone fences—that was a prospect no county in England could match.

"August might be too soon," she said cautiously. "With the house sitting empty so long, we must allow plenty of time for our preparations."

"Shall we say September, then?" There was no mistaking Kilwarden's eagerness.

"We mustn't take you away from your English harvest." Cecilia smiled up at him demurely. "I'm sure your tenants would sorely regret your absence at so crucial a time of year. But after the harvest is over—" She stopped abruptly, as though the idea had come as a bolt from the blue. "What a perfect solution! Our cub-hunting season starts in early October. The very thing; we'll make it a hunting party. How pleased our neighbors will be when the new Lord Kilwarden rides out with the Kilwarden pack!"

A shadow of doubt ruffled Kilwarden's forehead. "For myself, I should like nothing better. But what of Aunt Lydia and Constance? Won't they find it quite dull at that time of year?"

Cecilia was taken aback. In her zeal to impress Kilwarden, she'd completely forgotten the distaff side of the party. "Dull? Not a bit of it," she answered boldly. "Aunt Lydia's often told me that she'd love to go hunting again. It was only Sir Edgar's wish that kept her from joining the field with the Quorn or the Pytchley."

"Really? That's very surprising. I had no idea she cared that much for the sport."

"Naturally, Cousin Constance is adamant against it." Cecilia made haste to change the subject, not wanting to delve too deeply into Lady Annesley's supposed love for hunting. "But then, dear Constance is opposed to most forms of entertainment. However, I have some plans which should keep her happily occupied as well."

Francis smiled down at her with wry amusement. "It's hard to imagine a *happy* Constance. But considering the way her spirits have improved since you've come to London, I'm sure you'll be able to keep her less miserable than usual."

"You do agree then?" Cecilia said eagerly. "The house party is set for mid-October? You won't regret it, I'm sure. Hunting in Ireland is a far more challenging sport than it is in England."

"So I've heard from some of my friends. It's a tempting proposal to dangle before a sportsman. But before we make the decision, we must think a little more about ways and means. What will we do for horses? Shall I bring my own string across? They might have a stormy passage at that time of year."

"No need for that." Cecilia's mind was awhirl with elation. "We can borrow some from the neighbors. Count O'Hanrahan, I'm sure, would be glad to oblige us. Wait 'til you see how his Daybreak takes the fences! Or his chestnut mare, Disturbance. I'd match those two against anything here in Lady deRoos's stables."

Kilwarden was finding Cecilia's elation contagious. The hunting party seemed more and more attractive. And she'd already proved herself an excellent judge of horseflesh. "If *you* say they're excellent hunters, I'm sure I won't be disappointed. But what makes you so sure that the count will fall in with your wishes? Your other neighbors as well; perhaps they won't share your enthusiasm? Remember the very cool welcome I received on my previous visit."

Cecilia was sorely tempted to throw caution to the winds and explain Mr. Quinlan's share in that lack of a welcome. But with this enticing prospect almost within her grasp, she knew she must tread more carefully than ever. "I've been hoping to have a chance to explain that unfortunate matter. The sad truth is that someone made a mistake. Not one of the guests on your list received your invitation, and the three who ventured to call to bid you welcome were turned away from your door—apparently on your specific instructions."

"I never gave such instructions." Kilwarden looked truly appalled. "What an arrogant boor they must think me! The servants must have misunderstood Mr. Quinlan's orders. Since I don't speak their difficult language, I had to rely on him to transmit my intentions."

When all the house servants speak English as well as myself? Only the sight of his evident distress restrained Cecilia from denouncing the odious Quinlan. He looked extremely perturbed about the alleged "mistake." "I've attempted to smooth things over," she hastened to reassure him. "I've explained to them all about your intended dinner, and assured them their cool reception was some sort of mistake. They told me they quite understood, and would not let one unfortunate lapse affect their relations with you. Even the count's formidable temper appeared to be mollified, especially when I explained how much you love hunting."

"I'm extremely pleased to hear it. Just the other day at my club, I heard his name mentioned by someone who served with him in the Austrian forces. He is said to be a man of considerable valor—and considerable temper as well."

Cecilia smiled. "His bark is worse than his bite. I feel quite certain you'll find him extremely congenial."

"I'm sure I shall." Kilwarden smiled warmly. "Especially since you'll be presiding over our meeting. I'm inclined to believe that the most unlikely companions would quickly become congenial in the warmth of your presence."

Cecilia acknowledged the speech with a heartfelt smile. "I sincerely hope I shall justify that faith," she said demurely. "The matter is settled, then? We're all to be at Kilwarden by the fifteenth of October?"

"The fifteenth of October," Kilwarden assented firmly. "Provided, of course, that your aunt and cousin agree. They didn't accompany you this afternoon? Perhaps I should call and give them the news at once."

"Leave the fête before it's begun? Oh, Francis, you couldn't do that." Cecilia had no doubts at all of her aunt's acceptance. But first she would have to confess her gentle deception in the matter of that alleged secret passion for hunting.

To her great relief, he was easily persuaded. "I suppose it would be impolite to leave this early. Especially since I'm invited to dine with the royal party. Will you and Miss Stowe consent to accompany me there? I'm sure I can arrange for your invitations."

"To dine with the King himself!" exclaimed Cecilia. "Oh, Francis, how wonderful! The perfect climax to my delightful Season in London."

He smiled and offered his arm. "Shall we go see what's happening down at the river pavilion?"

She looked around for Miss Stowe, and found her a stall away, apparently still absorbed in her study of horseflesh. "Dear Miss Stowe," trilled Cecilia. "You'll never believe what's happened! We've been invited to dine with the royal party. And Lord Kilwarden is coming to hunt in Ireland. Won't that be a grand surprise for Mr. Barlow?"

As the two Irish ladies, escorted by Lord Kilwarden, emerged again into the sunlight, Sir George Damien stepped from the shadow of Roman Oak's stall. What a fortunate chance that he'd come to size up the stallion before placing his bets. He'd finally seen through the game that sly minx was playing. She'd been *using* him for her own cunning purpose, using him as a decoy to challenge Kilwarden's interest. Now that she had her quarry, she thought she could cast him aside.

The cold eyes narrowed to slits. The fleshy jaw jutted grimly. *No one plays such games with Sir George Damien.* It was time that presumptuous girl was taught a lesson—and he knew the perfect way to go about it. When she took to the field in Ireland next October, the proud Miss Annesley would be riding for a fall.

Chapter 8

"Have you heard the latest delicious morsel about Lady Brandon?" Lady Headfort's high-pitched voice strained to be heard over the rattling coach wheels. "Those letters her husband found from Mr. Lamb? As I've always told my Lucinda, such peccadilloes are bound to come to light sooner or later." She cast a fond glance at her daughter, who was gazing dreamily out the window, completely ignoring the other three occupants of the handsomely-appointed traveling carriage. "Still, one must admit, it makes one regard the lady with a certain interest."

Lady Lydia Annesley leaned back in the jolting coach and stared glumly out at the mountain landscape. Good Lord, would this silly woman never stop talking? As if the long journey wasn't fatiguing enough, with that execrable inn last night in Bangor, and the dismal ordeal of the crossing yet to come.

It was all her own fault, of course. If she hadn't been so keyed up with anticipation, she'd never have dropped the fatal remark. But how could she have dreamed that this rattlebrained bore and her daughter would be visiting Ireland during October, too? As it was, she'd been taken off guard, and had accepted the invitation to share the Headfort carriage on the journey to Holyhead. If she'd only had time to think, she would have chosen the public stagecoach as the far lesser evil.

Now that she'd *had* time to think, she was growing surer and surer that there was something very strange about the situation. Lady Headfort's sly smile, oozing with some hidden triumph, and those assessing glances she kept casting toward her Lucinda—she'd seen them before, playing an arch obbligato to a breathless account of some splendid forthcoming offer, an offer which thus far had never materialized. One would almost think she'd invented her Irish cousin and this opportune invitation to spend the hunt season thirty miles from Kilwarden House and its highly eligible master. But that was absurd; the cousin was perfectly real. His traveling carriage would meet Lady Headfort at Kingston. The wearying bore and her daughter would drive off to this obscure place called Killashee, while she and Constance pursued their journey in peace. No doubt the girl would turn up in her hunting pink; thirty miles wasn't far for riders to come to a meet. Kilwarden would be obliged to invite her to dinner, perhaps several dinners, even a ball or two. What a slender foundation for all those maternal hopes!

She was sorry for poor Lucinda. The girl was really quite pleasant when she was among other women. It was only when men appeared that she suddenly turned to a chattering, simpering doll. To think she'd once worried that Francis might find her attractive! Now she knew that was out of the question. Lucinda's contrived seductiveness could never compete with Cecilia's direct, sincere charm. If only the boy would let himself realize—but enough of that; if she dwelt too much and too long on her hopes for Cecilia, she might easily spoil things by pushing Kilwarden too fast. It was only a matter of time until nature would take its course—and now there was plenty of time, thanks to Cecilia's inspired idea of this Irish house party.

As she thought of Cecilia, serene and secure among her accustomed surroundings, a warm glow of pleasure suffused Lady Annesley's bosom. How delightful it would be, seeing the girl again. That sunny, outgoing nature, that flow of impetuous, high spirits! If only poor Constance could make herself half so attractive.

She checked her treacherous thoughts, casting a guilty glance at the pale, silent girl beside her, hands clasped round a book of devotions, lips moving in silent prayer. How ironic that she should feel so close to Cecilia, and so hopelessly far removed from her own flesh and blood. Why wasn't she weaving these fond maternal dreams for her own quiet daughter, devising some way to show her that the love of God need not rule out the love of a man?

Still, this trip might be of some help in that direction. Cecilia, she gathered from her daughter's ecstatic comments, had promised Constance to give her the longed-for chance of serving the poor. If the stories one heard were true, the sights and smells of an Irish peasant's cottage might help to dispel some of those pious notions. Ah, well, one could only hope...

A sudden thunder of hooves sent her gloomy thoughts scattering. She heard the raucous bray of the coaching horn, found herself sputtering and coughing, assailed by the storm of dust left in the wake of the shiny chocolate brown coach speeding past them. Lady Headfort was sputtering too, scrabbling in her lap for a handkerchief, while she turned her streaming eyes toward the girl beside her, her whole face alight with that sly, smug look of triumph. "The *Nimrod*," she announced. "It arrives in Holyhead at ten on the dot. We won't be far behind it. Isn't that delightful, Lucinda? Only three more hours 'til we board the packet for Ireland—on what may be the most momentous trip of our lives."

"Try to lie quietly, my poor Lucinda. All this writhing and turning only makes matters worse." Lady Headfort reapplied the handkerchief, soaked in eau de cologne, to her daughter's temples, trying valiantly to ignore the ominous warnings from her own queasy stomach.

"I shall die, Mama; I know I shall die." A sudden lurch of the ship set Lucinda's hands clutching at the sides of the hard, narrow bunk. "This horrible ship! I'm sure we're about to founder. I wish we *would* founder; I wish we'd sink straight to the bottom. At least I'd be out of this terrible misery."

"Nonsense, my dear. The ship is perfectly safe. We've only a few more hours 'til we land in Ireland, and all this agony will be quickly forgotten."

"But I don't want to land in Ireland. It's a horrid country. This whole expedition is utterly, utterly mad."

"Mad? You call it mad? This unparalleled chance to interest Lord Kilwarden?"

"I'm tired of your schemes to interest Lord Kilwarden. If they didn't succeed in London, they'll have no chance at all in that wild, savage country. Oh, why didn't we stay in London, with that charming Sir Arnold DeVere calling twice every day, and all those delightful young men to waltz with at Almack's!"

"I've told you a hundred times, Sir Arnold DeVere is a pauper, compared with Kilwarden. As for Almack's, you know very well those young men aren't serious."

"Neither is Lord Kilwarden," wailed Lucinda. "I managed to dance with him at every ball last Season—but he showed the same attention to twenty others."

"That's just the point, don't you see?" Lady Headfort's voice was rich with confidence. "Out here in Ireland, there will be no distracting *others*."

"How can you say that, Mama? Surely the Irish gentry must have plenty of daughters. You've been talking for weeks about the lively hunt dinners and balls we'll be attending. Won't the Irish young ladies be there in throngs, all of them quite aware what a good catch Kilwarden would make?"

Lady Headfort waved her hand in a contemptuous gesture. "A pack of provincial belles, dressed in last year's fashions, with their awkward rustic manners. What chance have they against your London polish? Kilwarden's a civilized man, who can have his pick of all London. He'd never tie himself down to some Irish bumpkin. Besides, you'll have one great advantage over all the rest; you'll be living under the roof of Kilwarden House. Think, my dear, of the opportunities! The chance encounter on the stairway coming down to breakfast, the request for his help in choosing a book from the library, the pot of tea at dawn after the ball guests have left. Propinquity, my dear, propinquity! That's the secret of half the matches the world calls brilliant."

Lucinda's eyes brightened a little. "Yes, that *would* be an advantage," she admitted. "But how can you be so sure that we'll stay at Kilwarden House? We may very well find ourselves marooned thirty miles away with your cousin, Sir Arthur."

"Leave that to me, my dear. I wangled Sir Arthur's invitation smoothly enough. And he really did offer to send his carriage to Kingstown. Lady Annesley need never know I refused it. She will simply see us stranded on the wharf. Since she's already shared *our* carriage on the trip from London, she will feel herself strongly obliged to return the favor."

"But once we arrive at Kilwarden, surely we'll be expected to go on to Sir Arthur's at Killashee?"

"Now, now, Lucinda; don't worry your pretty head. I assure you I'll manage somehow to stay at Kilwarden. If worst comes to worst, I'll feign illness—but I doubt it will come to that, especially if we arrive there before Lord Kilwarden. Miss Cecilia Annesley is a trifle naïve; she will easily be convinced it's her duty to keep us."

"Lady Annesley, however, is scarcely naïve. Won't she see straight through you? I think she's already guessed at part of your plan."

"Who cares for my dear friend Lydia's good opinion? It's Kilwarden's opinion we're after. That part of the business, my dear, is up to you. Try to rest a bit now, and conserve your strength. You must be at your very best when Kilwarden first sees you beneath his ancestral roof."

"There, there, my beauty. I know you're in misery. Only a few hours more, and we'll be in Ireland." Lord Kilwarden stroked the big bay's heaving flanks and murmured soothing endearments into his twitching ears. He felt a pang of remorse at the handsome beast's suffering. Perhaps he'd been wrong to bring his own hunters across. Celilia's plan of borrowing from the neighbors might have worked out very well. Hadn't some of the best English hunters been bred in Ireland?

He'd almost been persuaded to follow her plan til he cast his mind back over Mr. Quinlan's reports. Lord Cornelius's stable of hunters had obviously been a sorry collection; they'd gone for some thirty apiece in the auction at Dycer's. The horses he kept for racing seemed scarcely better; though listed as thoroughbreds, they'd fetched less than one might have paid for a common post horse.

"So you're bound for Ireland too, my dear Kilwarden." A familiar voice sliced through the fetid air of the shadowy hold. Kilwarden, startled, raised his eyes to the neighboring stall, and dimly discerned Sir George Damien's florid features peering at him over the glossy back of a chestnut gelding. "You've come for the hunting season? That bay of yours looks well able to take those Irish stone fences."

Kilwarden felt a wave of dislike surge up through him. He forced himself to suppress it. Sir George was a pleasant fellow, and had always been very friendly. His rakish reputation was no excuse for not being civil.

"Yes," he admitted, with a stiff attempt at a smile. "I thought I'd see what sport my new estate offers."

"A very pleasant surprise." Sir George beamed genially. "We'll be riding together then. I'm sure we shall have some good runs. There are several excellent packs in the country around Kilwarden."

Kilwarden stared at him dumbly, not quite believing his ears. He'd given Cecilia carte blanche to invite whomever she wished—but he'd scarcely expected Sir George to be one of her guests. Aunt Lydia must have been right; Cecilia must have hopes of a serious offer. But why on earth, in that case, had she not forewarned him? If things had progressed as far as this invitation, surely it was time he had a talk with the man.

Recovering his wits, he tried to make light of the matter. "A pleasant surprise for me as well, Sir George. It seems Miss Annesley's kept us both in the dark as to her list of house guests at Kilwarden."

"Miss Annesley?" Sir George seemed amazed. "I'm afraid you've misunderstood me. That estimable young lady has nothing to do with my coming to Ireland." The broad, ruddy face looked distressed and embarrassed. "Believe me, Kilwarden, much as I admire Miss Annesley, our relations have not yet reached the degree of intimacy where she might invite me as a house guest—especially without *your* consent. No, no, my dear sir; I'm visiting a neighbor of yours and kinsman of mine, Sir Jonah Boothby."

Kilwarden felt a gush of relief. So Cecilia hadn't invited him after all. But why should he be so pleased at that revelation? He should have known at once that so daring an indiscretion was not in her nature.

"What a pleasant coincidence," Sir George was rattling
96

on, "that Sir Jonah should invite me at this particular time. You mentioned Miss Annesley's house guests? I wasn't aware from her conversations in London that she and her mother still lived in the manor house."

"I've put Kilwarden House at those two ladies' disposal," said Kilwarden crisply. Now he was the one feeling embarrassed; that assumption about Cecilia's invitation had been a blunder. He cast about for a change of subject. "I met Sir Jonah last winter when I was in Ireland. As a matter of fact, he gave me an excellent dinner."

"I'll be bound he did." Sir George smiled knowingly. "Though I'd guess you dined in some very strange company."

"I wouldn't say that." Kilwarden's voice was frosty.

"Oh, come now, Kilwarden. I know my ambitious kinsman. Before the election last spring, he was courting every squireen from fifty miles round. 'Half-mounted gentlemen,' they call them in Ireland. Well-meaning fellows all, but with very rough manners."

Kilwarden felt a sharp distaste for the man's eagerness to denigrate his prospective host. "I enjoyed myself immensely. As I recall, he serves an excellent claret."

"Oh, yes; one can't fault his claret. And I must admit he keeps an excellent stable. That's why I brought only one of my hunters across. Sir Jonah was kind enough to offer a choice of mounts—as well as sending his traveling carriage to meet me at Kingstown. What a shame I didn't know we were traveling together. I could have saved you the trouble of bringing your own carriage from Kilwarden."

"I don't keep a carriage there." Kilwarden's tone was terse. "My agent, Mr. Quinlan, keeps one at my disposal in Dublin. However, just now that one is transporting some guests of mine down to Kilwarden. Lady Annesley and her daughter crossed by the steam packet several days ago. I shall go by post horse, leaving my groom to bring my hunters down by easy stages."

"My dear sir, that's out of the question. You must ride with me in comfort."

Kilwarden flinched away from the too-eager smile. "That's good of you, Damien, but I prefer to stick to the posters."

Sir George's smile changed to a chilly reserve. "You don't

care for my company, sir? I'm sorry to hear that. I was not aware I had done anything to offend you."

You kissed my cousin in Lady Annesley's garden. Kilwarden was startled by the vividness of the image. Good Lord, that was ages ago. Was he really still letting it turn him against Sir George? As Aunt Lydia had said, the man might have honorable motives. He didn't believe in this so-called coincidence that had brought him so close to Kilwarden House, or his overeager assurance that Cecilia played no part in his plans. But the courtship—if courtship it was—might still be in that tenuous stage where an anxious head of the family ought to tread softly.

"On the contrary, my dear sir," he protested warmly, "I find your company most agreeable. I was merely concerned that I might be imposing on you. I shall be delighted to accept your generous offer. Meanwhile, since we've a few more hours of this pitching and tossing, perhaps you'll share a bottle up in my cabin?"

As Sir George followed Kilwarden up the hatchway ladder, he allowed himself to relax in a smile of triumph. Things were working out just as he planned. It had been well worth those bribes to Kilwarden's servants to learn the man's travel arrangements. And he'd hit on the proper tone in discussing Cecilia—a feigned ingenuousness the man couldn't help but see through. He was already half convinced that his pretty cousin's wishes had something to do with Sir George's arrival in Ireland. It wouldn't take long to paint in the rest of the picture—a devious minx, keeping a secret suitor on the string, while publicly encouraging another's addresses. If he gauged Kilwarden aright, that would put paid to any thought of a marriage. Serve the ungrateful girl right; it would teach her not to play games with a man like George Damien.

Chapter 9

"Hark, Mama! I think I hear hoofbeats." For the twentieth time that evening, Cecilia dropped her book and ran to the drawing room window. She peered out into the blackness. Her heart skipped a beat as she saw what seemed to be some sort of moving figure on the broad graveled avenue that led to Kilwarden House. But a few more minutes' inspection brought the now familiar pang of disappointment. It was only a drooping beech branch, tossed by a gust of wind.

Lady Margaret looked up with a smile from the fireside table where she and her sister-in-law were sharing a late pot of tea. "You're imagining things, my dear. I'm sure Lord Kilwarden has stopped at some inn for the night. He'd not be so rash as to ride through this fearful storm. Isn't it time you took to your bed, so you'll be fresh and bright to greet him tomorrow? I'm sure Lucinda and Constance have long since dropped off to sleep."

"I'm much too excited to sleep," protested Cecilia. "You know what it means to me to see Cousin Francis back at Kilwarden House."

"It means a great deal to us all." Lady Annesley's smile held a world of secret meaning. "And Kilwarden himself was very eager to get here. He was mightily vexed at the business which kept him in London and prevented his making the crossing along with us."

A pang of alarm shot through Cecilia's bosom. "Crossing the Irish Sea in this fearful storm! Pray God he comes to no harm."

Lady Lydia smiled at her indulgently. "The storm didn't break 'til nearly mid-morning, Cecilia. Francis was certainly safe on the quay by then. He had probably already started his ride to Kilwarden. I hope he was wise enough to take shelter and wait for the tempest to blow itself out."

"Such unusual weather for this time of year." Lady Margaret's forehead furrowed in distress. "What a blessing it broke before Lady Headfort set out for Killashee. The roads must be impassable in this downpour."

"Yes, wasn't it fortunate?" Cecilia tried vainly to make her voice sound as enthusiastic as her mother's. She remembered the shock of dismay she'd felt at seeing Lucinda and her mother step out of the carriage yesterday evening. For a moment she'd thought they'd come at Kilwarden's request, and had been surprised at her own resentful anger. Why should it gall her so, the thought of sharing Francis with our other guests, even this shallow rattlebrained girl who obviously regarded her as some sort of country bumpkin?

Now that the facts had been explained, she still found it hard to feel cordial toward Lucinda. Lady Headfort's invitation from this Irish cousin seemed a transparent pretext; during her season in London she'd noticed the way Lucinda was wont to appear "by accident" wherever Lord Kilwarden happened to be. She wished she knew what Aunt Lydia thought of the matter. Was she really pleased that the miserable weather would keep Lucinda here for another few days? Perhaps she had planned the whole scheme with Lady Headfort. Though she'd never spoken about it, Cecilia was sure she'd like to see Francis married. The Annesley name was dangerously close to extinction. Judged by the standards of London, Lucinda would make him a very acceptable wife. Pretty, vivacious, equipped with an adequate dowry—what more could a gentleman wish for? Cecilia thought the prettiness artificial, the vivacity rather painfully contrived. But perhaps she was judging too harshly. Others, Mama included, evidently found Lucinda quite charming.

Dear, warmhearted Mama! Cecilia's lips curved in a smile. How lovely it was to see her bustling about, once more in her old domain, taking such obvious delight in serving her guests. Nothing could please her more than to have every bedroom filled, plus some pallets on the ballroom floor for impromptu arrivals. No wonder she'd pressed Lady Headfort so warmly to stay for a week or two, not noticing how Cecilia blanched at the thought. Since it clearly gave her such pleasure, what was the point of objecting? The fear that she'd have to share Francis's attention? But surely she didn't expect the poor man to talk about farming all night and day. If Lucinda kept him amused—even charmed—so much the better. Under her spell, he might lengthen his stay in Ireland. And wasn't that the point of her whole careful scheme—to keep him here at Kilwarden long enough to see for himself what his tenants needed?

She was startled out of her musing by the unmistakable sound of coach wheels on gravel. She ran to the window again. This time it was no illusion. Old Thady, lantern in hand, was already out on the portico steps to greet the arriving carriage. She gasped as she saw the emblem on its door. "Sir Jonah's coach!" she exclaimed. "Why in the world is he out on a night like this?"

Lady Margaret peered at her over the back of the sofa. "That *is* very strange," she agreed. "Perhaps it's this awful storm that's driven him here. You know how quickly the Togher reaches flood tide. Maybe the bridge to his place was washed away, and he found himself marooned on our side of the river. Oh, dear; I must go bid him welcome and see that he has a bed. Wasn't it lucky I had the back bedrooms aired out as well as the front ones!" She hurried out to the pillared entrance hall, leaving Cecilia with her nose still pressed to the glass.

Before old Thady could get the near coachdoor open, a supple figure emerged from the other side and came around into the circle of light. Cecilia felt a chill pass through her, as though a bolt of cold lightning had rooted her to the spot. Francis! Could it really be he? She'd imagined it every day for the past three months—Kilwarden's master, mounting those wide front steps. She'd seen herself greeting him, welcoming him into the house she hoped he would make his own home. Now he was here, no longer a creature of dreams but a man of flesh and blood. What was the matter with her? Why was she standing here like a lifeless statue, with a

101

giddiness in her head and the floor inexplicably shifting under her feet?

She felt a gentle hand touch her shoulder lightly. "Come along, my dear," murmured Lady Annesley. "Isn't this the moment for which you've been waiting?"

The kind, quiet voice miraculously gave her back the power of motion. She hurried out into the hall, just in time to see two men step through the big front door. At the sight of the second figure, her hand flew to her mouth to stifle a gasp of dismay. That odious man! What on earth was he doing here? She stopped short where she was, lingering in the shadow of one of the marble pillars.

Lady Margaret quickly moved forward to greet Kilwarden. He returned her greeting with obvious pleasure, then indicated the man who stood beside him. "I hope you don't mind, Lady Margaret. I've invited Sir George Damien to spend the night here."

"You know there's no need to ask, Francis. Of course he must stay." Lady Margaret beamed at the prospect of one more guest. Then a sudden thought seemed to strike her. The beaming smile faded, giving way to a look that seemed strangely apprehensive. "*Damien,* did you say?" She seemed to have trouble forming the words. "I once knew an *Osbert* Damien. A very gallant soldier, attached to the Austrian forces."

Sir George bowed and smiled, acknowledging the tribute. "My uncle, Lady Margaret. As you say, a most gallant soldier."

Lady Margaret turned visibly paler. Her face was grave and thoughtful. "You are doubly welcome here," she told Sir George. "Sir Osbert Damien was a very close friend of—of a member of my family. I mourned his death as though he had been a brother."

Sir George looked surprised. "Are you sure it's the same Sir Osbert we're speaking of? My uncle, I assure you, is still very much alive."

Lady Margaret seemed taken aback. "Could there be two Sir Osberts? The one I knew was killed at the battle of Aspern."

Sir George looked puzzled for a minute. Then his expression cleared. "Ah, yes, I remember now. I was only a lad at the time, but I do recall that we had a report he was killed. That report, however, turned out to be mistaken. He had merely been grievously wounded, and lay ill for six months in a Viennese convent. Then after the French took Vienna, he chose to stay on as a private citizen. It was only a few years ago he returned to England."

The color rushed back into Lady Margaret's cheeks. "Sir Osbert is still alive?" Her voice rang out clearly, almost filling the big entrance hall. "What marvelous news, Sir George. If you knew what this means to me—"

"Margaret, my dear, won't all this wait for tomorrow?" Cecilia was startled to see Aunt Lydia move swiftly to Mama's side, as though to intercept some desperate *gaffe*. "These two gentlemen of ours have had a fatiguing day. If you'll let me instruct the servants—some food, perhaps; hot water; a fire in their bedrooms—"

Lady Margaret blinked dazedly, as though coming out of a trance. Then she became all business, aglow with hospitable zeal. "Yes, yes; of course. What am I thinking of? The fires are already laid. I'll have some food brought to your rooms. Francis, you know your way to the master bedroom. Sir George, if you'll follow me, we'll soon have you settled and warm. What a blessing I kept to my dear Cornelius's habit. 'Keep all the bedrooms ready,' he used to tell me. 'There's always room for another guest at Kilwarden.'"

Cecilia watched the four of them mount the graceful staircase, Lady Margaret reassuring Sir George about the next day's weather, Lady Annesley murmuring something to her nephew about the presence of Lucinda and Lady Headfort. Only after they had all disappeared from the upstairs landing did she move from her shadowy refuge behind the pillar.

If only she'd known in advance that Sir George was arriving with Francis! She might have prepared herself, and been able to welcome him in a dignified manner, instead of hiding away like a silly schoolgirl. A black wave of disappointment engulfed her. She's been looking forward so long to her cousin's arrival, imagined herself making such pretty speeches, pictured so often Francis's look of pleasure. Now that long-awaited occasion had come and gone—and she
103

might as well have been fast asleep in her bedroom for all the notice Kilwarden had taken of her.

And who was at fault for that unhappy state of affairs? Surely it wasn't fair to place all the blame on Sir George. Perhaps Kilwarden himself had insisted he come here. Why he should do such a thing she couldn't imagine, especially when he'd been so perturbed by that scene in the garden. But surely even the arrogant Sir George would not have presumed to invite himself to the house.

Still, Kilwarden *had* said he was merely to stay the night. That implied he must have been driven here by the storm. Perhaps he would be on his way early next morning. She sincerely hoped he would; in fact, she'd make it her business to see that he left as soon as the storm abated.

But what if Mama had already asked him to lengthen his visit? On the strength of her old acquaintance with his uncle, she seemed to be treating him as a long-lost relation. Still, she'd surely understand Cecilia's position, once she told her how he had forced his unwelcome attentions.

She found herself stifling a yawn, and realized she was almost dropping with tiredness. It had been a taxing day—struggling to entertain the supercilious Lucinda, placating Constance's zeal to be out on errands of mercy, constantly on edge for Francis's arrival. A few hours of sleep would cast a new light on things. Perhaps if she came down early enough to breakfast, she might have a chance to speak to Francis alone. And the weather was bound to clear soon; there were already three or four meets fixed for the coming week. Once out in the hunting field, all these annoyances would fall into perspective. And that, after all, was the next step in her campaign—to show Kilwarden's new master what marvelous sport it was to hunt in Ireland.

Kilwarden finished the last of the excellent pheasant, and flung himself down on the bed, looking appreciatively around the master bedroom. Quite an improvement here since his last visit. The spotless carpet had regained its jewel-like colors, the scars in the bedstead had been cleverly smoothed away, a mountain of blazing turf was making the spacious room a haven of warmth. Cecilia, evidently, had been as good as her word. She and Lady Margaret must have taken the servants in hand and managed to bring them up to English standards.

The thought of Cecilia stirred up disquieting feelings. How strange her behavior had been—hiding behind that pillar instead of coming forward to bid him welcome. He realized now how much he'd been looking forward, during these past few months, to seeing his cousin here in her proper surroundings.

Sir George's arrival had obviously come as a shock. In the one glimpse he'd had of her, she had seemed very pale. A rush of emotion at seeing a favored suitor? Or a fit of embarrassment at seeing that suitor arrive with the head of the house, a dreadful uncertainty as to what secret hopes might have been revealed?

Yes, there clearly was something between them. She had probably confided her feelings to Lady Margaret; that's why she'd given Sir George so effusive a welcome. That business about her possibly knowing his uncle merely made a convenient fiction to explain why she greeted him like a second mother.

Damn the man! I won't have it! That arrogant rake is not good enough for Cecilia! Kilwarden flung himself angrily off the bed and strode to the narrow window, staring moodily out over the long line of beeches. He was surprised and shocked by the strength of his own reaction. What right had he to decide who deserved Cecilia? She had a mind of her own. If she was in love with Sir George, why should he interfere? This business of falling in love was notoriously chancy. Some very improbable matches often turned out very well.

He saw his scowling face reflected back by the glimmering window glass. *All the same, I don't like it.* He spoke the words aloud, then looked guiltily around as if wondering who might have heard him. Thank God for these good, thick walls; the old house was solidly built. One could play the fool in one's bedroom and no one need be the wiser.

He moved away from the window and methodically started undressing. He was overtired, that was all. A good night's sleep would put things in better perspective. Perhaps if he went down early tomorrow morning, he could speak to Cecilia alone. No, damn it all, he'd forgotten: that silly Lucinda Headfort was here in the house. If she kept to her usual form, she'd be lying in wait to ambush him on the stairway.

And *there* was another mystery; how had she managed to join this hunting party? No doubt it was part of Aunt Lydia's machinations. The woman could never resist the chance to matchmake.

He arranged himself for sleep, heaving a sigh of tolerant resignation. Delightful creatures, the ladies, but one couldn't afford to get tangled up in their schemes. The weather should clear tomorrow. If he could borrow a hunter, he might try a few fences. Soon the hounds would be out, with the field in elated pursuit, men in a world of men, all these pestilent quirks of emotion dissolving away in the soft October mists.

The flurry of servant's activities dwindled away into silence. Kilwarden House composed itself for the night. One single window disclosed a glow of lamplight. In Lady Margaret's bedroom, two anxious women discussed a long-buried secret.

"I had hoped we need not speak of these ancient troubles, but this business about Sir Osbert introduces a new element into the situation." Lady Annesley paused, as though fearing to give offense. "Would it give you great pain to discuss this vexing question? You must be aware that I already know your secret. At the time of Cornelius's marriage, the Annesley family spent hours discussing the fact that his intended bride had just borne a fatherless child."

Lady Margaret's chin rose proudly. "Fatherless, *then,* to be sure. Cecilia's father, my dear husband Harry, had been killed at Aspern."

Lady Annesley's face grew soft with commiseration. "You found yourself in a very difficult plight. My dear Margaret, I hope you'll be frank with me. That highly unlikely story of a secret marriage—"

"I realize that no one believed me." Lady Margaret's eyes were dark with remembered pain. "But there really was a marriage. I was at school in Vienna when I met Harry Reynolds. We fell in love at first sight. We would have consulted our families, but there wasn't time; he already had his marching orders. We were married in proper fashion at our embassy in Vienna. Then Harry was killed, and I came back to England to give birth to Cecilia. I assumed my parents and friends would understand. I almost gave way to despair when I found they refused to believe me."

"You can hardly blame them, my dear. You had nothing to back up your story. No witnesses, no marriage certificate."

"Cornelius believed me." Lady Margaret's voice was full of quiet pride. "It was only his faith and love that kept me alive through that bitter time."

"I have always admired Cornelius for standing up to the wrath of the Annesley family. He sacrificed a great deal out of love for you. Of course it would have been hopeless to stay in England after your marriage. Your story was widely known; Society would have never accepted you. And so he chose to bury himself at Kilwarden."

"Bury himself!" Lady Margaret's voice was scornful. "He didn't see it that way, and neither did I. We had a wonderful life here at Kilwarden."

"It may seem so to you, but the world doesn't see it that way. To transport himself from the center of civilization to this rural backwater—London would think that a kind of premature death."

"What would Cornelius have done in that *civilized* London?" Lady Margaret's eyes flashed with unaccustomed fire. "He'd have wasted the rest of his life as a moneyed idler, a titled drone with no overriding purpose except the pursuit of amusement. Kilwarden provided him with a reason for living. He found a half-ruined estate full of starving tenants. His skill and perseverance helped to build it into a thriving prosperous place. If only those absentee drones would follow his example, this much-talked-of *Irish unrest* would no longer plague our country."

"An eloquent speech indeed," murmured Lady Annesley. "I begin to see where Cecilia learned her opinions."

"Cornelius reared Cecilia as his own daughter. It is scarcely remarkable that she should share his opinions."

"She obviously worships the memory of Cornelius. Have you ever told her he wasn't her natural father?"

"Cecilia knows nothing about that part of my life." Lady

Margaret's air of assurance faded abruptly. Her voice took on a tone of apology. "If I'd been able to prove it—that I was really married, I mean—but Cornelius thought it best not to stir up old scandals."

"Do you think that was fair to Cecilia? To hide her true parentage? It might mean a great deal to her to know her real family."

"Her real family chose to disown her." The pain was back in Lady Margaret's eyes. "Mr. Reynolds, my dear Harry's father, refused to even receive me. He wrote me a cruel letter in which he implied I was merely after his fortune, and derided the fact that I offered no proof of the marriage." A wondering look spread across Lady Margaret's face. She raised her head and stared at her sister-in-law with an air of challenge. "But now I *do* have proof! Sir Osbert Damien witnessed that marriage of ours. Surely his word is enough to convince the doubters."

"A witness? After all these years? No wonder Sir George's news made you so happy."

"It seems like a gift from Heaven," said Lady Margaret, "especially in our present unhappy straits. Once Mr. Reynolds learns that Cecilia is his only son's legitimate child, he'll surely have no objection to sharing with her part of his ample fortune."

"What about the scandal? Don't you think it may come as a terrible shock to Cecilia?"

"If Cornelius were still alive, I would let things stay as they were." Lady Margaret's face was alive with new resolution. "Or if there was still room for doubt about the marriage. But now that the requisite proof is so close at hand— I'll talk to Sir George tomorrow, and ask his advice on how best to approach his uncle."

"You'll do no such thing, my dear Margaret. The man's an unprincipled rogue. I can't imagine why he's appeared here out of the blue, but I'm sure he's up to no good. Who knows what he'd do with such delicate information? I fully agree that you ought to approach Sir Osbert—but you mustn't breathe even a hint to his devious nephew."

Lady Margaret looked at her perplexedly. "I must take your word on that matter, my dear Lydia. I'm sure you're wiser than I in such matters. But how *shall* I approach him? I might write him a letter—but that seems so cold and unfeeling."

"In affairs of this kind, the less put on paper, the better. What's called for on this occasion is a personal visit from someone close to your family."

Lady Margaret's face brightened. "Of course! We'll ask Kilwarden. He'll be glad to do it, I'm sure, for Cecilia's sake."

Lady Annesley assumed a bland, wide-eyed expression, while she rapidly calculated some subtle matters of timing. "No, I don't think that's wise. Kilwarden is too straightforward. He's quite incapable of any deception."

Lady Margaret flushed. A hurt look crept into her eyes. "So you still believe it's a matter of deception? Surely you don't think I'd use Sir Osbert to buttress a falsehood? He *was* our witness, I tell you."

Lady Annesley looked contrite, and placed a consoling arm around the perturbed woman's shoulders. "I didn't mean it that way. It's Cecilia I'm thinking of. We must keep the secret from her a little longer. It will be enough of a shock to find that she wasn't really Cornelius's daughter. We mustn't add to her burden with any lingering doubts about her legitimacy. That's why I hesitate to tell Kilwarden. He'd never be able to keep the secret from her."

"I see what you mean," agreed Lady Margaret. "You're right; she mustn't know until we're sure of our proof."

"Don't you have some friend here whose discretion you can trust? Perhaps that young curate who came to dinner tonight?"

"Mr. Worsley? Heaven forbid! He couldn't handle this matter. That sensitive soul would be shocked to the core by any such topic as *illegitimate birth*. No, what we really need is a man of the world who can talk to Sir Osbert as equal to equal—"

She stopped abruptly, a sudden surge of elation flooding her eyes. "Of course! The very man! Count O'Hanrahan would be delighted to help. He may already know Sir Osbert, since they fought in the same campaigns. I'll send him a message the very first thing in the morning and ask him to call here.

We have a perfect pretext—Cecilia's arranged with him to provide us some hunters."

"You're sure he won't drop some dangerous hint to Cecilia?"

"The count is the soul of discretion. Cecilia won't know a thing 'til the proof is certain and Mr. Reynolds's acceptance is fully secured. It's all settled, then, my dear Lydia. Would you care to talk to the count when he comes tomorrow?"

"I'll leave that to you, since it's rather a delicate matter. Besides, it might be well if I lured Lady Headfort out on some pleasant walk when the count is expected. The woman's a veritable ferret at digging out gossip; she'd surely sense that there's something exciting afoot and give herself no rest 'til she learned your secret."

"I forgot about Lady Headfort." Lady Margaret looked worried. "She's almost the same age as we are, is she not? Do you think she remembers the gossip about me in London?"

"She must have heard some of the scandal at the time of your marriage, but I'm sure she doesn't remember—not yet, at least. Otherwise, she'd be brimming over with hints and insinuations. Let's hope her formidable memory remains unawakened."

"It's not that a little more scandal would matter to me. But for Cecilia's sake—"

"Exactly, my dear sister Margaret. And now, for Cecilia's sake, let's both get some sleep. In the delicate business we're just about to embark on, it's quite essential that we have all our wits about us."

Chapter 10

"Please stop your scolding, Mama. I couldn't endure that horse for another minute." Lucinda Headfort gave a vicious tug to her scarlet coat, stripped it away from her shoulders and flung it down on her bed with a petulant gesture.

"After all I've told Kilwarden about your love of hunting, it really looks very strange that you leave for home as soon as the hounds throw off. You used not to be so timid when you were out with the Quorn."

"But this is far rougher country than Leicestershire. Those awful stone fences put me in fear of my life. It's all very well for Cecilia; she's been jumping them ever since childhood. Compared to her, I look quite ridiculous."

Lady Headfort gave a sigh of exasperation. "If you'd only try, Lucinda. I declare, you're doing nothing to advance our plans. Last night at dinner you ignored Kilwarden completely and wasted all your charm on Sir George Damien."

"Sir George is very amusing. At least I don't have to fight for his attention." Lucinda picked up an ivory-backed brush and moodily began to brush her hair. "We've been here a week, and Kilwarden has scarcely seen fit to acknowledge my presence. He seems to have eyes for no one but Cecilia. A blind man could see that much. We might as well give up and go on to Sir Arthur's. It's obvious that we've long outstayed our welcome."

"I don't agree. Cecilia finds many pretexts to snare his interest. You could do the same, if you'd only try. Those early morning rides of theirs, for instance—if you'd rise early enough to go down to the stables, you could easily manage to make a third in the party."

"And spend two more hours on a horse? I couldn't stand it. You know I detest the beasts. I only learned to ride because you insisted. Besides, I've nothing to use for conversation. Cecilia plays up to the hilt this pretext of advising Kilwarden about his estate. Of course we're both aware it's all a ruse, just like her silly pretense of not wanting a husband."

"I agree the minx's motives are quite transparent. But I'm not at all convinced that she's succeeding. He may be quite fond of Cecilia—but that doesn't mean he's about to make her an offer. Lady Annesley was quite certain he wouldn't marry a cousin."

Lucinda flung down her brush with an impatient gesture. "Do you really believe what that devious woman tells you? She's obviously trying to snare him for Cecilia. Look at the way she's pretended to relish hunting. I think she detests the saddle as much as I do, but pretending a passion for sport means Cecilia can join the field at every meet, not being obliged to stay at home with her guest."

Lady Headfort's face darkened. "She certainly does appear to favor Cecilia," she said in a musing tone. "I wonder why? You'd think her own daughter would be her first concern."

Lucinda shrugged in contempt. "She's given up any hopes she had for Constance. She knows that prudish miss could never attract Kilwarden. But she'd like to keep all that wealth in the Annesley family. That's why she champions Cecilia—points out her accomplishments, accompanies her in the field, spends hours and hours in conference with her mother. Meanwhile she lets her own daughter ramble around unattended with that milksop curate."

Lady Headfort smiled wryly. "I'm sure the young lady's quite safe, playing the ministering angel with Mr. Worsley. I must say the role she's adopted seems to suit her. The way she came in to dinner last night, pink-cheeked and bright-eyed. I've never seen her look so animated."

Lucinda gave a delicate shudder. "A very fatiguing way of improving one's looks, poking around in those noisome peasant hovels. Her conversation is just as dreary as ever.

I swear, if it weren't for Sir George, I should never survive these boring dinners."

"How many times must I tell you not to waste your time on Sir George? You know you've no chance with him. The man is determined to marry a great deal of money."

"So I had always thought when I saw him in London. But now I begin to wonder. Why did he choose to come to this part of Ireland? It obviously had something to do with Cecilia. Their manner when they're together is very strange. When Kilwarden's around, he makes a great show of pretending to ignore her, yet he's always finding a pretext to meet her alone. Yesterday, for instance, he lured her down to the stables, pretending he wanted advice on a limping horse. And now that Sir Jonah has lent him that hunting lodge, he keeps inviting her there to advise him on furnishing it."

"Cecilia, from all I've seen, appears to loathe him. She allows him the barest minimum of conversation."

"Mama, we already know how cunning she is. Perhaps this frosty manner is merely another pretense. It doesn't appear to dampen Sir George's devotion. He spends far more time at Kilwarden than he does at Sir Jonah's."

Lady Headfort cocked her head in a thoughtful fashion. "If Kilwarden suspected Cecilia was playing some game—pretending to loathe Sir George while secretly leading him on—it might do something to lower the high esteem in which he holds her."

Lucinda's eyes lit up with malicious glee. "It certainly might, Mama. If he found his high-minded cousin was stooping to such an intrigue, he might see her less as an angel and more as an ordinary woman. I'll drop him a few hints; shall I? I have no hopes at all it will win me Kilwarden—but at least the attempt will keep me from dying of boredom."

"Don't give up on Kilwarden too quickly, my dear. I still have a great deal of faith in propinquity. He may not be caught in Cecilia's net much longer. You do your bit toward disillusioning him—while I take some steps of my own that may quite disabuse Kilwarden of any thoughts about marrying his cousin."

Lucinda's eyes narrowed with suspicion. "What's all this mystery, Mama? I know you're up to something. That cat-lapping-cream expression means you're on to some juicy gossip."

Lady Headfort beamed at her indulgently. "Don't bother your pretty head, my dear Lucinda. It's better you shouldn't know, until I'm sure of my facts. I've just sent a letter to one of my friends in London. If her answer confirms my suspicion, this campaign of ours will take on a new burst of life. No, I won't say another word. Let me send up your maid to start arranging your hair. Cecilia may have the advantage when she's on horseback, but when our hunters come back to dinner and dancing, you'll quite outshine our rustic Irish hostess."

The grand saloon of Kilwarden House had been cleared for dancing, the magnificent Wilton carpet rolled up, the mahogany parquet floor waxed to a lively sheen. Two hundred wax candles struck rainbow sparks from the crystal waterfalls suspended from the plaster-wreathed ceiling, while astonished plaster cherubs gaped from each corner at the rhythmic melee surging below them. Two long lines of flushed, laughing dancers advanced and retreated, advanced and retreated, then shouted and cheered and stamped as each couple in turn, arms entwined, pranced from the head of the line to part again at its foot.

Sir George Damien watched from the sidelines, sipping a glass of port, the barest trace of a smile curving his fleshy lips. So the pretty minx and Kilwarden were partners again. What was it she intended? A wordless declaration to the county that she was back in command at Kilwarden House? Very well, let her have her hollow moment of triumph. It wouldn't last very much longer. Already Kilwarden was starting to grow suspicious. Last night when he'd found them together in the little alcove, comparing the swatches of silk he'd brought as samples, there had been a questioning look in his lordship's eyes. He'd covered it up with an overly cordial greeting, but he'd seemed withdrawn and bemused for the rest of the evening. The seed of doubt had been sown and had taken root; tomorrow's business should bring the crop to full blossom.

He shifted his gaze around the noisy room. Ah, there she was, Cecilia's would-be rival. She was watching the happy pair with a sour expression. Drained of vivaciousness, the little, sharp-boned face looked almost ugly. She didn't relish being left on the sidelines. He saw two of the country bumpkins who posed for gentlemen here eyeing her covertly; a few minutes more and she'd be back on the floor. Now was the time; she was clearly ripe for suggestion. A few words in her ear, and tomorrow's success was assured.

He edged around the room 'til he stood beside her. She flashed him a dazzling smile, her beauty restored by the thought of a man's attention. Murmuring a few words of greeting to Lady Headfort, he seated himself so that only Lucinda could hear him.

"I'm surprised you're not dancing, my dear Miss Headfort. Back in London I scarcely ever saw you so quiet."

Lucinda fluttered her fan, shrugging delicately. "These rude country dances are not to my taste, Sir George. In London, such romps are confined to the nursery."

"Lord Kilwarden seems to enjoy them greatly. Back in England, I thought him rather a sober dog, but here he kicks up his heels like a newly weaned colt."

"Indeed, he does seem quite changed." Lucinda drawled the words in affected boredom. "We're quite inundated with sermons about the excellence of everything Irish—Galway oysters, Belfast linen, Donegal woolens—the list is endless."

"With a certain Irish young lady capping the list of delights?" Sir George gestured with his chin toward the lithe auburn-haired girl on the dance floor. "He seems to be well on the road to acquiring an Irish bride."

Lucinda's eyelashes fluttered with mock amazement. "You say that with such approval. Have your own interests in that quarter faded so quickly?"

A hooded look came over Sir George's eyes. He gave her a wary glance, then ostentatiously looked at the space around them, as though to make sure there was no one within hearing distance. "May I speak to you frankly, Miss Headfort, as friend to friend?" His voice dropped to a whisper, delivered within two inches of Lucinda's right ear. "My affection, once given, does not fade away so quickly, especially when it finds such an ardent response as it has in this case. Miss Annesley and I are deeply in love. My family, unfortunately, are strongly opposed to my marrying a penniless girl. Until we can win them over, we must keep our love a secret from the world."

This time the startled Lucinda did not have to feign amazement. "Dear me, how very romantic. Do tell me more, Sir George. You suggest that Cecilia reciprocates your affection. I should never have guessed that from her distant manner toward you."

Sir George's face seemed to darken with self-reproach. "How I hate the need for us both to behave so falsely. Especially when it involves so fine a man as Kilwarden. I fear he'll be hurt and angry when he finds all her friendliness toward him has been mere deception, intended to cover up the true state of her heart."

He shot an appraising glance toward the wide-eyed Lucinda, and seemed to hesitate a moment as though wondering whether to share a further secret. "I take a tremendous risk in telling you this." The words were rapid and breathless, obviously impelled by desperation. "But I've often sensed in you a kindred spirit. May I be assured that I can trust you with the very delicate matter I am about to impart?"

"Your secret is safe with me." Lucinda gave him a tremulous, soulful smile. "I have nothing but sympathy for your situation. It must be terribly galling to be in each other's presence, yet not be able to openly share your affection."

"How well you understand our misery. So near, and yet so far—an intolerable state of affairs. We had hoped to snatch some moments when we were out hunting—briefly detach ourselves from the rest of the field, find some refuge where we could be alone. When Sir Jonah so kindly agreed to lend me his shooting lodge, we were sure we could somehow manage a rendezvous. But Kilwarden's attentiveness had dashed all those hopes. He's always literally galloping at her heels. We were growing desperate when Miss Annesley hit on the notion of a picnic. I'm to extend the invitation tonight at supper."

"A picnic!" exclaimed Lucinda. "What a lovely idea. It will make such a pleasant break from all this hunting. Where are you and Cecilia planning to take us? I hope it's a place we can reach without too much riding."

"No riding at all, dear lady. You'll go part of the way in a carriage, the rest by boat. Sir Jonah's shooting lodge is on Inishcleraun—the peasants around here call it the Holy Island. A most picturesque little place, full of all sorts of ancient ruins. With some slight assistance from you, we can manage to have our party so well dispersed that Cecilia and I can snatch a few moments together."

"Assistance? What sort of assistance?" Lucinda's eyes were sparkling. "I'll do anything in my power to help dear Cecilia. So long as it's not really wicked, you understand. You won't require me to tell any outright falsehoods?"

Sir George drew himself up as though his pride was offended. "My dear Miss Headfort, I would never ask you to lie. All we require of you is that you attempt to distract Kilwarden's attention. I'm sure such a charming young lady knows many ways of accomplishing that maneuver. I shall give you a little signal when we're ready to slip away. Your task is to keep him with you and the rest of the party."

Lucinda's eyes sparkled. "What an exciting intrigue! I shall certainly do my best. If necessary, I shall ask Mama to help me."

Sir George looked alarmed. "Please don't mention our little secret to anyone else. If Kilwarden got wind of it, he might become quite vindictive toward his cousin."

"I realize that, Sir George." Lucinda's eyes were bright with resolution. "I won't take the slightest risk of harming my dear Cecilia's reputation."

"I knew I could trust you, Miss Headfort." Sir George made a little bow. "And now, if you'll do me the honor? I believe it's time for us to go in to supper."

The big front door clanged shut behind the last of the lingering guests. Cecilia sighed—half in relief, half in contentment—and flung herself wearily into a comfortable armchair. Lady Margaret smiled at her over the rim of her teacup. "A marvelous evening, my dear. All our friends were in excellent spirits. A few of them told me it reminded them of the old days, when Kilwarden House was the social hub of the county."

Cecilia gave her a little smile of agreement. "And how

117

nicely dear Francis played his role as our host. He wasn't nearly so stiff as he used to be. I believe he's becoming used to our Irish humor. When he led the gentlemen back to join the ladies, I noticed that he and the count were roaring with laughter."

"Yes, the count has quite taken to him." Lady Margaret lowered her eyes to hide a secret smile. "He's doing his best to persuade him to stay at Kilwarden."

Cecilia's eyes opened wide. "Is he really, Mama? I hadn't realized that. When he told us about his coming trip to England, I was half afraid he might take Kilwarden with him."

"He wouldn't find it easy to tear the dear boy away. He's become such an ardent convert to our style of hunting."

"Yes, he has, hasn't he." Cecilia smiled blissfully. "I was counting on that. We've had some excellent runs these past few days. If the weather continues with this convenient dry spell, I'm sure he'll decide to stay 'til the end of the season."

"Only 'til the end of the season?" Lady Margaret smiled at her archly "Your little campaign hasn't progressed further than that? After all those morning rides you've been taking together I had hoped for some more permanent arrangement."

Cecilia suppressed a tremor of irritation. Dear Mama couldn't be blamed for seeing all the world from the matchmaker's angle of vision. "I think I have made progress. He's been quite impressed with all Papa's drainage projects. Now if only I could convince him that the roads and houses and all Papa's other improvements weren't really a waste of money. The wages he paid all came back to him in the rents— and kept his tenants healthy and contented."

A look of sadness passed over her mother's face. "In those days, of course, the rents were reasonable. They hadn't been raised to these present impossible heights."

"He won't even discuss the rents. Mr. Quinlan has him convinced that his rates are no higher than those of the other landlords. He thinks our tenants object because they're lazy. If only he'd talk to some of our hard-working people—Sean Ryan, for instance, or Peadar Rua Martin! He'd soon be convinced that they're working twice as hard as his English tenants—with nothing to show for their labors but the constant threat of eviction."

"It really is a pity he's so stand-offish. I suppose that's the English way. But our tenants are used to your dear Papa's genial manner. They remember how every complaint got a hearing from him. Bridie says she's afraid they're beginning to dislike Francis. She's heard people say that the new master has no heart, that he's just a money-grubber like that hateful Sir Jonah."

"Oh, dear! Things are worse than I feared. Are they really comparing Francis to that awful man?"

"It's most unfortunate that Kilwarden insists on inviting him to the house. All of our people remember quite clearly that your father refused to let him set foot on Kilwarden land. They see his presence here as an ominous sign."

"One really can't blame them for that," exclaimed Cecilia. "I can scarcely stand it myself, seeing that greedy face at our dinner table. But since Sir George has become such a friend of Kilwarden's, I suppose his unpleasant kinsman can't be excluded."

Lady Margaret's eyes brightened with pleasure at the mention of Damien's name. "Sir George is always so pleasant. I quite enjoy having made his acquaintance. I can't think why you and Lydia detest him so."

"Mama, I'm surprised at you. After that dishonorable incident in Aunt Lydia's garden—"

"A stolen kiss? Is that so dishonorable? I really think you're making too big a fuss. From all I've seen of him here, he seems to have learned his lesson. I'm sure you would have informed me of any improper advances."

"He *seems* to be behaving quite properly. But I still feel there's something strange about his actions. He seems to keep thinking of pretexts to get me alone—that lame horse of his, or some book he wants to show me. It's always some innocent matter, so I'd look ridiculous if I refused him."

"That seems quite usual behavior for a young gentleman who finds a young lady attractive. Perhaps it's the only way he can have a few words with you in private. The way Kilwarden is always hovering around you—"

"Kilwarden doesn't *hover*." Cecilia's voice was edged with

irritation. "He pays me no more attention than he does Lucinda or Constance. As for Sir George, he makes only the most trivial comments when we're alone."

"He hasn't tried to make any unwelcome advances?"

"I must admit he's been the soul of discretion." Cecilia forced out the words reluctantly. "All the same, I still don't trust him. Why has he come here at all? The last time I saw him in London, I made it quite plain I wished nothing to do with him. And yet he comes down to Kilwarden—"

"Not really to Kilwarden, my dear. And Sir Jonah *is* his kinsman."

"A kinsman he's visited once in the last ten years. Why should he visit him *now*, just at the time we've arranged our hunting party? And why has he made such an effort to win Kilwarden's friendship? When they were in London, they scarcely knew each other."

"Really, Cecilia, I think you're too suspicious. There's nothing discreditable in trying to make new friends. And it *was* very kind of him to arrange with Sir Jonah for the picnic tomorrow on Inishcleraun. I've always wanted to see those three old churches. They're said to be quite well-preserved. But of course your dear father would never set foot on that island, because of his quarrel with Sir Jonah."

The wistful look in her mother's eyes went straight to Cecilia's heart. "You do love to poke about in those mouldering ruins! Is that why you positively leapt at Sir George's suggestion?"

Lady Margaret looked slightly abashed. "Perhaps I was a little precipitate. But it did seem to me a picnic would be an amusing diversion. You and dear Lydia, of course, are quite engrossed in your hunting. But it's been rather dull for some of our other guests. Lucinda and Lady Headfort are dying for some amusement. And exploring those old churches would provide a welcome new interest for your cousin Constance."

"I don't know that Constance wishes to go on the picnic. She seems quite eager to proceed with her errands of mercy."

"I'm sure she is, my dear. And Mr. Worsley would gladly accompany her. But they've already spent far too much time alone together. People are beginning to talk. I've hesitated to interrupt your enjoyment, but you really ought to give up a few days of hunting to see that your cousin is properly chaperoned."

Cecilia couldn't suppress a burst of laughter. "Good heavens, Mama. Don't tell me you're worried about Mr. Worsley's motives. She's as safe with him as though he were her brother."

"I doubt that Constance regards him as a brother. Have you *looked* at her lately, Cecilia? Have you seen the light in her eyes, the way she blushes, the dreamy smile that lingers around her lips? She's the perfect picture of a young girl falling in love."

"Constance in love with Henry? You can't be serious."

Lady Margaret looked slightly affronted. "I'm not quite so ancient, my dear, that I don't know young love when I see it. *You* may not have been attracted to Mr. Worsley, but a young lady with Constance's pious disposition might find him the perfect answer to all her prayers."

Cecilia was gripped by a spasm of consternation. Her mother was right. She had been very self-centered. If she'd been paying the slightest attention to Constance, she'd have seen for herself the direction matters were taking. A most satisfying direction it might prove to be—but Mama was correct in pointing out the need for discretion.

She smiled at her mother with twinkling, affectionate eyes. "My precious Mama! That matchmaker's heart of yours must be swelling with pleasure. Constance went through a whole London Season without the slightest sign of falling in love. Then she comes to what Francis calls 'this rural backwater' and instantly succumbs to the blind boy's dart."

"Do you really find that so strange?" Lady Margaret beamed at her fondly. "I've seen this sort of thing a score of times. That's one of the reasons I used to love giving house parties at Kilwarden. They're a perfect method of bringing young couples together."

Cecilia gave her a smile of impish amusement. "I'm sure Lady Headfort thinks so. But I don't think Lucinda agrees. She appears to have quite abandoned her pursuit of Kilwarden. I expect she'll be off very soon to search for a husband elsewhere."

"You say that with such satisfaction. Almost as though she were your rival."

"My rival!" Cecilia's cheeks flamed. "Why, Mama, you know that's not so. I haven't the slightest thought of marrying Kilwarden. Besides, as he's already told us, our close relationship makes it out of the question."

"If you really believe that, my dear, then you really aren't being fair to poor Lucinda. By encouraging him to spend all his time with you, you don't give her very much chance to impress him. One might even accuse you of playing the dog in the manger."

On the verge of an indignant protest, Cecilia checked herself. She might not like Lucinda, but the girl *was* a guest of hers. She had a perfect right to Kilwarden's attention. "Dear Mama, I'm so ashamed," she said contritely. "I haven't been a very thoughtful hostess. I shall try to make amends, beginning tomorrow. The picnic's a perfect solution; it will give me a chance to see that Lucinda has plenty of time alone with Kilwarden. And I'll persuade both Constance and Henry to take a little time off from their charitable errands. With half the county coming, there'll be plenty of chaperones to ensure discretion."

Lady Margaret beamed at her. "There's a generous child. I knew you'd see reason. Now, it's time we were off to bed. We must be up bright and early for Sir George's delightful outing tomorrow morning."

Chapter 11

Kilwarden stifled a sigh, and cast a hasty glance around the grassy hollow. What a boring expedition this had turned out to be. And yet everyone else seemed to be full of high spirits. The count and Miss Stowe were surrounded by a chattering group down by the lake shore. Lady Headfort and his Aunt Lydia could be glimpsed at intervals in a neighboring grove, apparently quite entranced in gathering assorted bits of the native vegetation. And somewhere up in the woods that covered the island, the rest of the picnic party—Cecilia and her mother, Constance and her curate, and the genial host who'd organized the picnic—were presumably deep in their study of still another pile of distinguished old stones.

Lucinda Headfort smiled at him coyly, as she took another sip from her glass of wine. "How kind of you, Lord Kilwarden, to stay behind and provide me with company. I'm sure you were longing to visit those other old churches. But after that delicious luncheon, I was much too contented to stir from this heavenly spot."

"There's no kindness involved, I assure you. It gives me great pleasure to share this prospect with you." Kilwarden forced himself to return her smile. He was vaguely aware of the fact that his sitting here *tête-à-tête* with the coy Lucinda was no mere accident. Who had maneuvered them here? Lucinda herself? That scheming mother? No, it had been Cecilia; when she'd gone wandering off after lunch, she had virtually ordered him to amuse Lucinda.

Not that he really minded. He knew nothing at all about

ancient Irish churches. It was pleasant enough sitting here with Lucinda; he'd been paired off, in the past, with far less attractive companions. It was true he was finding it hard to follow her conversation, but that was probably the fault of Sir George's excellent Madeira.

"I know what you're thinking." Lucinda's tone was teasing. He looked at her guiltily. Had his inattention really been that obvious? "You're thinking all this is a waste of good hunting weather. Admit it, now. Wasn't I right? Your mind is miles away, hearing the call of the hounds, seeing a fox streak across some rocky outcrop."

Kilwarden smiled sheepishly. "You've caught me out, Miss Headfort. I find it hard, with the glorious sport we've been having, to spend even one day out of the saddle."

"I quite understand, Lord Kilwarden. But I can't help being pleased that Sir George provided this pleasant change of pace. I quite enjoyed inspecting Sir Jonah's lodge this morning. Sir George has had it done up nicely, don't you agree? I suppose that's the fruit of our dear Cecilia's counsel. Especially that blue and silver bedroom, so much like her own boudoir at Kilwarden House. Of course, they've been thick as thieves over this project."

Kilwarden looked surprised. "Have they, indeed, Miss Headfort? I wouldn't have thought that. My cousin's manner when she addressed Sir George has always seemed remarkably distant."

Miss Headfort laughed, an affected, silvery trill. "Surely you've learned, Lord Kilwarden, that young ladies have different manners for different occasions? Perhaps she is rather reserved when you are present. At other times, I assure you, she permits herself to display some distinctly warmer feelings."

Kilwarden stirred uneasily. He knew he ought not to be discussing Cecilia's "feelings," especially with this rather malicious young lady. But he couldn't resist the opportunity to learn more about how things stood between Sir George and his cousin. "I had been aware, back in London, that Sir George was most attentive to Miss Annesley. But from all I've seen of them both since I came to Ireland, I had become convinced that there was no longer any attraction between them."

Lucinda flashed a brief, mysterious smile. "They *have* been very discreet, especially Cecilia. I'm sure the rest of the family are as much in the dark as you."

"As much in the dark about what?" asked Kilwarden sharply. "I can't believe Cecilia would do anything underhanded. She always seemed an especially candid young lady."

"Yes, she does *seem* to be, doesn't she?" Lucinda shifted her eyes away from his and gazed dreamily out across the water. "And yet—that shooting lodge does set one thinking. The bedroom, for instance—it seemed more like a lady's boudoir than a huntsman's refuge. And I find it rather strange that Sir George had our luncheon served down in this hollow. Wouldn't it have been more convenient to have it up near the lodge? And the way dear Cecilia insisted so strongly that you stay down here with me, when she and Sir George went up with the exploring party."

"What on earth are you saying, Miss Headfort?" Kilwarden glowered at her. "You're not suggesting a ... a *rendezvous?*"

"A *rendezvous?* Heavens, no! Where did you get that idea? Oh dear, it's all my fault." Lucinda's eyes grew misty with contrition. "I've let my silly tongue run away with me. A thousand pardons, my dear Lord Kilwarden, if anything I may have been babbling about could have led you to think so harshly of poor Cecilia. I assure you, the idea is quite ridiculous. Let us drop the subject. The little exploring party will no doubt return any minute, and the sight of Cecilia put *both* our minds at rest."

As though her words were a cue, a shout rang out below them. "Here they come at last, our intrepid explorers!" Count O'Hanrahan was scrambling to his feet, hurrying up toward the little hill behind them. Kilwarden found himself following him eagerly toward the spot at the top of the hill where three weary figures had just emerged from a tangle of underbrush. He realized now how much he'd been missing her. How refreshing it would be, after all those insinuations of the malicious Miss Headfort, to hear Cecilia's lilting, melodious voice, happily describing the latest ruins ...

Why were there only three figures making their way down the hill—a man in sober black, a woman in white and violet, a young lady in apple green? Where was the stocky man in the tightwaisted Newmarket coat who had led the little group off on this exploration? And where, for Heaven's sake, was the girl in that very attractive yellow chintz day dress?

As Lady Margaret came closer, he saw her beaming smile turn to apprehension. "Cecilia isn't here yet? But she started back almost half an hour ago! Sir George was showing her back by another path. I do hope she hasn't met with some accident. The paths are so rough—they haven't been used for years."

"I'm sure there's nothing at all to worry about." Kilwarden could hear it clearly, the insinuating note in Lucinda's voice. "After all, Sir George is with her, isn't he?"

Without conscious thought, Kilwarden found himself speaking. "Sir George is not familiar with this island. The two of them may have lost their way. I'll go up myself and try to find them. No, please don't come with me, Mr. Worsley. It's your turn to stay here and help entertain the ladies."

Without waiting for Worsley's answer, he set off up the hill, trying to remember which path they had taken this morning. The broad path from the hollow diverged just beyond that stony outcrop above him. One fork was the path to the ruined church, the one the exploring party had just come down on. The other was the one that led to his destination—that luxuriously-furnished lodge, the little stone house with the blue and silver bedroom.

"Are you sure this path leads down to that little hollow?" Cecilia paused in a clearing to look around her. She was almost sure now they'd taken the wrong turning somewhere. This path kept going uphill; that grassy hollow of theirs had been close to the shore. To reach it, they should have been going steadily downhill.

And yet, this path must lead somewhere. It seemed to be newly cut through the underbrush. And Sir George was striding ahead with such confidence, as if he were very sure of his destination.

She should never have let him split up the exploring party. They should have all stayed together, gone back by the tried-and-true path by which they'd come up. But he'd arranged things so very deftly, playing up to Mama's reluctance to leave the ruins, Henry and Constance's absorption in each other. And her own impatience as well; she'd had quite enough of poking around in old ruins. A short way down had seemed a veritable godsend.

He was looking back at her now, having come to a stop at the turn of the path ahead. "Sir George," she called, "this path doesn't go to the hollow. Shouldn't we look for another one, going downhill?"

A strange smile, almost a grimace, spread over his face. "Come along," he said brusquely. "I've found a landmark you're sure to recognize."

She knew what the "landmark" must be before she saw it—the low stone building with the trampled mud around it, the freshly-cut turf piled at its further end. She'd smiled and praised his progress when she saw it this morning; told him how glad she was for the work he'd provided for some of Sir Jonah's tenants. But that had been this morning, with her family and friends around her. Now she was here alone with this devious rake, who was smiling at her in a way that turned her to ice.

She stood stock still on the edge of the clearing and eyed him warily. "What is the meaning of this, Sir George? Why have you tricked me into coming here?"

Sir George feigned a look of surprise. "How can you speak of tricks, my dearest Cecilia? You've made your wishes quite clear; now we're alone together, won't you drop all these coy pretenses?"

Cecilia gazed at him in rising horror. "What's all this talk of pretenses? You know I sincerely detest you."

A lazy smile flickered in Sir George's half-closed eyes. "What a very strange girl you are. You keep insisting that you detest me—and yet you flirt with me so delightfully every evening."

"I *don't* flirt with you, Sir George. Since you're my cousin's guest, I have to be civil at dinner. But you've surely observed that I avoid you as much as I can. Were the choice mine alone, I would cut you off altogether."

Sir George pretended that he was greatly amused. "Don't you think you're overdoing these maidenly protestations? It's been clear to me from the start that you're longing for my caresses. Now we're alone you can lay aside all pretense. I assure you, your passion for me is fully requited."

"Have you gone mad, Sir George? I've just told you I detest you—"

"Enough of this badinage." Sir George was no longer smiling. He took a step closer to her and stared down into her eyes. "Let's not waste time bandying words. We have only a few stolen moments to spend together. You'll come with me now, into that pretty bedroom, the bedroom I furnished for you with your favorite colors." He reached out to clasp her waist and draw her to him. She stayed in his arms for a moment, frozen with horror. Then she wrenched herself from his grasp and stumbled blindly back toward the little path, running as fast as the clutching shrubs would let her. She heard his heavy footsteps pounding behind her. Her skirt snagged itself on some brambles; she heard the chintz tear as she jerked it free. But the instant's pause was enough for her pursuer. She felt his heavy hand grasping her shoulder. He wrenched her around to face him, snatched her up in his arms, and started carrying her back toward the shooting lodge. She opened her mouth to scream, but he was too quick for her; his hand clamped over her mouth, almost smothering her.

"Don't be a little fool," he muttered angrily into her ear. "I'm not going to harm you. Why not cease this silly struggling and enjoy our brief time together?"

She shook her head wildly, trying to break his grasp. He laughed at her useless struggle and clasped her tighter. They were at the door of the lodge now. He gave it a vicious kick. It opened before him. With a mounting sense of panic, she saw the obsequious servant scuttle along the hall ahead of them and throw open the door to the blue and silver bedroom.

Sir George strode into the room. The door slammed behind them. He tossed her onto the brocade-canopied bed, then went back to the door and turned the key in the lock.

"Now you may scream if you like, Miss Annesley. No one can hear you through these thick stone walls."

She scrambled to a sitting position and glared at him fiercely. "How dare you do this, Sir George! You can't keep me here forever. Don't you know what will happen to you when my family and friends learn what you've done to me?"

He flung himself into a chair and regarded her with bland amusement. "Just what have I done to you, Miss Annesley? I've responded to your entreaties to bring you here, and locked the door—on your instructions—to safeguard our *rendezvous* from prying servants."

Cecilia was stunned for a moment. What brazen arrogance! "Do you think they'll believe your lies? Of course they won't. They know me too well for that. They'll never believe I came here willingly."

Sir George arched a quizzical eyebrow. "I shouldn't count on that if I were you. After all, it's my word against yours. I intend to tell a very convincing story. Your family and friends will pity you when they hear it—an infatuated young girl, who didn't quite realize the risk she was running. Of course, I'll manfully shoulder my share of the blame. But the men, at least, will understand my position. What man could turn down so tempting an invitation? No doubt Kilwarden will banish me from his house. But he won't go further than that; he won't want the scandal that calling me out would bring."

"You don't know my cousin Kilwarden," Cecilia said staunchly. "He'd never forgive this assault on his kinswoman's virtue."

Sir George's eyes widened in pretended amazement. "My dear Cecilia, is that why you're so upset? Believe me, I wouldn't dream of assaulting your virtue. I haven't the slightest intention of touching you further."

Cecilia's mind was numb with incomprehension. She'd assumed when he took her by force, there could be only one end to this awful encounter. But now she wasn't so sure. His promise about her safety had the ring of truth. And he *hadn't* attempted to touch her since they'd entered the bedroom. Why had he brought her here, then? What did he have to gain by casting this horrid blight on her reputation?

As if he had read her thoughts, he gave her a knowing smile. "You're wondering why I've gone to all this trouble? Simply, my dear, to teach you a little lesson. You played a game with me, using me as a pawn to secure your king. Now

I'm playing another game to snatch that king from you. You won't have lost your virtue when you leave this house, but you will have sadly tarnished your reputation. That's all that's necessary. You may say good-bye to your dreams of a match with Kilwarden."

"A match with Kilwarden! Now I *know* you must be mad. I've never even thought of such a thing."

"Spare me your protestations." Sir George's voice was heavy with contempt. "Your motives are quite transparent to everyone except your poor, besotted quarry. You've had your eye on your cousin ever since you met him. Why else would you have arranged this hunting party? Only so he could see you riding to hounds, showing yourself an expert at the sport he loves. And the poor fool has taken the bait. For all I know, he may already have made his offer. But he'll quickly withdraw it, after the sordid events of this afternoon."

Cecilia's mouth was dry with apprehension. Sir George had clearly gone mad. No sane mind could have conceived such a distorted picture of her intentions. There was no point in trying to reach him with explanations. Her only hope now was to somehow escape from this room and rejoin the people who loved her in the sane, bright world below.

"I see it's no use to protest." She made her voice meek and demure. "Since you've told me this much of your purpose, perhaps you'll be kind enough to explain the rest. How long must I remain here as your prisoner?"

A glint of triumph sparked in Sir George's eyes. "I'm glad your good sense has reasserted itself. I found all those angry denials most fatiguing. Your imprisonment, as you call it, will not last very much longer. In less than an hour, I'll unlock that bedroom door. It won't take us long to make our way down to the hollow. Your family and friends will be wondering what has delayed you. The explanation we give will be up to you. You may simply say that we happened to lose our way. Of course, it's highly doubtful that they'll believe you, but—"

The sound of knocking startled them both into silence. Sir George turned his head to listen. Then a triumphant smile spread over his face. "Excellent timing, truly. We have a visitor, Miss Annesley. I fear we must end this pleasant *tête-*

à-tête. With your permission, madam." He stepped to the door, turned the heavy key, and flung the door wide open. Then he stepped back toward her with a sweeping bow. "After you, Miss Annesley."

Cecilia needed no second invitation. She jumped from the bed, plunged out through the open door into the hallway—and came face to face with a grim-faced Lord Kilwarden.

A flood of relief surged through her. "Oh, Francis," she cried, "thank God you came in time." She would have flung grateful arms around his neck, but his look of shock and reproach brought her up short.

For a moment he stood there in silence, obviously struggling to find the appropriate words. When he finally spoke, his voice was ominously calm. "I'm surprised to find you here, Miss Annesley. I sincerely hope, Sir George, you can give me some satisfactory explanation."

"You see, Cecilia," Sir George said accusingly from behind her shoulder, "I warned you we were staying away too long. Our absence was bound to be noticed."

"I was tricked into coming here!" cried Cecilia shrilly "Please don't believe one word this monster tells you."

"Try to be calm, my dear." Sir George's voice was unctuous and soothing. "You know I won't give you away." He stepped in front of her, addressing himself to Kilwarden. "If the young lady chooses to claim that we came here on my suggestion, I shall not be so impolite as to accuse her of lying. Believe me, Kilwarden, I am as concerned as you that your cousin's behavior should not be the cause of malicious gossip."

"Francis, don't listen to hir   You know I'm incapable of the vile things he's implying!"

Kilwarden stared back at her with a gaze of ice. "We will discuss your surprising behavioɪ at another time and place, Miss Annesley. Our first concern now is to ameliorate the harm you have already done to your reputation."

"You're quite right, Kilwarden. Naturally, we must provide some innocent explanation for our long delay in rejoining the picnic party. May I suggest that Miss Annesley might pretend to have sprained her ankle?"

"I won't do such a thing!" Cecilia's eyes sparkled with scorn. "I won't tell lies to conceal your criminal actions."

"My dear Miss Annesley, I ask you to reconsider." Kilwarden spoke with exaggerated patience, as though he were humoring a rebellious infant. "I believe Sir George's suggestion is a very good one. You may count yourself lucky that he seems to be willing to join me in shielding you from the natural results of your indiscretion."

"My indiscretion!" echoed Cecilia blankly. Then the full force of his words came home to her. "But I've told you that he's the culprit. Do you really believe all those lying insinuations? You'd take the word of this notorious rake against the heartfelt plea of a member of your own family?"

Kilwarden's cold eyes swept her from head to foot. With a sickening lurch of her heart, she realized how she must look to him at that moment—disheveled hair falling about her face, her ragged gown wrenched halfway off one shoulder. Through a maze of shame, she heard his measured words. "I fear I may have allowed our family connection to cloud my judgment where you are concerned. Nevertheless, I shall do my best to safeguard your reputation. It should be easy enough to feign an injury."

Cecilia drew herself up stiffly, resisting the futile impulse to pull her gown back into place. "My conscience forbids me to connive at such a falsehood."

Kilwarden gave a sigh of exasperation. "Then we will simply say you both became lost in the woods."

"No! I'll proclaim the truth!" A rising tide of anger was filling Cecilia's bosom, buoying her up, giving her the courage to stare Francis straight in the eye. "He tricked me by saying he knew a short way down. He overpowered me and carried me into the bedroom. Then he locked the door—"

"Such a romantic imagination." Sir George's suave drawl cut smoothly through her tirade. "Why don't you complete your schedule in true novelistic style by accusing me of tampering with your virtue?"

Still watching Francis's eyes, Cecilia saw an arrow of pain shoot through them. She felt her own face flame, and almost shouted at him in her desperation. "No, I haven't said that. Even you couldn't be that vile a monster."

"I thought as much," purred Sir George. "Unlike your

other wild charges, that accusation would be susceptible of actual proof."

"We're wasting time," said Kilwarden brusquely. His face was white and taut, his eyes averted. "It is true, Miss Annesley, that I can't require you to tell an outright lie. But as head of the Annesley family, I do have a right to command your silence. We will go down to the hollow now. I shall make some explanation to our friends and neighbors. Sir George, of course, will quit this part of the world immediately. There will be some gossip, no doubt, but without his presence to feed it, we may hope it will quickly die down.

"I shall go with the greatest pleasure." Sir George gave a little shrug. "I've had quite enough of impetuous Irish young ladies."

"On my cousin's behalf, Sir George, I must ask you to remember how secluded a life she has led. If she lacks the discretion one finds in English young ladies—"

"This is really too much!" All of Cecilia's anger returned in a mighty wave. "You dare to apologize for me to this vile conniver? You have gone too far, Lord Kilwarden. If it weren't for the rest of the family, I would leave your house instantly. As it is, I am forced to be civil, and continue to play my role as hostess. But from this moment on, I shall no longer consider you a friend of mine."

Kilwarden's only answer was a curt nod of the head. He turned away abruptly and started down the well-trampled path that led away from the turf pile. Sir George, with a mocking smile, stepped aside to make way for Cecilia to follow Kilwarden. She heard his sibilant whisper as she passed him. "My game, just as I told you. I seem to have swept the board."

Seething with silent rage, Cecilia followed her stiff-backed cousin down the path to the hollow.

Chapter 12

"If you really believe that, Francis, you're a thousand times more a fool than I thought you." Lady Annesley, erectly posed for battle, glared at her nephew from one of the big leather armchairs in the Kilwarden House library. After several vain attempts to speak to him alone, she had finally waylaid him this morning just as he was leaving the house to attend a steeplechase in nearby Ballymahon. Now he was warming his hands at the little fireplace and making a sulky attempt to defend himself.

"How can you say that, Aunt Lydia? I met her coming out of the fellow's bedroom."

"And jumped immediately to the worst conclusion, without even listening to Cecilia's side of the story."

"I admit I was somewhat hasty. But at the moment, my chief concern was the need to preserve her reputation."

"And so you told that highly improbable story of finding the two of them lost somewhere in the woods. As if anyone could be lost on that tiny island. It was obvious to us all that you must have found them in some scandalous situation. And now, having made things a hundred times worse for Cecilia, you stand there and tell me that further discussion with her would be quite futile."

Francis glanced at her irritably. "What can I do, Aunt Lydia? She's refused every invitation to discuss the matter, avoids me like the plague, has even given up hunting. For the last three days I've scarcely seen her; apparently she's been out with Mr. Worsley, making charitable rounds among the tenants."

"That seems to me quite understandable. Your hasty conclusion that she was the one in the wrong must have seemed an intolerable insult. Perhaps if you sent her a written apology—"

Francis stared at his aunt in consternation. "An apology? Surely you can't be serious. It's she who owes *me* an apology, for soiling the family honor."

"And what about Sir George Damien? Are we to believe that he's the soul of virtue? That notorious rake whose amorous exploits are the talk of London?"

"I hold no brief for Sir George. I've always thought him something of a scoundrel. But that doesn't excuse Cecilia's part in the matter."

"Well, I'm glad you haven't taken complete leave of your senses. You admit the man's a scoundrel. Then why on earth did you bring him here to Kilwarden, and force your innocent cousin into his company?"

Francis's jaw set grimly. He had the look of a man about to shoulder an unpleasant burden. "I'm sorry to tell you this, my dear Aunt Lydia. Your innocent Cecilia had a great deal to do with bringing Sir George to Kilwarden. I'm sure they had things all arranged between them. Perhaps she even wrote him my traveling plans, so that he could trick me into bringing him here."

Lady Annesley stared at him, openmouthed. "For heaven's sake, Francis, who has been feeding you this ridiculous porridge of lies? That sly Miss Headfort, perhaps? I wouldn't have thought even she could invent so preposterous a story."

"No one needed to tell me. I could see it myself. She looked shaken to the core the night he arrived. And since then, her manner toward him has been so awkward. The blindest man could see there was something between them."

"Of course there was something between them, you egregious fool! On Cecilia's part it was bitter detestation. If you'd taken the slightest trouble to inquire, you'd have found that she shuddered whenever he crossed the threshold. She had already told me in London how very much she disliked him. But since you seemed to regard him as a friend, she had to

136

do her best to be civil to him. As for Sir George, one can easily guess his motives. You saw him force himself on her that night in my garden."

"Force himself on her?" Kilwarden's tone turned ominously quiet. "Would you say that again, Aunt Lydia? That wasn't the way you described the passage to me. You had me believing it was all part of love's young idyll."

Lady Annesley's eyes shifted uneasily. "I realize now I should have been more candid with you, Francis. When you first told me what you had seen, I really thought that there might be a match in the making. But one frank talk with Cecilia disabused me of that notion. Ever since that night in my garden, she's done her very best to have nothing to do with the man."

Francis's eyes were full of astonishment—and something else, a kind of dawning elation. "You really might have told me," he murmured softly. "You would have saved me a great deal of needless worry."

Lady Annesley gazed at him with shrewd, knowing eyes. She still felt a little guilty. She had misled him about the situation, hoping to fan his jealousy of Sir George. It appeared that her little ruse had achieved its intended effect—though Kilwarden, as yet, did not fully understand his own feelings. Now she felt obliged to do something to repair the harm her devious matchmaker's game had done to Cecilia. "I hope you'll forgive me, Francis," she said contritely. "I was less than honest with you. Now that I've told you the truth, I can see you believe me. Whatever Sir George was up to that day of the picnic, you must accept that Cecilia was totally innocent."

Francis was almost laughing with relief. "If you only knew how happy you've just made me! I could never conceive how a girl of Cecilia's good judgment could have anything to do with a man like that scoundrel. I should have trusted her more, and followed my own intuition. But it's all come clear to me now. I'll go find Cecilia at once, and beg her pardon. I hope she'll listen to me."

Lady Annesley beamed at him. "I'm sure she will, Kilwarden. She's more hurt than angry, I'm sure. If you have any trouble, I'll put in a word or two for you. If I'd been more honest with you, this would never have happened."

Kilwarden acknowledged her offer with a grateful nod as he hurried out of the library to look for Cecilia. He found her in a little cloakroom just off the entrance hall, arranging the voluminous hood of a black wool Kinsale cape to protect her curls against the chilly November breeze. "My dear Miss Annesley," he said breathlessly. "I'm so glad I found you. I hope you will grant me the favor of a few minutes' conversation."

Cecilia gave him a cold, hostile look. "Some other time, Lord Kilwarden. I am on my way to meet Mr. Worsley. We have several very sick tenants to visit today."

Kilwarden was taken aback. "Surely you're not going to miss the steeplechase? You told me last week you were looking forward to it."

"Since then I have had it brought home to me how much of my life I have wasted in shallow diversions. I've neglected our tenants for far too long." With chin held high, she moved past him toward the door to the hall.

"Cecilia!" he cried, "I beg you to listen to me. I've come to apologize."

She paused abruptly, just as she reached the door. Then she turned back and faced him, her face still impassive, waiting silently for him to continue.

"Will you ever forgive me, Cecilia—I've been such a fool— I realize now I should never have doubted you." The words tumbled out in an eager torrent. "I am sure you were innocent of any wrongdoing. It's quite clear to me now that Sir George was up to some mischief. I blame myself for inviting him here in the first place."

The ghost of a smile illumined Cecilia's eyes. "This is very gratifying, Lord Kilwarden. I am glad you no longer think me a fallen woman."

"I have never considered you *that,* and I never could. I merely thought you'd committed an indiscretion. Even for that, I was ready to make allowance, since I thought you had set your heart on a match with Sir George."

"A match with Sir George!" Cecilia was clearly astonished.

"Where on earth did you ever pick up that preposterous notion?"

Kilwarden nobly forbore to mention Aunt Lydia's name. "Some piece of gossip or other I heard in London. You know how people talk."

"You should never have listened to them." Cecilia was horrified. "To think you could make your decisions on any such basis!" Her eyes grew wide with dawning comprehension. "Is that why you asked him here? To promote my chances of winning him for a husband?"

Kilwarden nodded apologetically. "I blame myself for that. I thought you wanted him here. I disliked the fellow intensely, but I told myself I must think of your future welfare."

"My welfare, sir?" Cecilia's voice was shrill, on the edge of hysteria. "Is this what you mean by my welfare? You'd marry me off to any rake or scoundrel? But of course you would; I should have realized that. Your only concern is to get me off your hands. Then you'll have done your duty as head of the family, and can return with an easy conscience to your revels in London."

Kilwarden winced inwardly under her angry tirade. "I'm afraid I've explained myself badly—"

She cut him off before he could finish the sentence. "You haven't a trace of any real feeling for me—any more than you have for your poor, unfortunate tenants. Your only concern is to spare yourself any trouble. Let Quinlan run the estate, let Sir George take care of Cecilia. Let them all go down to perdition, so long as you can claim you have done your duty."

Kilwarden's face turned stony. "Miss Annesley, you really aren't doing me justice. I don't intend to shirk my duty toward you—"

"You have no duty toward me." Cecilia was almost shouting. "I here and now absolve you of any such duty. When I want a man to marry, I won't ask you for advice. You've already proved you're completely devoid of good judgment by trying to foist that odious rake upon me. After all, it's my whole future we're talking about. Henceforth I shall take full charge of my own affairs, without any more disastrous 'help' from you."

Whirling away from Kilwarden, she flung open the door to the entrance hall—and collided with a wide-eyed Constance, knocking her to the floor. She slammed the door shut and knelt down to help her cousin. "What are you doing here?" she muttered between clenched teeth, as she pulled the girl to her feet and rearranged the black hood on her pale blond curls.

"How could you say all those terrible things to Kilwarden?" Constance's eyes were dark with accusation. "Have you no thought of the poor souls depending on us?"

Cecilia abruptly ceased her ministrations and hurried away across the polished oak floor. When she reached the big front door, she cast an angry glance back over her shoulder. "We have work to do today," she said in an icy voice. "Let us not stand here discussing my private affairs."

She pushed the front door open. Constance scurried across the hall and managed to get through the door just before it closed. At the foot of the wide stone steps, Cecilia's little phaeton was waiting for them. Constance clutched at Cecilia's arm, preventing her from starting down the stairway. "Your private affairs are not the important issue. You *must* make friends with Kilwarden for the sake of the peasants. You were doing so well, Cecilia. He was beginning to listen. Now you throw away your advantage for a personal whim."

Cecilia turned on her, eyes flashing with fury. "Not another word, Constance. Save your sermons for Maire O'Rourke, though I doubt she'll pay them any more heed than I will. There's no use expecting Kilwarden to understand. I was a fool to waste so much of my time. If we want any help for those who depend on us, we must henceforth count on our own unassisted labors."

The improvised steeplechase course had been laid out a few miles east of the market square of Ballymahon. When Kilwarden reached the grassy hill where the race was to start and finish, he found it thronged with carriages of every description, surrounded by a larger crowd who had come on foot. A holiday atmosphere hung over the busy scene, as the spectators watched a lone gentleman rider taking a few practice jumps, or pushed their way through the mob to buy ale and gingerbread at the makeshift refreshment stands, or risk half a crown or a shilling at the betting tables.

Infected by the general gaiety, Kilwarden felt a perceptible lightening of his downcast mood. What a zest for living they had, these Irish. Peasant and gentry alike, they seemed to have the gift of casting away all care and enjoying the moment. Half of the men in this crowd, he supposed, had scarcely two ha'pennies to rub together—and yet here they were, making their miniscule bets with each other, as excited and full of anticipation as though they were staking a fortune.

Scanning the gaily-dressed occupants of the carriages, he was startled and pleased to find how many people he knew. He smiled and bowed to acknowledge a score of greetings—heartfelt shouts of welcome, not the bored, supercilious gestures he might have received from his usual cronies at Newmarket.

"Hallo there, Kilwarden! What in the devil's name has been keeping you?" Count O'Hanrahan's round face beamed at him from inside the wooden railing of the improvised weighing circle, the two white tufts of hair jutting out over his ears like the horns of an owl. "Come in and join us here. The last of the riders is just about to weigh in."

Kilwarden ducked under the railing and stood beside the count, who was peering in a businesslike way at the balance arm of the scales. "Sorry I'm late," he murmured. "Some last minute business..."

The count dismissed his excuses with the lift of one bushy eyebrow. "Don't give it a second thought, dear lad. You've plenty of time. But where is our charming Cecilia? Haven't you brought her with you? Surely Lord Corny's daughter wouldn't miss this sterling event."

"I pressed her strongly to come," Kilwarden said stiffly, "but Miss Annesley, it seems, had a prior engagement. She's out with Mr. Worsley, visiting some of my tenants."

The count's rosy face crinkled up in an impish smile. "So that's the lie of the land. She's givin' a bit of help to Mr. Worsley. I've thought for some time there was something afoot between him and your family. Of course, he's as poor as one of the mice in his church, but he might make a very good match for a certain young lady we're both concerned with."

Kilwarden was thunderstruck, but tried not to show it. Henry Worsley had seemed to him just part of the household trappings of his estate. Could what the count was implying really be true? Could that drab, pious young man have engaged the serious affections of his sparkling cousin?

"Young Worsley seems pleasant enough." He kept his expression impassive. "If my cousin consults me about him, I certainly won't let his poverty count against him. But I scarcely think it's time yet to talk of a match."

Count O'Hanrahan laid a waggish finger beside his nose. "It may be a good bit later than some of us think. When these spry young fillies take the bit in their teeth, there's no stopping them. Young blood fires up quickly, Kilwarden. Old campaigners like us are prone to forget that."

The Count gave Kilwarden's shoulder a comradely squeeze. Kilwarden answered him with a sickly smile, finding himself at a loss for a suitable comment. He didn't much like being classed as an "old campaigner." Surely he hadn't grown callous to the tender emotions? Then why had he been so blind to this state of affairs? And why, now that it was revealed, did he find himself overwhelmed with this flood of disagreeable sensations, as if some giant's hand was crushing his rib cage and a cold gray fog wrapping itself around his brain?

He felt the count's genial gaze upon him, and guessed that he must be presenting some sort of spectacle. A sudden outbreak of cheers from the crowd outside the railing gave a welcome excuse to change the subject. "Look there, O'Hanrahan. They're leading out the horses. A magnificent lot, I must admit. Whose is that lovely bay gelding, the one in the green and white colors? He seems too good for such a provincial meet."

"You've made a good choice there, Kilwarden. That's Mr. Barlow's Othello. Wait 'til you see him taking the jumps today. Old Corny certainly bred a winner in that one."

Kilwarden was startled. "That horse was bred at Kilwarden? You surprise me, Count. From what Mr. Quinlan told me, the horses he sold to Mr. Barlow weren't in that class at all. A few old hacks, ready to send to the knacker."

Now it was Count O'Hanrahan's turn to look startled. "He told you that, did he? Something smells fishy here. Othello is certainly no more than a three-year-old. And Corny himself schooled him to steeplechasing. He *was* a bit lame when Barlow put in his bid. No doubt that's why he was sold here at home, instead of being sent up to Dublin. The horses that were auctioned at Dycer's must have brought double the price that Barlow paid."

Kilwarden's eyes grew narrow with calculation. "Do you happen to know," he asked in a quiet tone, "how much Mr. Barlow paid for that lovely beast?"

"One hundred and fifty pounds, and cheap at the price. He's already won half of that back in prizes, and he's only begun to make his mark as a racehorse." He paused for a moment, regarding Kilwarden shrewdly, noting the sudden firmness of his jaw, the look of cold anger filling the deep-set gray eyes. "Oh, oh," he said, "did that rascal try to bilk you? How much did *he* tell you Barlow paid for the nag?"

"Twenty apiece for the three 'old hacks' he bought. The ones that were auctioned at Dycer's he said fetched fifty apiece."

"Hell's cauldron!" exclaimed the count. "The man's a thief and a liar. Not one of those horses fetched under three hundred."

"Are you sure of your figures?" Kilwarden's brow furrowed in thought. "But I saw those accounts myself, signed by the auctioneer. And stamped with Dycer's seal; I can swear to that. Quinlan couldn't have made them up himself."

"Could he not?" The count cocked an eyebrow. "I wouldn't be too sure. Dycer himself is an eminently honest man. But some of his underlings may be bribable."

"I can't believe it." Kilwarden was shaking his head in bewilderment. "I'm sure there's been some mistake. I'll write to Quinlan today and ask for an explanation."

"I wouldn't do that, dear lad. Let's not be so hasty. It might be well to be armed with some solid proof. If I might make a suggestion—let me talk to Dycer tomorrow when I'm up in Dublin. I'll have a few hours there before the steam packet leaves. I know the old gentleman well. I'm sure he'll agree to let me look over his books. If there's been some skullduggery, I'll get his statement in writing. Then we'll decide together how to deal with Quinlan."

Kilwarden turned to him with a grateful smile. "An excellent suggestion, O'Hanrahan. Please write me immediately after you've talked to Dycer."

"I'll do that, of course." The count's eyes grew thoughtful. "But tell me, Kilwarden, haven't you had your suspicions? From the talk that one hears in these parts, Mr. Quinlan's reputation is not of the best."

Kilwarden appeared chagrined. "I've heard those rumors, sir, but I gave them no credit. I thought them merely the work of dissatisfied tenants."

The count eyed him diffidently. "Dissatisfied tenants. Ah, yes. Does it never surprise you, Kilwarden, that all of your Irish tenants seem to have cause for complaint? Surely that's not the case on your English estate. A few malcontents, no doubt, but aren't the majority of them tolerably happy?"

"The cases are scarcely alike. Everyone knows that Irish tenants are always complaining."

"Everyone?" The count loaded the word with a world of meaning. "And who is *everyone,* pray? All of the Irish landlords, or merely the rack-renting landlords who live in London?"

Kilwarden flushed. "Do I take it, sir, that you're lumping me with those landlords? In that case, I'd like to suggest that you may be wrong. My rents are reasonable; most of them haven't been raised since Cornelius's time." He realized that he wasn't being quite honest. "Of course," he said hurriedly, "there are some cases in which the land is improved—"

"Never mind about the improvements. That's an arguable matter. But what of the fees for new leases, the penalties for not paying the rent in gold, the demands for meat and corn to supply the Great House?"

Kilwarden felt a thrill of alarm. He'd shrugged off this sort of talk when it came from Cecilia. He'd thought her regard for her tenants had made her too sympathetic to unfounded complaints. But here was this knowledgeable man, a landlord himself, making the same kinds of charges.

"Perhaps I should have looked further into the matter. Miss Annesley has tried to persuade me to do so."

"You'd do well to listen to her when it comes to Kilwarden's tenants. In Lord Corny's time, they were far less *dissatisfied*, to put it mildly. I know we all tend to discount the opinions of women on business—especially charming young women. But you'll find this particular lady has a very shrewd mind as well as a beautiful face. No more of that now; I didn't mean to offend you. But sometimes a little plain speaking is needed between friends and neighbors."

"I agree, sir, completely. I hope you will always feel free to give me advice. I am sure I could have no better guide to the conduct of my affairs."

The count seemed to smile to himself, as though savoring a hidden jest. "Hell's cauldron, dear lad, you'll find I am full of advice. When I come back from England, I hope to have somewhat more to say about your affairs. But let's leave all this for the moment. The horses are ready to start. I'll be damned if I'll let *good advice* spoil an excellent horse race."

Chapter 13

Cecilia leaned over the wan, emaciated figure on the straw pallet and put out a hand to test the old woman's forehead. Her face grew bright with relief. "Her skin is moist," she said. "I believe the fever has broken."

"Thanks be to God!" exclaimed Constance. "Perhaps now Maire will join with us in a prayer of thanksgiving." She turned to the black-coated man standing beside her. "Mr. Worsley, will you be so kind as to lead us?"

Cecilia glanced apprehensively at the still form on the pallet, hoping Maire wasn't about to burst out in a colorful exposition of her feelings about being prayed for by the Protestant curate. "Later, dear Constance, later. Just now what she needs is rest. Remember, we've still a number of tenants to visit. "We'll see Stella Ryan next, to find out how that new baby is faring."

Constance's eyes brightened, like a hound picking up a fresh scent. "I always look forward to seeing dear Stella. We had such an edifying conversation a few days ago. She's beginning to understand the privilege God has bestowed on the poor and needy."

Cecilia turned back to the silent old woman, suppressing a little grimace. Despite her dutiful reading of Hannah More's tracts, she could not bring herself to agree that poverty was a blessing. And no matter how Henry argued the healing power of prayer, she still had a great deal more faith in a bowl of good porridge.

A gust of wind down the rudimentary chimney sent the

white flaky ashes of the turf fire swirling into the room. Constance was seized with a sudden fit of coughing. Henry Worsley quickly offered an immaculate handkerchief, then hovered solicitously over her as she dabbed away at her streaming eyes.

Cecilia looked up with a frown, fearing the sound of the coughing might waken Maire. "Dear Constance," she said, "you must think of your own health as well. Why don't you let Mr. Worsley take you outside for a breath of air? I'll wait a few minutes with Maire til I'm sure she'll continue sleeping."

Constance, her eyes still streaming, nodded in gratitude, and let the attentive curate shepherd her out the door. The crisp fall air was a welcome relief, after the smoke and smells of the tiny cabin. She pulled up the hood of her Kinsale cape to shield her curls from the breeze and took a few deep breaths, smiling with pleasure. How good it was to be out in the sunlight again. Surely these small dark cabins could not be good for sick people? But of course, the poor were different. They were used to these conditions. If one tried to give them such boons as a few more windows, the change would only make them more discontented.

"I'm so glad you're feeling better, Miss Annesley." The curate retrieved his handkerchief, and tucked it neatly away in an inside pocket. "I do so admire you for subjecting yourself to our primitive conditions. I'm sure you must be longing to get back to civilized London."

"Not at all, Mr. Worsley. The past few weeks have been the happiest in my life. To be allowed to minister to the poor has always been the dearest wish of my heart. I'm sure you understand how joyful it makes me. After all, you've devoted your life to helping all these poor souls."

"Of course; of course." Worsley seemed a trifle embarrassed. "Naturally, all this is a part of my lonely calling. Though I must admit, it tests my strength at times. I find myself growing weak and faltering."

Constance gazed at him with admiring eyes. "Such a noble soul as yours could never be weak!"

Henry Worsley acknowledged her words with a deprecating smile. "I have felt a new access of strength these past few weeks. It has been very heartening to me to be helped in my labors by so expert a handmaid."

"You do me too much honor, Mr. Worsley. I am only a novice worker in the fields of the Lord. Cecilia is much better than I am at tending the sick."

"Your cousin, of course, is an angel. But I fear there are a few gaps in her spiritual education. She is excellent, as you say, in tending the poor sick bodies. But when it comes to the spiritual side of existence, your understanding far surpasses hers."

Under his admiring gaze, Constance grew pink with pleasure. She looked up shyly at him, noting how smoothly the pale shining hair was brushed back from his forehead. With that stern sweet look on his face, he was really quite handsome...She reproached herself for the worldliness of the thought. What did outward appearance matter? That noble soul of his was his real attraction.

"How very kind of you, Mr. Worsley. I've been inspired by your example. I believe I've learned a great deal these past few weeks about how to speak to the poor in an edifying manner." She hesitated a moment, then plunged bravely on. "I had thought of asking Mama if I might continue my labors here for the rest of the winter."

His look of sudden delight almost dazzled her. She felt her cheeks flaming, and shifted her eyes away in embarrassment.

"Do you really mean that, Miss Constance? I sincerely hope so. Your companionship would be such a comfort to me."

The unprecedented use of her Christian name startled Constance so that she had to look back at him. She found he was blushing just as fiercely as she was. He took her glance for reproof and started apologizing. "Forgive me, Miss Annesley. I know I shouldn't presume to be so familiar."

The dazzling smile gave way to a look of abjectness. The sudden surge of a feeling she had no name for gave Constance the courage to reach out her hand to him. "Dear Henry," she said, "you could never presume. I feel as close to you as if you were my brother."

The curate's eyes grew bright with joy and wonder. Bereft of words for a moment, he gazed silently into her eyes, the strength of his grasp almost crushing her hand. "A brother?"

he murmured softly. "I wish I might hope to be something closer than that."

Constance could feel her heart pounding. Could it really be true? Was the dearest wish of her life about to be granted? She gazed at him dreamily, her astonished heart full of thronging pictures. Henry and she together, praying beside an endless procession of sickbeds: Henry at the back of a schoolhouse, watching admiringly while she taught the village children to read the Bible; Henry and she in some rose-covered cottage, a cradle by the fire, a simple meal, prepared by her hands, on the table...

The pictures faded abruptly. She looked up at him in alarm. "Oh, Henry," she said. "I shall have to learn how to cook."

He looked nonplussed for a moment, then burst into a peal of laughter. "My dearest one, does that mean I am accepted?"

She smiled at him in rueful embarrassment. "Good gracious, I'm afraid I must seem quite idiotic. Of course you're accepted, Henry." The grip on her hand grew tighter. She looked down at it in surprise, as though she'd just realized he was holding it. "I'm sure this is all quite improper," she said hastily. "Perhaps you had better let go of my hand at once. Then we must go find Mama to ask her approval."

Reluctantly, Henry let go of her hand. He gazed down at her with a mixture of fondness and apprehension. "I know that's the proper thing, but it frightens me, rather. How do you think she'll take it? She may not like the thought of your marrying a penniless curate."

"Oh, no; I'm sure you misjudge her." Constance was trying to convince herself as well as Henry. "I know she appears very worldly, but she's always said I may make my own choice of a husband. And I do have a moderate fortune, quite large enough to support our simple existence."

Henry's face brightened a little, but he still looked doubtful. "Then, too, there's the fact that we'd be living in Ireland. She might find it very upsetting to have her daughter so far away from London."

Constance felt a chill in the space where her heart had been pounding. "I hadn't considered that. She seems to be really enjoying her Irish visit. But of course, she's too fond of London to live here permanently. And she has often spoken of wanting her grandchildren around her. It's been such a disappointment that I was her only child—"

She broke off abruptly, not wanting to say too much on that painful subject. To her great relief, Cecilia chose that moment to emerge from the cabin. "My darling Cecilia," cried Constance, "you'll never guess what's happened! Mr. Worsley and I—" She was going to say "are engaged to be married," but she realized with a pang that was not quite the case. There was still this troublesome matter of parental assent.

Cecilia didn't need to hear the end of the sentence. She had only to take one look at their two flushed, tremulous faces. "I'm so glad for you both," she said warmly. "I have never seen any two people so obviously made for each other."

"I am very pleased to have your approbation," said Henry, a little stiffly. "Perhaps you might give us some useful counsel on how to approach Lady Annesley?"

"Oh, yes, Cecilia!" Constance's eyes were shining with newfound hope. "Mama is so fond of you. I'm sure you could help us deal with her objections."

Cecilia looked surprised. "What objections could she possibly have? You know she's not a stickler for wealth and rank. And she does respect your opinions, although they're different from hers. I'm sure she'll be delighted that you've found someone who shares them so fully."

"That's exactly what I told Henry—I mean, Mr. Worsley. But I *am* afraid she'll object to my living in Ireland. She may consider the separation too drastic."

Cecilia looked grave for a moment. Then her face brightened. "Need you necessarily live in Ireland? If that's her only objection—"

"But I love it in Ireland," cried Constance. "I've been happier here than in any place I know. Surely no country on earth could give such scope for my charitable duties. And Henry, of course, is devoted to Kilwarden and its people."

Cecilia suppressed an indulgent smile. "Constance, my dear, I know you're happy here now. But it *is* a different life from the one you're used to. I fear once you've settled down to married life, you'll find a great lack of conveniences here in our rural backwater." She turned to Worsley, raising a quizzical eyebrow. "Would you really be desolated, Henry, to leave Kilwarden? In the past, I seem to remember, you had other ambitions."

Henry's face turned a shade or two pinker. "As a man of God, I go where duty calls me. It is true I have sometimes hoped that duty might call me to some wider sphere of usefulness. There's not much chance for advancement here in Ireland."

"There, Constance, you see? You must think of Henry's future. He would have far more scope for his talents if you lived in England. And I'm sure you'd be happier living close to your mother."

Constance had her own private doubts about that, but she felt it was scarcely the time to voice them. And of course, as Cecilia said, she was used to England. That rose-covered cottage, for instance—she realized now that was a purely English invention. She hadn't seen even one such edifice since she'd come to Ireland.

"My darling Cecilia, you're as percipient as ever. Of course it's my duty to Henry to urge him to come to England. But how would he go about finding a suitable living?"

Cecilia couldn't suppress a small chuckle of pleasure at being so easily able to answer that question. "The simplest thing in the world. You have only to ask Cousin Francis. I happen to know there's a very good living vacant, down on his estate in Buckinghamshire."

Constance was too excited to wonder why Cecilia had been discussing vacant livings with Francis. "Oh, Cecilia, that's wonderful. It seems like a gift of God. Henry, you must go immediately and ask him. Once our home in England has been assured, Mama can have no further objections."

Henry looked pleased, but not quite so pleased as Constance. "We mustn't approach Kilwarden too hastily. He may already have someone in mind. Perhaps, Cecilia, you could feel him out?"

"Oh, yes, Cecilia, I'm sure he'd listen to you—" Constance broke off in mid-sentence, obviously remembering the scene in the Great House that morning.

Cecilia was careful to keep her face impassive. "At the moment, as Constance knows, I'm not on the best of terms with Lord Kilwarden. If you wish, however, I'll try to do what I can."

"Oh, no, Cecilia, I wouldn't dream of putting you to that trouble. Mr. Worsley will speak for himself. Won't you, Henry?"

Henry Worsley looked distinctly uncomfortable, but rose manfully to Constance's expectations. "It is really my place to speak to him. Since his lordship is head of your family, it is only proper that I inform him of our intentions." He glanced anxiously at Cecilia. "Have you any opinion, Cecilia, as to whether he'll object to my marrying your cousin?"

"If we have Mama on our side, he'll have to give in," Constance broke in eagerly. Then her bright smile faded. "Oh dear, it's all such a muddle. Mama's consent depends on our living in England. And that depends on your getting that English living. So Cousin Francis is really the key to it all. Let's go together, Henry, and see him at once. I can't bear another minute of this suspense."

Henry gave her a look of husbandly sternness. "I'm sure that would strike his lordship as a far too impetuous mode of procedure. I have a better suggestion. I shall wait to speak to him until after the service next Sunday. Meanwhile I shall be preparing a moving sermon on the duties of property owners toward the Established Church."

Cecilia, who thought that approach not likely to be successful, ventured a cautious protest. "I'm sure there's no need for such arduous preparation. Won't you just ask him straight out? Then we could make the announcement at the hunt ball this Saturday night. I'm sure all our friends and neighbors would be delighted to drink an engagement toast."

Following Henry's lead, Constance turned a reproving gaze on her cousin. "What a frivolous notion, Cecilia. What do we care for such things as *announcements* and *toasts*? I'm sure dear Henry is right. We must wait until next Sunday. I hope I may have your promise that you won't drop any premature hints to Mama or Lord Kilwarden?"

Cecilia was extremely reluctant to make any such promise. She was perfectly sure no good could come of postponement. The demand that she hide the secret from the family went painfully crossgrain to her forthright nature. But the plea in Constance's eyes was too strong to resist.

"Very well," she said slowly. "I'll keep your secret 'til Sunday. But not a day longer, mind you. I don't like keeping secrets from Lord Kilwarden."

Kilwarden, riding homeward after the race, paused on the crest of a rise to survey his domain—the rolling pastures, still green in early November; the rich dark soil of farmland awaiting the plough, the gray-brown little hills ringing him round, with the darker brown slashes where turf had been freshly cut. There was only one blemish to mar his growing delight with his Irish estate: those tumbledown stone cabins— hovels, really—strewn over the countryside in random fashion. He gave a deep sigh of frustration. How could this small world of his ever hope to prosper while its lazy, ungrateful tenants wallowed in filth and rags?

A flicker of motion off to the left of the road caught his attention. He saw two black-clothed figures emerge from one of the cabins. Despite his distance from them, he recognized them at once—and was gripped by an unaccountable feeling of irritation.

The black-coated man was standing very close to the lady in the hooded Kinsale cape. He saw her lift her face to him, as though in surprise. Then she put her hand out impetuously; it was seized at once in what was clearly a lover's gesture.

A wave of pain and loss swept over Kilwarden. He spurred his horse to a canter, and quickly moved away from the intimate scene. The canter turned to a gallop; in a few minutes more he was back at Kilwarden House. Lady Annesley, snug in her drawing room armchair, laid aside her book as she heard him enter the hall. To her great surprise, he didn't come in to greet her. She heard his footsteps running up the stairs, and then the slamming door of the master bedroom.

She turned to the other occupant of the elegant room, still placidly occupied with her embroidery. "Very unusual behavior, is it not, Lady Margaret? What can have happened to make Kilwarden so angry?"

Chapter 14

Cecilia folded the ends of the white lace falling tucker and pinned it with the shell cameo brooch which had been Lord Corny's favorite. Then she stood back to survey the effect in her mirror. She felt a small flutter of pleasure. The lilac tabernet gown with the stiff satin scrolls round the hem looked even more splendid here than it had in London. Perhaps she should have saved it for later on in the season. There were still a dozen or so hunt balls to come.

But not another one here at Kilwarden. Not this year. Perhaps not ever. The nagging, inward voice dampened her festive mood. She dropped wearily into the chair by her dressing table, oblivious of the way she was rumpling her skirts. What did it really matter, all this splendor? The twenty-foot dining table, gleaming with linen and silver, waiting for the sumptuous feast which Sheila Reilly had been preparing for days? The hundreds of new wax candles in the grand saloon, highlighting the decorations of rich autumn foliage? The dusty bottles of claret, disinterred from the cellar and lovingly polished; the hogshead of whiskey set up in the billiard room?

She knew what the guests would think. She could already hear their exclamations of pleasure. "It's just the same," they would say, "just as it used to be in Lord Corny's time." But it wasn't the same at all. It could never be. The old Lord Kilwarden had been genial and expansive, exuding a warmth so cordial that even the dourest guest found his spirits uplifted. The new Lord Kilwarden was an unfeeling tailor's dummy, with a cold and distant manner that turned one's blood to ice...

You know that's not so, Cecilia. Francis's manner may not be so exuberant, but he's already made firm friends of most of our neighbors. He's not cold and icy to them, only to you. And whose fault is that, my haughty, ill-tempered miss? If you hadn't turned down his apology so rudely...

For the twentieth time that day, Cecilia surveyed the dismal events of that week. Kilwarden had been avoiding her like the plague—barely civil at meals, ignoring her presence in the drawing room after dinner, not deigning to speak when they passed on the stairway. She'd even abandoned her shepherding of Constance, hoping to mend the breach in the hunting field. But there, as at home, the iciness had persisted.

And of course, he was perfectly right to treat her so coldly. Her conduct toward him had been abominable. What on earth could have impelled her to lash out at him in that execrable way? What right had she to be angry simply because he had paired her off with Sir George? Why should he care who she married? She'd only come into his life a few months ago, as an awkward burden to be somehow disposed of. She'd go out of his life just as quickly. If he stayed here even as long as the end of the season, it wasn't because he enjoyed her company. It was only because he'd discovered what marvelous sport this corner of Ireland offered.

But even that wouldn't draw him back next year. Not when it meant putting up with that barbarous Irish cousin, who'd flared up at him like a spitfire when he was trying his best to make amends....

A wave of desolation swept over Cecilia. She leaned on her dressing table, burying her head in her arms, the lilac-clad shoulders heaving with huge racking sobs. She'd never see him again—that pleasant, gray-eyed host smiling quietly at her from the head of the table; that lithe scarlet-coated horseman, soaring over a high stone fence beside her; that supple, light-footed partner, gilding a boisterous evening of country dancing with the same elegance that had captivated Almack's.

The sobbing went on and on; she was powerless to stop it. She knew her reddened eyes and puffy eyelids would spoil the whole effect of the splendid gown. But what did it matter? What did anything matter? With Francis once more a stranger, what was the point of living?

Through the sound of her sobs, she heard a knock on the door. She tried to ignore it, but the knocking grew more insistent. She snatched a handkerchief, doused it in eau-de-cologne, and dabbed furiously at her eyes. "Come in," she called, turning away from the door to hide her ravaged face. She saw the servant's reflection in the mirror. He was trying not to look curious, but obviously was embarrassed by her strange demeanor.

"What is it?" she said in a choking voice.

"It's his lordship sent me, miss. He says I'm to tell you it's very important. He asks will you be so kind as to grant him an interview immediately. He's down in the library now, awaiting your answer."

A surge of hope burned its way through Cecilia's veins. What could it mean, this summons? Was he giving her a chance to atone for her rudeness? Or did he intend some final, curt dismissal, perhaps the news that he was leaving for England?

She stumbled to her feet, no longer troubling to hide her face. "Tell Lord Kilwarden I'll be with him very shortly."

The servant nodded and closed the door discreetly, as Cecilia turned back to her dressing table, assessing its restorative tints and unguents like a general preparing his troops for battle.

The servant's report that Cecilia was on her way set Kilwarden pacing again. He had thought his course of action was fully decided. Now he found himself wrestling once more with his strange repugnance to give his approval to the match with Henry Worsley.

Hang it, what did he have against the man? The Church, after all, was still a gentleman's calling, despite the rough diamonds one found in some pulpits these days. His manners were excellent; his moral character above reproach. He shared Cecilia's devotion to the poor.

And yet, he couldn't help thinking the match disastrous. The crux of it was that he didn't think Henry deserved her.

She seemed made for a far better fate than settling down as the wife of a country curate. She ought to have a husband who could dress her in style, provide her with an elegant setting, give her the chance to indulge her passion for hunting. She had proved already that she could shine in London. She'd be wasted, spending her life in the provinces. Of course, she'd probably not like to leave Ireland completely—but a suitable husband could work out some congenial pattern— say four months in Ireland, four months in London, four months somewhere in England, Buckinghamshire, for instance...

He jerked to a halt in front of the marble fireplace and stared at himself in the mirror that hung above it. Good Lord, was *that* the root of all this malaise? That he secretly wanted to marry Cecilia himself?

For a moment or two he let himself imagine what life would be like for the two of them. A throng of delightful images assailed him: Cecilia, bright-eyed and laughing at the foot of a dinner table; Cecilia galloping over the countryside, her whole being attuned to the cry of the eager hounds; Cecilia, radiant in yellow net over white satin, lifting her face to him on some shadowy terrace...

He cut off those thoughts abruptly, all too aware of where they were going to lead him. The thing was impossible. He had always known that. How had he let himself grow so fond of the girl?

He squared his shoulders, still watching himself in the mirror. *So there you are, you sly rascal; I've caught you out. You won't play the dog in the manger any longer. Whatever hidden regrets you may let yourself harbor, you won't let them hinder your duty toward your cousin.*

A gentle tap on the door made him swing around quickly. As Cecilia entered the room, he caught his breath in wonder. She was more beautiful tonight than he'd ever seen her. He forced himself to keep his face impassive, not let his eyes betray how enchanting he found her. "That's a very attractive gown." He managed to keep his voice level. "I believe it's one I've seen you wear in London."

Cecilia's heart lifted at the mildness of his tone. At least he didn't intend to read her a lecture! "Yes, it's one of my favorites. I wore it the first night you danced with me at Almack's."

Kilwarden sketched a bow. "I'm honored that you should remember the occasion."

Cecilia flushed. Had she given herself away? She couldn't bear him to guess that she remembered every moment they'd spent together. She found that she was unable to meet his eyes, and railed at herself for being a foolish ninny.

Kilwarden was too involved with his own disturbing thoughts to notice anything strange about her manner. He forced himself to get down to the business in hand. "I summoned you here this evening, Cousin Cecilia, so that I might apologize. I've behaved atrociously toward you these last few days."

"Oh no, Francis, no!" exclaimed Cecilia. "I am the one who ought to apologize. That hysterical outburst of mine the other morning—I've been full of remorse ever since. How could I ever doubt that you have my welfare at heart?"

"I insist that I should bear at least part of the blame." Francis was doggedly trying to get to his point. "I've been most insensitive toward your tender feelings. I can quite understand your hesitation to turn to me for advice in your choice of a husband."

Cecilia was overcome with mortification. "Those wild words I shouted at you! Will you ever forgive me? I didn't mean them, of course. I fully acknowledge your role as head of the family. If the question of choosing a husband ever arises, you may be assured I will eagerly seek your advice."

Kilwarden felt himself growing unbearably tense. He drew a deep breath, hoping it would relax him. "I'm extremely gratified to hear you say that. I hope I may justify your trust in me. In your current situation, for instance, I believe I might be able to remove some obstacles for you."

"My current situation? What on earth do you mean?"

Kilwarden's tone turned apologetic. "I hope you won't think I'm intruding. I couldn't help seeing you with Mr. Worsley. Purely by accident, you understand. I was overjoyed to see how things stood between you. He's a fine young man, and I'm sure he will make you happy."

For a moment, Cecilia's mind was numb with incomprehension. Then she realized what must have occurred. Last Monday morning with Henry Worsley, Constance and she had both worn their Kinsale cloaks. That all-enveloping hood must have hidden her cousin's fair hair. Kilwarden had seen them together—perhaps at the very moment of Henry's proposal. They must have been holding hands, perhaps even kissing....

Cecilia's face flamed. "Appearances, sir, are not always to be trusted."

Kilwarden was stung by the acid edge to her voice. He told himself that he'd better start treading more softly. Like any young girl in love, her emotions just now were terribly volatile. "I really don't want to pry. I merely want to assure you that I'll help you and Mr. Worsley in any way that I can. There's a vacant living, for instance, of which I have the bestowal. If the two of you would consider leaving Ireland, at least for a time, it might give him a start on a very successful career."

Cecilia's mind was awhirl with conflicting emotions—delight at his generous offer, hurt and resentment at his pairing her off with Henry. Did he really think she could love so dull a man? But of course, the question of love didn't enter into the picture; hadn't she just decided that his only concern was to be rid of a burdensome duty?

If only she could explain, tell him that Constance was Henry's intended, not herself. But she'd given her word; there was no going back on that. Still, she had to make some kind of answer. If she remained stubbornly mute, he'd think she still clung to that mood of rebellion that had caused such a breech between them.

"I thank you with all my heart for that generous offer, Cousin Francis. But I'm sure you realize that I'm scarcely the proper person with whom to discuss it. I trust in due time Mr. Worsley and you will be able to settle the matter between yourselves."

Kilwarden felt a hollow sensation in the pit of his stomach. Cecilia's words had banished his last faint hope that he might have somehow misread the situation. Cecilia saw the shadow clouding his eyes. "You look troubled, Cousin Francis," she said hesitantly. "I hope nothing I've said has given offense."

Kilwarden arranged his features into a mechanical smile. It was now high time, he decided, to change the subject. "Not at all, not at all," he said briskly. "I am somewhat troubled, it's true, but it has nothing to do with your marriage. I've had some disturbing news about Mr. Quinlan."

"Really?" Cecilia affected a casual air. "I hope the poor man's not ill? Much as I dislike his methods, I don't wish him any harm."

"I'm beginning to share your opinion about his methods." Kilwarden paused for a moment, obviously wondering whether to confide in Cecilia. Then he appeared to reach a firm resolution and plunged into a startling speech of apology. "After the way I've brushed off all your warnings, it goes against the grain to admit this to you. I fear you were quite correct in describing the man as a rogue and a scoundrel."

His rueful words sent Cecilia's spirits soaring. Was her moribund campaign about to be resurrected? Was there still some chance to avert the total disaster that threatened Kilwarden's tenants? "I am surprised to hear you say that, Cousin Francis." She was trying to keep the excitement out of her voice. "May I inquire what has caused you to change your mind? But perhaps you think that question too presumptuous."

"It's not presumptuous at all. You have every right to know what I've discovered. You've been doing your best ever since the day I met you to open my eyes to Mr. Quinlan's crimes. I was a fool not to listen to your advice. From now on, I assure you, I shall eagerly listen to whatever you choose to tell me."

"I'm sure you know how very happy that makes me." Cecilia gave up the attempt to hide her elation. "Do tell me, Francis, what caused you to change your mind? Can't you see I'm dying with curiosity?"

Francis took a letter out of his pocket. "This has just come from Dublin, where Count O'Hanrahan was making some inquiries on my behalf. You may as well read it yourself. I'm sure it won't surprise you. There can be no further doubt that the man is a thief and a scoundrel."

Cecilia took the letter and scanned it quickly. "I don't understand," she said. "The count merely quotes the prices for Papa's three steeplechasers. Four hundred pounds seems a little too high for Regal. Salamander is a better jumper, and he only fetched three hundred and fifty."

"The account Mr. Quinlan gave me of that transaction showed each of those horses going for fifty pounds each."

"Good heavens!" exclaimed Cecilia. "So Quinlan put the difference in his own pocket. But wasn't he taking a terrible risk? What if you'd asked to see the papers from Dycer's?"

"I'm not quite *that* much of an innocent. I did ask to see those papers. The rascal produced them. They looked authentic enough. I've seen Dycer's seal before, since some of my own horses had passed through his hands. And Dycer, of course, has a spotless reputation. But now it appears some underling produced false copies, no doubt upon receipt of a suitable bribe."

"That explains the count's last paragraph. I wondered why he should mention that a clerk of Mr. Dycer's had just been dismissed."

Kilwarden gave a nod of grim satisfaction. "One rascal has got his deserts. The principal culprit remains unscathed. But not for long, I assure you. I have already sent off a letter to Mr. Quinlan, summoning him to render a full accounting. Not just about the horses; that's a minor detail. But now that I know he's a thief and a liar, I'm going to investigate *all* his accounts. I need your help in that, Cousin Cecilia. All those fees and exactions you've told me about—they never appeared on the books, so I thought they didn't exist. I believed you had been deluded by your crafty tenants, playing on your womanly sympathies."

"My crafty tenants! Those miserable, overworked wretches? If only you'd speak to them, Francis, learn to know them. They could tell you far better than I how Quinlan has soueezed the life out of your estate."

"I can see the mistake I made in refusing to hear their complaints. I intend to remedy that as soon as I can. Meanwhile, I ask your help in confronting Quinlan. We'll face him together, question every account, go over all the leases, find out the reason for every change of tenant. You'll be there to supply all the damning details. I know what a marvelous memory you have for these things." He checked himself, and gave her a diffident glance. "I hope I'm not asking too much of you. It may be a very unpleasant encounter. That rascal will know he's fighting for his life. If you prefer, I'll confront him by myself—armed, of course, with your valuable information."

Cecilia looked up at him with an impish smile. "Don't you know me better than that? I assure you, I'm more than a match for Mr. Quinlan. So long as Kilwarden's landlord is by my side, I could wrestle a cave full of lions—figuratively speaking, that is."

Kilwarden smiled down at his newly-acquired accomplice. "I hope it won't prove to be quite that strenuous an effort. But all this will have to wait for a few more days. Meanwhile, we have our dinner guests to think of." He looked guiltily at the clock, and saw it was almost time to go in to the table. He moved quickly to the door and opened it for her. "If you'll allow me, dear Cousin, we shall go partake of Sheila's glorious cooking. After which, I devoutly hope, you'll overcome your distaste for 'shallow diversions' and let me lead you out in the first quadrille."

Cecilia acknowledged the barb with a little *moue,* and happily took the arm he proffered. "Lead on, Kilwarden," she said. "Speaking of 'strenuous effort,' you won't know what 'strenuous' means until you've survived your first Kilwarden hunt ball."

"You must be very proud of your Lucinda." Lady Margaret shifted her gaze from the roomful of dancers to exchange a maternal smile with Lady Headfort. "She's quite the belle of the ball. Each time the music stops, she's surrounded by handsome young men demanding to be her next partner."

Lady Headfort's answering smile had a little hint of sourness around the edges. "I'm very pleased to see her enjoying herself. The poor girl has had a rather thin time of it lately. Much as I like and admire your worthy nephew, I fear he has sadly neglected his duties as host."

Lady Margaret looked a little apologetic. "It *is* rather naughty of Francis to dance with almost no one except Cecilia. I really ought to go have a word with him, ask him to dance with some of the local ladies. But I must admit I've been feeling greatly relieved to see them together. This past week I thought I detected a distressing coolness between them. But perhaps that was all in my imagination."

"There's certainly no coolness tonight. He's scarcely looked at anyone else." Lady Headfort tried to sound as though that fact pleased her as much as it obviously pleased Lady Margaret. Good Lord, what a fool of a woman. *A certain coolness, indeed!* Didn't she realize how close her daughter had come to total disaster? If it hadn't been for Kilwarden's intervention, the girl would have been easy prey for that cunning Damien. She wouldn't have thought anyone could be so naïve as to swallow his facile talk of a secret engagement. That was certainly one of the oldest tricks in the book. Still, what did the old saw say—"like mother, like daughter." Lady Margaret, given her own impetuous nature, was scarcely equipped to constrain others' rash behavior.

It wasn't fair; it really wasn't fair. She'd spent half her life shaping Lucinda into an elegant, irreproachable lady. By rights, she should be the one in Kilwarden's arms instead of this so-called cousin of dubious morals. What would it take to open his eyes to the dreadful mistake he seemed perilously close to making? Perhaps it was time to use that damning letter from Lady Maxbury. Once he knew the girl was a bastard, he would surely banish her from his life altogether.

She felt a pang of regret about Lady Margaret. At her time of life, the disgrace would be hard to bear. Still, she had to think first of her own Lucinda's welfare; if it took that last dreadful stroke to win her Kilwarden's attention, then the blow must fall, regardless of whom it hurt.

Her fertile mind started sketching an alternate plan. She was sure she knew why Kilwarden had relented. It all came back to his ardent passion for hunting. That icy coldness—so promising for Lucinda—had begun to thaw when Cecilia came out with the hounds. The hunting field was where his heart would be lost or won—by a girl who could chase a fox to catch a husband. Lucinda could share that sport if she'd only try. Cecilia's skill in jumping might outshine hers, but that shouldn't keep her out of the field completely....

What if Cecilia wasn't there to outshine her? The insidious thought seemed to leap at her out of nowhere. Once it had made its entrance, it refused to be banished. *The thing would be easy to do. Of course I don't wish the girl to be seriously hurt. But wouldn't a few bumps and bruises heal much faster than the harm that might be done by that damning letter?*

Lady Headfort, stifling a few stray qualms of conscience, devoted herself to considering ways and means.

Chapter 15

"A most persuasive sermon, Mr. Worsley." Kilwarden pressed the curate's hand warmly. "And now, I trust, you're coming back to the Great House to join us for luncheon? I've already sent the two carriages back with the ladies. Perhaps you and I could ride up to the house together."

Henry Worsley's heart started thudding painfully. He knew he ought to be seizing this heaven-sent chance to broach the subject of marriage, but all his well-prepared phrases seemed to have flown out the window. He had planned to invite Lord Kilwarden into the sacristy, in order to raise the delicate matter in private. But Kilwarden was already mounting, clearly eager to be on his way. "I'll join you with pleasure, my lord. It will only take a few minutes to store my vestments." He scolded himself as he hurried back into the church for the fawning servility with which he had spoken. That was scarcely the way to approach his prospective in-laws—as though he were some improvident beggar humbly asking for crumbs from their table.

He forced himself to take his clerical robes off slowly, resisting the impulse to hurry back to Kilwarden. When he finally emerged from the church, he felt more in command of himself. Kilwarden, he was glad to see, didn't look especially impatient. He kept his horse to an amble as they moved away toward the house. Henry matched his pace, reconsidering his approach. Perhaps it was just as well that he hadn't yet spoken. The thing could be done much more smoothly up at the Great House. The sight of Constance over the luncheon table would no doubt fire him with new resolution. And then, with Kilwarden relaxed over port and cigars...

"I am led to believe there is something you wish to discuss with me, Mr. Worsley." Kilwarden's quiet statement seemed to shatter the silence between them like the blast of a shotgun. Henry did his best to rise to the challenge.

"As a matter of fact, Lord Kilwarden—I realize you may think me very forward—but since a certain young lady has done me the honor—" Henry paused, gulped, fell silent again, trying vainly to make some use of his paralyzed tongue.

Kilwarden sighed to himself. Why couldn't this clumsy young man get on with the business? "That certain young lady has already spoken to me." He forced what he hoped would pass for a cordial smile. "I must tell you at once that I approve the match heartily. I'm sure she'd mentioned to you the living in Buckinghamshire. It's yours if you choose to take it. As your future cousin by marriage, I hope you'll allow me to help you to this extent."

Henry's disabled tongue was startled back into life. "What a generous offer, Lord Kilwarden. I don't know how to thank you sufficiently. Not just for the living, though I must admit it will be extremely helpful. But of course, the inestimable gift of Miss Annesley's hand far surpasses any material satisfaction." A delicious warmth was suffusing Henry's veins, as he felt all the well-polished phrases seeping back into his mind. Just as he was opening his mouth to continue the speech, Kilwarden cut him off with an impatient gesture.

"There's no need to thank me for that. It's not my gift to bestow. Miss Annesley has made her choice; I am pleased to confirm it. I trust you will do your best to make her happy."

Mr. Worsley felt his nascent pleasure invaded by a tiny tremor of apprehension. Kilwarden's words had been cordial, but something about his tone hinted at disapproval. Constance had already warned him that her titled cousin shared her mother's worldly predilections. No doubt he had wished her to make a far grander marriage. Still, now his consent was secured, what did it matter if it was a trifle grudging? There was plenty of time in the future to prove that even a lowly curate could be a good husband. "I sincerely intend to make Miss Annesley happy. Since our interests in life are so convergent, that sacred task should present no great difficulty."

"Ah, yes. Your interests in life." Kilwarden nodded glumly. "I realize how much you share Miss Annesley's devotion to my tenants. I hope you won't find it too much of a wrench to transfer that devotion to my other tenants in England."

"Miss Annesley was quite reluctant at first." Henry jumped at the chance to exchange confidences. "She finds such scope here, you understand, for her special gifts of spiritual counseling. However, I was able to persuade her that an equally fertile field awaits her in England. And of course, she is delighted at the prospect of living within easy reach of her own family."

Kilwarden felt a qualm of disquiet. He hadn't fully considered this side of the matter. Did he really want Cecilia living in Buckinghamshire? Now that he'd become fully aware of his feelings toward her, would he not find a continuing torment in having her near him as the newly-wedded wife of Henry Worsley? But surely he could quickly subdue those unsuitable emotions. And he'd be able to watch over her welfare, make sure she was really happy. "That, sir, is a two-sided pleasure—to have my cousin practically on my doorstep." He smiled genially at Worsley—a more genuine smile this time, as though he'd just reached some difficult decision. "Of course, Miss Annesley will have the run of my stables. I hope she will spare some time from her charitable duties to try out a few of my beasts in the hunting field."

Now it was Worsley's turn to register disapproval. "That's very kind of you, sir," he said frostily. "However I scarcely expect Miss Annesley to accept your generous offer. I'm sure she'll have far more serious calls on her time and attention."

Not even married yet, and already playing the tyrant. Kilwarden was shocked at the strength of his sudden anger. Would Cecilia let this clod deny her that favorite diversion? Would those sparkling high spirits of hers be damped down into pious meekness? What in the world was she doing, condemning herself to that drab half-life? Surely he ought to do something to prevent it. But what could he do? She had made the choice, after all. He had already given his formal consent. He could scarcely withdraw it now, much as he yearned to do so. No, better to get the whole thing over, make it irrevocable. Then he'd be better able to deal with his own unruly feelings.

"Everything's settled, then," he said abruptly. "When do you and Miss Annesley plan to be married? I presume you've already chosen a suitable date. Christmas, perhaps, or even a little sooner?"

Henry had the uncomfortable feeling that he was being hurried along toward a future he wasn't fully prepared for. "Well, actually, it isn't completely settled." He cast an embarrassed glance toward Lord Kilwarden. "I haven't yet spoken to Miss Annesley's mother. We thought it best—Miss Annesley and I—to approach you first, in this matter of the living."

Kilwarden's impatience was growing intolerable. "Yes, yes, of course. That was very prudent of you. That estimable lady, I'm sure, will have no objections. If you think it would help for me to put in a word—" He spurred his ambling mount into a trot. "If we hurry a bit, we'll arrive before time for luncheon. Perhaps we can take a few minutes to put the question before Lady Margaret."

Worsley quickened his horse's pace to match that of Lord Kilwarden. "I hadn't thought of approaching Lady Margaret." He was forced to shout to be heard above their hoofbeats. "I suppose, as Miss Annesley's aunt, she will also be concerned for her niece's welfare."

"Aunt? Did you say aunt?" Kilwarden reined in abruptly, bringing his horse to a standstill. Worsley, still trotting briskly, found himself several yards ahead of him on the road. He wheeled his mount and came back to face Kilwarden. The landlord's face had gone pale with astonishment, as though he'd just seen some ghostly apparition. "Do I understand you aright, sir? It's Miss *Constance* Annesley you wish to marry? It's Lady *Lydia's* permission we have yet to secure?"

"Of course. Whose else could it be?" Henry Worsley's bewilderment gave way to embarrassed comprehension. "You surely didn't think I meant Cecilia? She's a very fine girl, of course, and one of my dearest friends. But I trust you won't think me offensive when I say she's not serious enough for a clergyman's wife."

"My dear Mr. Worsley, I agree completely. My cousin Constance is far better suited for that kind of life." Kilwarden was beaming now, as though he'd just been informed of some bountiful stroke of good fortune. "Come, man, we're wasting time. Let's go up to the house and get this all settled at once. I'm sure Lady Annesley will be delighted—though not even she, I assure you, could be half so delighted as I am to be giving this particular cousin away in marriage."

In accordance with a custom begun by Cecilia's father, the third week of November began with a meet on the lawn of Kilwarden House. This had become a major social occasion, attracting a crowd of well-wishers from miles around, who enjoyed the champagne Lord Corny always provided, while preparing to cheer the horsemen on their way.

This particular Monday morning, the new Lord Kilwarden was seen to be smiling broadly as he proposed a toast to the happy couple who would, he informed his neighbors, be married in late December. While the cheering crowd were downing their glasses, Kilwarden made his way to the portico of the Great House, from which Lady Annesley was surveying the lively scene. "My dear Aunt Lydia," he murmured into her ear, "may I offer you my own private congratulations? It must give a mother's heart great satisfaction to see her daughter so appropriately settled in life."

Lady Annesley looked archly up at her handsome nephew. "Judging from your demeanor, I'd say *your* pleasure was almost as great as mine. Is that merely relief that my Constance is finally disposed of? Or does your satisfaction stem from some more personal motive?"

Kilwarden made some noncommittal answer, averting his face from his aunt's perspicacious gaze. He was fully aware of the source of his satisfaction. He had hated the thought of seeing Cecilia married—to pious young Worsley or anyone else. The news that Constance, not Cecilia, was the curate's intended bride had come as a welcome reprieve. He did not wish, at the moment, to let himself consider the matter further. He knew all too well where such thoughts must lead. Cecilia might be still unattached and fancy-free, but that didn't alter the fact that she was his cousin, and therefore marriage to her was completely out of the question.

Lady Annesley, seeing her nephew's discomfort, tactfully abstained from pursuing the subject. "What a fortunate idea it has turned out to be, this house party of Cecilia's. I'm sure you are well aware that I had almost despaired of finding a husband for Constance. I had often been assured by other mothers that house parties provided a perfect climate for budding romances, but somehow I didn't foresee that my serious Constance would reap any such benefits from our trip to Ireland." She let her gaze shift for a moment to Lucinda Headfort, noting how striking she looked in her scarlet coat. That petulant frown, though, was rather a pity. Lady Headfort must have laid down some ultimatum to induce her daughter back into the hunting field. Lady Annesley allowed herself a wry smile of satisfaction. No doubt that frustrated mother was seething with disappointment at having to drink engagement toasts to someone else's daughter.

She glanced back at her silent nephew, wondering if he had noticed Lucinda's presence. But he was preoccupied with other matters. "As you say, Aunt Lydia, it has proved to be a very fortunate expedition. Fortunate for me, as well as for Constance. I owe Cecilia a debt of gratitude for opening my eyes to the way my agent has been mismanaging my estate."

Lady Annesley did her best to conceal her surprise. She had thought her niece had abandoned that campaign of persuasion. What could have happened to bring it to life again? "So you think there is some good reason to distrust Mr. Quinlan? Cecilia's convinced you that you should dismiss the man?"

Kilwarden's gaze shifted evasively. "I'm not sure I'll go that far. I must wait until Quinlan comes down here to answer my questions. Suffice it to say that I'm giving Cecilia's complaints my full attention. I should have done so much sooner, but it took the count's letter to finally open my eyes."

Lady Annesley's mind was awash with consternation. Had the count gone back on his promise? He'd assured Lady Margaret that she'd be the first to know. Now it seemed he'd revealed his delicate mission to Francis. But what did all this have to do with Mr. Quinlan? "You—you've heard from the count directly?" she managed to stammer. "But that seems impossible. He's scarcely had time to conclude his business in England."

Kilwarden stared at her blankly. "The count told me nothing of any business in England. It was what he discovered in Dublin that opened my eyes to Mr. Quinlan's guilt. Still, I mustn't prejudge the man. I'm expecting him here at Kilwarden by the end of the week. After he's had the chance to defend himself, I may make some drastic changes in my future plans for Kilwarden."

Lady Annesley smiled with secret relief and satisfaction. So Cecilia's secret had not yet been revealed. How neatly these separate strands were knitting together! By the end of the week, there should be some news from England. If that news was what she hoped for, it might change Francis's future plans even more drastically than he expected. "I'm sure your future holds all sorts of exciting changes," she said enigmatically.

Francis gave her a puzzled glance, as though he was just about to ask what she meant. A sudden flurry of cheers from the crowd below them brought a precipitate end to the conversation. "They're cheering the Master, Mr. Barlow. He must be about to propose the stirrup cup. If you'll excuse me, Aunt Lydia, I must go find my horse and take my place in the field."

Still glowing with secret satisfaction, Lady Annesley watched Kilwarden stride toward his horse. Cecilia's handsome mare, Dido, was standing nearby. Francis helped her into the saddle, then sprang up onto his own sorrel gelding. The servants were rushing around, filling the champagne glasses of all the riders.

"A quick find and a rousing chase!" Mr. Barlow, beaming, shouted the final toast. As the field around him joined in the three times three, the whippers-in unleashed the eager pack. They streaked off down the avenue of beeches, past the little gatehouse, across the road and into the field beyond. Here they milled around in confusion for three or four minutes, while the riders reined in their mounts, watching the hounds in eager anticipation.

Then Rival, one of the leading hounds, lifted up his head

with a clarion call, and the whole pack was off behind him, noses close to the ground, soaring across fence after rocky fence, with the galloping hooves of the hunters thundering behind them.

The fox quickly led them out of the level farmland into a gray-brown ridge of heather-clad hills. The going was rougher here, full of hidden pitfalls. Most of the horsemen held their mounts to a canter. Kilwarden alone plunged recklessly ahead, almost overriding the hounds in his zest for the chase.

Cecilia, dropping back to the rear of the field, saw the pack split up into two separate halves, which then streamed off in opposite directions. She looked toward the Master, waiting to follow his lead. Mr. Barlow, after a moment of hesitation, wheeled around and followed the hounds to the left of him. Cecilia realized why he had made that decision. The group of hounds on the right were heading toward the little foothill where Kilwarden's land touched that of Sir Jonah Boothby. A four-foot fence ran along the boundary line—a treacherous fence, one of the worst in the county, with a wide, concealed ditch on the further side. To a hunter who wasn't familiar with the country, the bracken-filled ditch would appear to be solid footing.

She spurred her mount to a gallop, intending to catch up with Mr. Barlow. A flicker of movement halfway up the neighboring hillside caught her attention. She pulled up her horse abruptly, straining to recognize the two lone horsemen who had cut themselves off from the larger part of the field.

One, she saw by his cap, was Jack Burden, the whipper-in. That explained his defection; he intended to gather in the divergent hounds and bring them back to join the rest of the pack. The other rider was the overeager Kilwarden. He must have been too far in front to see what had happened, and was riding close on the heels of the errant hounds, not realizing that the field was no longer behind him.

Cecilia made an instant decision. She knew the whipper-in would shout Francis a warning—but what if he didn't hear it, or chose to ignore it? An appalling vision sprang vividly into her mind: a fallen horse writhing in pain on the ground, Francis's crumpled figure pinned beneath it. She wheeled her mount to the right, and pushed the mare to her limits. The distance between herself and the racing Kilwarden remained distressingly wide. With growing fear and horror, she saw the boundary fence on the crest of the hill, watched Kilwarden sail over the one low gray stone barrier that remained between himself and that treacherous hazard.

She spurred her horse on even more desperately. Now she was nearing the low stone fence he had just cleared so effortlessly. She could feel the mare's powerful muscles gathering for the jump. She loosed the reins, her eyes still fixed on Kilwarden, automatically giving the well-trained mare its head. As the horse rose up into the air, she felt a sharp jolt— and then, inexplicably, the horse was no longer beneath her. She felt herself being flung toward the rocky hillside; saw, for the briefest of instants, the earth rushing toward her. Then she was hurtling into a funnel of blackness, and then there was nothing, nothing, nothing at all.

"Hold hard, Lord Kilwarden! 'Ware ditch!" The whipper-in's shout reached Kilwarden's ears just as he came within jumping range of the treacherous fence. He reined in his horse so abruptly that the bit drew blood from its mouth. The horse whinnied sharply in protest at this unaccustomed roughness. Kilwarden stroked the beast's mane, murmuring words of comfort into its ear, then turned in his saddle to question the whipper-in. He was astonished to find that he was alone on the hillside. The hounds he'd been following so intently had disappeared over the crest of the hill. Their excited baying drifted back to him, rapidly fading away into the distance.

He realized at once what must have happened. The hounds had divided, and the rest of the riders had followed the other half of the pack. But the whipper-in wasn't rounding up the defectors, as Kilwarden would have expected. He had ridden back in the other direction, toward the little stone fence he'd just cleared a moment before. Beside the fence stood a riderless horse, whinnying in panic. Kilwarden felt a jolt at the pit of his stomach. There was no mistaking the beast's identity: Cecilia's black mare, Dido.

He spurred his own mount into motion, and a few seconds later leapt down from his saddle to join the hunt servant, now kneeling in frightened concern beside the crumpled figure sprawled on the rocky hillside.

Jack Burden looked up at him with a worried frown. "I'm afraid Miss Cecilia has taken a very bad spill. I can't understand it, sir. Dido should have taken that little fence without any trouble."

Kilwarden reached out to touch the still, white face, then parted the auburn hair to find the ugly gash, the blood congealing now in a sticky mass. Sick with dismay, he laid his ear against the front of the scarlet jacket. When he heard the steady thump of her heartbeat, he drew a deep breath of relief. He kept his head pressed against the still figure a few moments longer, reassured by the gentle rise and fall of Cecilia's breathing.

He raised his head and looked at the worried hunt servant. "Her heart is strong, thank God. But that wound on her head may be very serious. There's no time to lose. You must find a doctor at once. I'll wait here with Miss Cecilia."

Jack Burden looked even graver. "We'll need some sort of help sooner than that. The nearest doctor's at Mullingar, a good forty miles from this place."

"Surely you can find one closer than that!" Kilwarden's tone was rough-edged with frustration. "Where is the man whose subscription I pay? Quinlan told me his name—Kierney or Tierney, or some such thing."

Jack Burden shifted his gaze in embarrassment. "We did have Dr. Tierney, back in Lord Corny's time. But he had to move away when the agent cut off his yearly payment—on your orders, my lord, or so we were led to believe."

Kilwarden suppressed an oath. He could remember quite clearly that page of Quinlan's accounts. "Dispensary doctor: thirty pounds." He'd been a little surprised the amount was so small. In Buckinghamshire, the doctor got twice that amount. But even this pittance had gone to line Quinlan's pocket, like the extra profit from selling the horses.

"I gave no such order," he muttered grimly. "But that's beside the point now. We must find some immediate help for Miss Annesley. Ride back as fast as you can and send some men with a litter to carry her back to Kilwarden House."

"Whatever you say, my lord." Burden touched his cap with

a respectful finger. "But it might not be wise to move Miss Cecilia so great a distance—not 'til we get her a doctor, that is. I'll send someone off to Mullingar right away. In the meantime, if I might suggest it, we could have her carried to Mrs. Mulvey's cottage. It's very close by, just a little piece down the hill."

Kilwarden couldn't conceal his disgusted grimace. His darling Cecilia in one of those dark, smelly cabins, exposed to all sorts of vermin, attended to by some slatternly crone? The whipper-in guessed what had prompted his look of distaste. "Mrs. Mulvey's cabin, my lord, is more substantial than most. And she herself is an excellent housekeeper and experienced nurse. Her own husband, Mairtin Mor, got a bad cut on the head from a loy during last year's harvest. 'Twas Sarah's good nursing that kept him alive."

"Perhaps you're right, Burden. I don't want to move Miss Cecilia any more than we have to."

Burden took heart from Kilwarden's encouraging tone. "All of us here, your lordship, would give our lives for the Princess. If I thought the course I've advised would bring her the slightest harm, I'd never have ventured to open my mouth."

"The Princess?" Kilwarden's brow creased in a puzzled frown.

"I'm sorry, sir; I meant Miss Annesley. The tenants all call her the Princess, have done for years. On account, you see, of being Lord Corny's daughter. But I beg your pardon, sir; all this means nothing to you. Shall I be off to get some men from the house?"

"By all means, Burden. Ride as fast as you can. I accept your suggestion. We'll take her to Mrs. Mulvey's."

He watched the whipper-in gallop away down the hill, then turned back to look at Cecilia. The pale wan look of her face tugged at his heartstrings. So they called her the Princess, did they? A fitting name for that lively, high-spirited girl who had so quickly established her rule over his affections. Now, waxen-skinned and unmoving, she looked like the sleeping princess of children's stories, awaiting the prince who would bring her to life again. Impulsively, he clasped one of the limp, cold hands, pressed his lips against the pale, unresponsive lips of the crumpled figure. "Cecilia," he murmured, "please don't die. You mustn't die. I want you to live with me for the rest of my life."

He kissed her again, this time more desperately. Surely now those closed eyelids would flutter open, those lavender eyes would glisten with instant pleasure, that enticing mouth would widen into a smile. He sat back on his heels and gazed at her anxiously, every sense alert for some sign of returning life. Any moment now she'd awaken; he'd hear her call out his name, see her hands move toward him in eager welcome.

But as minute slowly succeeded leaden minute, the only sound that came to Kilwarden's ears was the quiet sob of wind on the rocky hillside and, off in the distance, the mournful cry of the hounds.

Chapter 16

Kilwarden awoke with a start, peering into the blackness. For a moment, he couldn't remember where he was. Then a puff of flame stirred on the hearth, illuminating the big cast-iron pot that hung above it and the stark whitewashed walls of the little cottage. Kilwarden stretched and yawned, relieving the ache in his muscles induced by the hard wooden bench on which he'd been sleeping. Then, struck by a sudden foreboding, he groped his way through the door to the other room and stared at the shawl-clad figure beside the curtained box of a bed.

Sarah Mulvey heard the light tread of his stockinged feet. She rose from her stool and beckoned him over to look at the sleeping Cecilia. "She's much improved, sir," she whispered. "She's awakened two or three times, and taken almost the whole of a bowl of broth. Now she's sleeping better, more natural-like."

Kilwarden leaned in through the parted calico curtains, dimly discerning Cecilia's face. She did look more like herself, less like a waxen image. He turned back to Mrs. Mulvey. "Please go and take some rest. I'll sit with her for the next few hours. You must be exhausted, watching here all through the night."

"Arragh, not a bit of it, sir. I'm fresh as a daisy. 'Tis yourself should be getting your proper amount of rest. You didn't drop off to sleep 'til well after midnight."

"Please, Mrs. Mulvey." Kilwarden adopted a gentle, coaxing tone. "Won't you please humor me? I don't want your strength undermined. We don't know how long this vigil will last. Miss Annesley may need many more days and nights of your expert nursing."

"Ah, well, if you're going to insist, I might stretch these old bones out for an hour or two. It won't be long at all 'til the sun will be up, and the children back from the neighbors', clamoring for their breakfast. Take this little stool, sir, poor hard thing that it is. I'll fetch you some good strong tea before I go off to sleep. 'Twill revive you a bit, after your fitful night."

"No, no, Mrs. Mulvey; that's really not necessary." But Mrs. Mulvey was already in the kitchen, wetting the earthenware pot and ladling in her last precious spoonful of tea. He reminded himself that he must send back to the Great House for some provisions. When Cecilia had first become conscious, well into the previous night, Mrs. Mulvey had given her the last drop of milk in the cottage. The broth that had followed had come from a neighboring tenant. So had the tea, of which he'd gulped endless cups as he counted the weary hours 'til the doctor came. Mrs. Mulvey, he'd noted, had drunk none herself, and had divided the fresh-baked oat cakes brought by another neighbor between himself and the children, apologizing profusely because she had nothing better. Her heartfelt generosity had made him feel small and ashamed, remembering all the times he'd parroted Quinlan's talk about "ungrateful tenants" and "greedy peasants."

How much he had learned in this single day and night of anxious vigil! Mrs. Mulvey had been reluctant to let anything slip which might be construed as complaining, but he'd slowly coaxed out the details of her difficult life. The two-roomed, well-built cabin—its stones bonded by mortar instead of clay daubing—had been built by her husband a good ten years before. The timber for the steeply-pitched rafters had been a free gift, cut from Lord Corny's plantation of American fir trees—that plantation now ruined for lack of adequate fencing. There had been free straw, too, back in Lord Corny's time, supplied from the well-managed farm that adjoined the Great House. Now the roof had begun to leak, but Quinlan was selling the straw at prohibitive prices, and her husband, Mairtin Mor, had gone off on a fifty-mile trip to the neighboring county in order to earn some money mending a road.

The potato crop this year had been less than they hoped for; still, they'd had to bring a tenth of the crop to the Great House. Mr. Quinlan, it seemed, shipped a steady supply of that staple to merchants in Dublin.

They'd managed to raise two pigs, which was one more than most of their neighbors, but they'd had to sell one to pay the renewal fee when their lease ran out. Even at that, they'd almost lost their land; they'd needed an extra half-crown to pay the penalty fee for not giving the agent his rent in golden guineas. Mrs. Mulvey had saved them from the brink of disaster by selling an old velvet cloak of Lady Margaret's that had served for years as the children's blanket.

And these were the "shiftless wretches" Quinlan complained of; the "lazy idlers" who "expected the landlord to feed them." He berated himself for ignoring the truth so long. That precious girl lying there on the bed had done her best to dispel his ignorance. She'd tried to explain how her father had managed to soften the burden imposed by too many people on too little land. But, blinded by prejudice, he'd refused to listen. He was ready to listen now, ready and eager. Once Cecilia recovered, he'd prove that to her.

Once she recovered...*If* she recovered...A lightningbolt of pain lanced through his chest. She must recover! She must! He couldn't imagine what life would be without her.

He drew a deep breath, hoping to calm himself. Of course she was going to recover. Hadn't the doctor said so? Clutching for comfort, Kilwarden tried to remember his words exactly. He'd commended Kilwarden for bringing Cecilia here, instead of trying to take her back to the Great House. He'd praised the way Mrs. Mulvey had dressed the wound, cleaning it carefully with soap of her own manufacture, wrapping it in a bandage torn from the freshly washed gown of her youngest daughter. He'd spoken comforting words about youth and resilience, while warning against any premature attempt to move the injured girl. "A day or two. Three at the most. By the end of the week, she'll be up and about again."

Kilwarden's muscles relaxed as the moment of panic receded. He heard a rustle behind him, and gratefully took the proffered cup of tea. A scurrying figure streaked in through the open doorway—one of the Mulvey children, coming home after his night in a neighboring cabin, sent there for the sake of Cecilia's privacy. "There's a man here to see your lordship." The child's treble voice was shrill with excitement. "It's Joseph Hines, old Mr. Barlow's chief huntsman. Will I tell him to come in to you? Or will you come talk to him outside the cabin?"

Kilwarden started to send the man away. At the moment he hated the very mention of hunting—that loathsome sport that had almost killed Cecilia. Then he caught himself up. It must be something important to bring the huntsman here at the crack of dawn. "I'll talk with him outside," he said wearily. The little boy hurried away to inform the huntsman. Kilwarden finished his tea, cast a last anxious glance at the sleeping Cecilia, then followed the child out of the cozy cottage.

The huntsman was shivering a little in the cold gray dawn, gazing up the hill toward the boundary fence. One arm was cradling a well-worn lady's saddle. He turned when he heard Kilwarden's step behind him. "I beg your pardon, your lordship, for disturbing you at such an early hour. But I thought you should see this. It's Miss Cecilia's saddle. One of your stableboys called it to my attention."

He turned the saddle over, displaying the broad leather straps that dangled from it. Kilwarden reached for the straps and examined the ends. "So that's how the accident happened," he muttered glumly. "The girth split down the middle, and the saddle slipped down to one side, causing Miss Annesley to lose her balance. Some groom has been guilty of criminal negligence. Whoever saddled the mare for Miss Cecilia should have seen that the girth was too worn to be safe."

"It wasn't a matter of wear, sir. The stableboy says that the girth strap was a new one, put on only last month at Miss Annesley's orders. If you'll look more closely, you'll see how clean-edged the split is—except for this little rough spot close to the end. Someone had cut it, sir, cut it half through with a very sharp knife."

"What a diabolical trick!" Kilwarden was livid with anger. "Who could have done such a thing? They must have known that a little strain would snap it." *What coldhearted wretch*

182

could have hated Cecilia so much? Or was it myself they hated?
Were they punishing me for being so bad a landlord?

The huntsman's face flushed as scarlet as his coat. "If you're implying it might have been one of your tenants, I will tell you straight out, sir, to put that thought out of your mind. They may seem to English eyes a very rough lot, but they'd never stoop to any such deviltry. Every last one of them loves and reveres the Princess. No one here would dream of doing her harm. Look, sir, there down the hillside. That crowd has been waiting all night to hear how she's faring."

He pointed to a spot lower down on the hill, where the morning ground fog was just beginning to lift. Through the shifting mist, Kilwarden saw the huddled shapes of some thirty people, clustering together around a tiny pile of glowing turf.

A warm tide of emotion flowed into his heart. These people loved Cecilia as much as he did. "Go tell them to come up here," he said to the huntsman. "No, wait a moment. It's time I made some amends for my long neglect. I shall go down to them and ask their forgiveness."

Ignoring the huntsman's look of astonishment, he strode down the hill toward the murmuring crowd. He heard the sudden hush that greeted him, and groped for the proper words with which to address his neglected tenants.

A burly red-haired man in ragged coat and trousers stepped forward from the group and tugged his forelock. "If you please, sir, your lordship, we've come to ask how the Princess is faring."

Kilwarden's gaze swept over the anxious faces. He saw some eyes that were bright with hope, others full of uneasy apprehension. "I am very pleased to be able to tell you that Miss Cecilia Annesley is out of danger. She is fully conscious now, and should be well enough to be moved in a day or two."

"Thank God for that, sir." The black-shawled woman pushed her way from the back of the crowd. "That darlin' girl is the jewel of our hearts. Last Bridget's Eve, when my mother lay sick with the fever, 'twas only the Princess's nursing that kept her alive."

"She's been like a guardian angel," broke in a stooped old man from the midst of the crowd. "Every week she'd come by with my bit of tobacco. 'I can't give you back your land, Sean *a vic*,' sez she, 'but at least you can have a cheerful pipe by your daughter's fireside.'"

"She brought me her own satin gown to cut up and make clothes for the children."

"She paid for my Liam's schooling, and found him a well-paid post in Mullingar."

"She brought my sick baby milk from her own Guernsey cow."

They were thronging around him now, each trying to outdo the last in praise of Cecilia's bounty. The red-haired man who appeared to be their spokesman stared with defiant calm into Kilwarden's eyes. "You hear what they say, Lord Kilwarden. There's a hundred others could add their own bit to that tale. Miss Cecilia has been our only ray of hope, all through these bitter months since Lord Corny died."

"Hush, Peadar, guard your tongue! His lordship will think we're after blaming him." A bony-faced woman tugged at the red-haired man's coattails. "Sure, don't we all know full well it's all Mr. Quinlan's doing?"

Peadar shook off her hand impatiently. "I'll say what needs saying, Nora Dugan. I'll speak the truth to his face, without fear or favor. If he wants to evict me then, I'll go with pleasure. But before I leave, I'll read him chapter and verse of the terrible desolation that's come down on Kilwarden."

"Have a care, Peadar Rua!"

"Peadar, don't be a fool."

A chorus of warning voices rose around him. The red-haired man silenced them all with a wave of his hand.

"I'll have my say. Let the devil himself try to stop me! You see, Lord Francis Kilwarden, what a miserable lot we look today—our clothes worn to tatters, the flesh melting off our bones. We didn't look so in Lord Corny's time. We had a landlord then who took thought for our welfare. Lord Corny knew land was too scarce, so he paid us good wages to help drain the bogland. Now your Mr. Quinlan raises the rent so high on that new-drained land that none of us can afford it. As a result, it's gone back to wasteland again. In Lord Corny's time, we could piece out our modest rent with all sorts of paid labor—keeping the fences mended and thinning the trees on his three plantations; building the roads for the parish, with himself paying half the expenses; digging stone from the quarry; tending the hothouse and gardens. Now Mr. Quinlan has cut out all those improvements, we have to trudge thirty miles to earn a few extra shillings."

Kilwarden remembered Quinlan's contemptuous words, condemning his Uncle Cornelius for "wasting money on all those expensive frills." Now he understood the true purpose of all those "useless improvements."

"If I had realized—" he began. But Peadar was in full spate now, and not to be interrupted.

"In Lord Corny's time, we didn't send half our food up to the Great House. It was he who sent *us* food, grown by well-paid men on his own private farm. Now there's some new exaction required every day—renewal fees, penalty fees, fees for the privilege of keeping a goat or a pig—and strange new taxes the government never heard of. In short, he's squeezed us so hard that the life's gone out of us all. I'm tellin' you now, Lord Kilwarden, if you don't pull the reins up tight on your Mr. Quinlan, you'll soon have no tenants at all here at Kilwarden. They'll all be wandering the roads, begging their food and shelter, or lying dead in the graveyard, their souls crying out a curse on their coldhearted landlord."

A gasp ran through the crowd. Kilwarden felt their frightened eyes fixed upon him, as though he were some angry Jove about to loose a thunderbolt of wrath. He reached out for Peadar's hand, and clasped it warmly in both of his. "You're a brave man, Peadar Rua. I thank you for speaking out. I fully deserve the reproaches you've heaped upon me."

The man looked surprised for an instant. Then the defiant look faded out of his eyes. In its place came a look of mingled hope and suspicion. The crowd had grown deathly silent. Kilwarden realized they were hanging on every word, and seized the moment to start his expiation. "I owe you all an abject apology." His eyes swept from face to face, noting the ravages of work and hunger. "I should have listened to you when you came to complain. But I had been told you were all connivers and liars, unwilling to work for a living, ungrateful, rebellious wretches who had to be ruled with an iron hand. I understand now how wrong I was to believe that. I have seen a tired, hungry mother watch through a sleepless night at Miss Annesley's bedside, drain the last drop of milk from her meager pitcher. I've seen the food that has come from the neighboring cabins—food sorely needed at home, as I'm now aware. I've seen the love and devotion that shine in your eyes when you speak of your Princess—and the shame and embarrassment you feel on behalf of your negligent landlord when one brave man dares to tell him the truth. For the first time today, I understand my new tenants—and the harm I've inflicted upon them through my callous neglect. I promise you this: Mr. Quinlan shall rule here no longer. Kilwarden has lacked a landlord for far too long. I shall do my best to follow my uncle's example. I shall have his daughter beside me as a guide and adviser, and eventually, I hope—"

He stopped speaking abruptly, overcome with dismay at the words he'd just been about to utter: *eventually, I hope, a closer relation than that.* A wave of despair made his mind go blank for a moment as he remembered the barrier that still stood between them.

He forced the thought back into the depths of his mind. There would be time enough in the future to face that dilemma. Right now his neglected tenants deserved all his attention.

He picked up the thread of his interrupted sentence. "And eventually, I hope, we shall restore you, Kilwarden's tenants, to the modest prosperity you knew in Lord Corny's time. We shall start to work on that task this very day. Not one man or woman of you will leave this place until he has spelled out in full the changes that must be made to keep him well-fed and thriving here at Kilwarden."

Chapter 17

Lady Headfort cautiously pulled aside the green brocade curtain and peered out through the tall, narrow window. No sign of the carriage yet, though Kilwarden had said they'd be back before midday. Perhaps the poor girl had taken a turn for the worse!

A tremor of guilt assailed her. If only she'd realized the chance she was taking! Who could have guessed the results of her innocent prank would be so disastrous? Still, the largest share of the blame must rest with Cecilia. If she hadn't ignored the Master's lead and galloped off on some mad whim into that rough stretch of country . . .

The rattle of carriage wheels cut short her musing. She pressed her nose to the pane, watching the crowd of servants erupt down the portico steps. Kilwarden leapt down from the carriage, waving away all offers of assistance. Before Cecilia's foot had touched the ground, he had scooped her up in his arms and was carrying her up the steps and into the house. There was no mistaking the look on the long, lean face. The man was head over heels in love with his Irish cousin.

Lady Headfort's mouth tasted like wormwood and ashes. So this was what her clever scheme had led to! All she'd intended to do was clear the stage a little, give Lucinda a better chance at Kilwarden's attention. What she'd actually done was to throw the cunning minx straight into his lordship's arms—a position of which she would surely take full advantage.

She hoped Lucinda hadn't observed the invalid's arrival.

The sight would make her more refractory than ever. Perhaps it would be best to yield to her petulant urging, and leave the scene of their unsuccessful foray. Given his present mood, Kilwarden was no longer an eligible prospect. But before they went, she must make one last attempt to put that devious young creature out of the running.

She patted the much-creased letter deep in her pocket. The time had come at last to explode that bombshell. No doubt Kilwarden would find it a crushing blow. But given time, he'd recover. Men always did, the shallow creatures. By next spring, when the next Season started, he might find himself in a more receptive mood.

She heard his unmistakable tread coming down the staircase. She waited expectantly for him to join her in the drawing room. She heard the sound of his footsteps dwindle away down the corridor, then the click of a closing door. She knew where he must be now—alone in the library. She had better seize her chance before one of those dreary dowagers came to forestall her.

She went quickly out into the hall and tiptoed down to the library door. She rapped on it softly, and heard Kilwarden asking her to enter. Firm in her resolution, she stepped into the room and shut the door behind her. "Lord Kilwarden," she said, "I apologize for this intrusion. I've come to say we must leave this house at once, myself and my daughter. To stay any longer might injure our reputation."

Kilwarden gazed at her in astonishment. What was this silly woman up to now? It was irksome enough that she had come barging in, when he wanted solitude to think through his dilemma. But now she was casting aspersions at his household, hinting at some unmentionable kind of scandal.

"Please explain yourself, Lady Headfort," he said in his frostiest tone. "You have made a rather remarkable accusation. After all, you've been my guest for nearly a month. Why do you suddenly find the experience so distasteful?"

"I'm sorry that I must be the one to tell you." Lady Headfort gazed up at him with tragic eyes. "I'm sure you've never been told the terrible secret. I only learned it myself a few days ago. If I'd had the slightest notion of the circumstances surrounding Miss Annesley's birth, I would never have let my

Lucinda make friends with her. My heart weeps for you, Lord Francis, when I think of the shame of it all. Lady Margaret must be completely devoid of conscience, passing her bastard child off as your cousin."

Kilwarden was thunderstruck. He stared at the grim-faced woman, bereft of speech for what seemed an eternity. When he finally spoke, his voice was crackling with anger. "How dare you make such an odious accusation! You surely can't bring the slightest evidence to support that vicious slur against Lady Margaret."

"You poor, deluded man." Lady Headfort's eyes were soft with commiseration. "Don't you know that all London was fully aware of the scandal? Lord Cornelius Kilwarden, taking a bride who had already had a child by some unknown lover? No wonder the Annesley family broke all relations and drove him into exile here in Ireland."

Kilwarden found it very hard to breathe. "You're speaking about Cecilia?" he managed to gasp. "You're telling me she isn't my uncle's daughter?"

"The girl who calls herself Cecilia Annesley does not have a single drop of Annesley blood in her veins." Lady Headfort's pitying smile turned to a sneer of triumph. She pulled a well-creased letter out of her pocket. "I don't wish to soil my lips with such sordid matters. If you wish further details, I suggest you peruse this letter from Lady Maxbury. Once you have read it, I'm sure you will feel as I do, and understand why we must take our departure."

Moving as though in a dream, Kilwarden took the letter from her outstretched hand. She gave a contemptuous sniff and made for the door; then cast a glance back over her shoulder, hoping to see his wrath turn to consternation.

Kilwarden was deeply absorbed in the damning letter. But instead of the look of horror she expected, his face was lighting up in a radiant smile. He looked up abruptly, feeling her eyes upon him. "Lady Headfort, I owe you my heartfelt thanks." He sprang from his chair and came toward her, eyes ablaze with elation. "I must go see Lady Margaret at once and make sure this is true. God forbid it may turn out to be merely idle gossip!"

The man has gone mad. Lady Headfort backed away from

Francis's outstretched arms, and hurriedly made her exit into the hallway. A few minutes later, she heard him bounding up the stairway. She sank into a drawing room chair, completely bewildered. She had been so sure that Kilwarden would be disgusted when she told him the sordid truth about the girl. Why had the man gone into such transports of joy when he learned that Cecilia wasn't really his natural cousin?

Kilwarden paused as he reached the second-floor landing, suddenly overwhelmed by compunction. Lady Margaret had kept her secret all these years. How could he burst in now and demand the truth? And yet that truth would determine her daughter's whole future.

As he stood there hesitating, his dilemma was solved for him. Lady Margaret hurried past him down the corridor, obviously on her way back to Cecilia's sickroom. He breathed a sigh of relief, strode down the hall in the other direction, and knocked resolutely on Lady Annesley's door. Gaining permission to enter, he drew a deep breath and stepped into the pink and white of the elegant bedroom.

His Aunt Lydia looked up in surprise, divining something portentous in his manner. "Just a word with you, Aunt Lydia." He paused for a moment, then plunged determinedly on. "It's rather a delicate question. It concerns the future happiness of a certain young lady whom I have always supposed heretofore to be my first cousin."

Lydia Annesley felt a sudden pang of dismay. "That pestilent Lady Headfort, I suppose? She's been scattering odious hints in all directions, but I didn't think she'd be crass enough to extend them to you."

"She has just informed me that she's forced to leave my household for fear of being tainted by our family scandal. When I inquired what she meant, she showed me a letter from Lady Maxbury, purporting to tell the truth about Cecilia."

Lady Annesley's protesting hand silenced him in mid-sentence. "Not a word further, Francis. She showed me that letter, too. It's an outrageous mixture of truth and lies."

"How much of it is the truth? I must know at once!" Kilwarden's voice was throbbing with impatience. "Cecilia's father, for instance. Is it true, as she says, that she isn't my uncle's daughter?"

"Please, Francis, not so fast! Let me assure you, there's nothing to be ashamed of. It's true that Cornelius was not Cecilia's father—"

"Stop! Not another word! That's the only thing I wanted to hear. I'm ready to face up to any amount of scandal, so long as I know Cecilia isn't my cousin, and that barrier no longer stands in the way of our marriage."

Lady Annesley gave a start of surprise. "My word, things seem to be moving quickly. Is that how matters stand now? You've already proposed and she's accepted?"

"No, I haven't proposed," Francis said brusquely. "Though I'll do so at once, if you'll stop evading my question. Is she or is she not Lord Corny's daughter? I don't give a damn if Cecilia's a bastard; just tell me straight out she isn't really my cousin."

Lady Annesley breathed a sigh of resignation. "Very well; I suppose it's high time to tell you the truth. Cecilia's real father was a gallant officer with the Austrian forces. His name was Harry Reynolds; he came from a fine English family—"

"That's all I need to know." Francis was at the door, his hand already clasped around the knob. "I'll go to Cecilia at once and ask her to be my wife. I can't wait another moment. I must have the matter settled."

"No, Francis, no!" Lady Annesley leapt from her chair and clutched at her nephew's sleeve just as he opened the door. "That poor, injured child knows nothing about this secret."

"She will hear it from my own lips, which will then meet hers in a kiss that will wipe out all shame."

"For heaven's sake, Francis, don't tell her now. There need be no shame at all, if you'll only be patient. Cecilia isn't a bastard; her parents were legally married. Please sit down here for a moment and compose yourself, while I sort the truth from Lady Maxbury's lies."

Reluctantly, Francis moved back into the room, flung himself down in an armchair, and waited for her to proceed. "Though most people in London refused to believe it, Lady Margaret was legally married to Captain Reynolds. Unfortunately, he was killed two months later, and Lady Margaret was left alone in Vienna, with no evidence to prove the fact of the marriage. When she came home to England, she went to plead with Captain Reynolds's father, swearing the child she was carrying was his legal grandchild. The old man turned her away for lack of proof. Cornelius, its seems, believed her from the start. To spare Cecilia from being touched by the scandal, he brought his bride here to Ireland, and let it be understood that the three-month-old child they brought with them was his own daughter."

"Aunt Lydia, I understand now why you stopped me. You think Lady Margaret should tell Cecilia herself. I implore you, then, please summon her here to discuss it."

"Francis, don't be so hasty." Lady Annesley glared at her nephew sternly. "Lady Margaret has suffered enough from this situation. I won't let you raise the matter with her at all, until the count writes us he's found proof of the marriage."

"The count?" Francis stared at her blankly. "Count O'Hanrahan, do you mean? How does he come into this whole affair?"

"Please stop all these interruptions and listen to me. One of Captain Reynolds's comrades-in-arms, Sir Osbert Damien, was the only witness at Lady Margaret's wedding. Until a few weeks ago, she supposed he was dead. When Sir George told her he was still living, her hopes of proving the truth sprang to life again. We asked the count to go over and speak to Sir Osbert. Any day now, we should have news from him."

"You trusted the count so much more than your only nephew? Surely as head of the family, I'm the person who should have approached Sir Osbert."

"I'm sorry, Francis. Perhaps we shouldn't have hidden the truth so long. But we feared you might drop some hint to Cecilia. The girl will be shocked enough to learn that Cornelius wasn't her natural father. We'll have to tell her, it's true, before she'll accept you. If you'll only be patient, wait 'til we have the proof that she's not a bastard."

Francis jumped up from his chair and paced up and down the room like a hungry tiger. "I simply can't bear it, Aunt Lydia. I just can't sit here, patiently holding my tongue. I've got to do something at once to get things settled." He came to a halt abruptly, obviously in the grip of a new inspiration. "I must leave for England at once. Give me the count's address there. No, never mind; I can track him down through his club. Not another word, Aunt Lydia. My mind is made up. If I leave here at once, I can sail by tomorrow's packet."

"But what shall we tell Cecilia? She'll want to know where you've gone. And that agent of yours, Mr. Quinlan. He's supposed to arrive before the end of the week!"

But Francis was already halfway down the curving staircase. A few minutes later, the front door slammed behind him. Lady Annesley stood there a moment, lost in thought. Then, suffused with an uneasy mixture of joy and misgiving, she went to join Lady Margaret at Cecilia's bedside.

"But why did he go? How long will he be away? Why didn't anyone tell me he was leaving?" Cecilia flung back the bedclothes and made her first try at climbing out of the bed. But her knees were treacherously weak; she gave up the futile attempt and let Constance's firm hand push her back against the heaped-up pillows.

"My dear Cecilia, please don't exert yourself. You're still very weak from that awful blow on the head. I don't know myself why Kilwarden left so abruptly, but I'm sure he had some good reason. No doubt in a day or two he'll be back to explain to us all."

"But surely someone must know! Why do they all act so strangely? Your mother bustles around with a secretive air, refusing to answer my questions. Meanwhile, my own dear mother scarcely comes near me. If it weren't for that chance remark you happened to drop, I wouldn't have even known that Francis was gone. And now you say Mr. Quinlan's expected this very evening."

"They were only trying to spare you, Cecilia dear. You mustn't worry your head about matters of business."

"All this secrecy only makes me more worried. What can Francis be up to, dashing away like that before Quinlan arrives? You heard them yourself, all those fervent promises—how we'd face Quinlan down together, force him to admit his injustice to our tenants."

"I assure you, it seems as strange to me as it does to you.

Mama cuts me off whenever I try to discuss it, and forbids me to even speak to Lady Margaret, saying she's under too great a strain from your illness. Mr. Worsley, too, seems quite perturbed. I fear he is somewhat doubtful of Kilwarden's intentions. After their first conversation, he's heard nothing further from him about that living."

Cecilia looked up in alarm. "Surely Francis wouldn't go back on his word. He knows your marriage depends on that living in England."

Constance heaved a sigh of resignation. "I sincerely hope so, but how can one ever tell? These shallow, worldly people, leading such heedless lives. Can one really trust them to keep a serious promise?"

"You mustn't call Francis shallow! He's the finest, most upright man I've ever known." Cecilia's angry retort caught Constance off guard. She looked at her in surprise, then lowered her eyes meekly. "A thousand pardons, Cousin. I didn't mean to denigrate his lordship. I'm sure he'll be back quite soon with some good explanation. Meanwhile, I beg of you to compose yourself. Your only thought now should be that of regaining your health."

"Oh, Constance," Cecilia groaned, "please don't join all the rest in treating me like a baby. Tell me the truth, only the honest truth—"

Constance's mouth firmed into a resolute line. "I always tell the truth so far as I know it. But I fear my conversation has made you distraught. I will leave you now, and let you get some sleep."

She rose from the beside chair and moved toward the door. Before she could touch the knob, the door opened by itself and little Peggy put her tousled head in. "Beg pardon, Miss Cecilia, but the post's just after arriving with a letter for you. Shall I bring it in now, or leave it for later?"

"A letter!" Cecilia felt a surge of elation. Perhaps all her doubts were about to be resolved. "Bring it in, Peggy. I want to read it at once."

Constance smiled, noting her cousin's quick change of spirits. "I'll leave you to read it alone," she said discreetly. "I hope it contains good news for all of us."

Cecilia forced herself to wait until the door had closed

behind Constance. Then she tore open the letter with trembling hands. A glance at the signature sent her hopes plummeting. She had been so sure the letter must be from Francis. But no, it was merely a note from Lucinda Headfort.

She crumpled it up in disgust, then smoothed it out again. She might as well see what Lucinda had to say. Probably just the standard note to her hostess, thanking her for that extended stay at Kilwarden.

Her eyes widened in surprise as she quickly scanned the one brief page of writing:

My dear friend Cecilia,

I hope I may call you my friend, after the grievous harm my own mother has done you. I was shocked and horrified when she told me about it. She, of course, believes she has acted rightly in bringing to light this long-buried family scandal. This older generation, with their smug code of rules! Let me assure you, Cecilia, that to an enlightened young person such as myself, the unhappy fact of your illegitimate birth could never prove a serious bar to friendship.

I realize that others, like Lord Kilwarden, are still in the grip of these ancient prejudices. Still, it *was* quite horrid of him to go off like that, after my mother's unfortunate breach of discretion. Perhaps once the first shock is over, he will relent a bit. Be assured that if I should see him during the coming Season, I shall do my best to plead your unfortunate case.

With heartfelt apologies,
and my thanks for all your
kindness,

Lucinda Headfort

Cecilia laid the letter down on the bedspread. She felt faint and dizzy, as though all the blood were draining out of her head. *Illegitimate birth.* What could the woman mean? She must have gone out of her senses, to make such an accusation.

An icy fear clutched at her heart. Did her mother know how brutally she'd been slandered? Was that why she seemed so evasive these last few days? *My poor dear mother. I must go to her at once. And Aunt Lydia, too. Surely she can think of some way to see this vicious wrong righted. Lady Headfort has to be forced to retract those lies...*

But what if it isn't a lie? Cecilia's head reeled again, awash with a sudden flood of remembered scenes. Lady Margaret, faced flushed with embarrassment, insisting that she could never go back to London. Aunt Lydia's look of wary caution, as she admitted that the family breach had been caused by her parents' marriage. Was this the buried scandal that had sundered the Annesley family? The fact that Cornelius Annesley's only daughter was not his daughter at all, but the child of another man?

She saw in a flash that this must be the truth. This was the hidden secret that had shadowed her mother's life. Now that secret had been revealed—and the revelation had brought the final downfall of all her hopes.

She took a deep breath, thinking it might help her return to coherent thought. A terrible sadness assailed her as she thought of her mother. How bravely she'd struggled to keep the truth from her daughter! And dear Papa as well; how he must have loved them both. He'd managed to give them a wonderful life at Kilwarden, away from that brittle, vicious world of London.

And then had come death, smashing that world apart. No, not death alone. It was *his* arrival that really started the damage. The secret that long ago had been laid to rest; *his* coming here had stirred up those ancient questions; *his* insistence had brought her to vicious London, then brought vicious London here to complete the disaster....

Her thoughts broke off abruptly as she heard Constance's step in the hallway. She still didn't look quite composed when Constance entered the room. But the girl was too intent on the news she was bringing to notice that.

"Mr. Quinlan has just arrived." Her eyes were bright with excitement. "Your mother has put him into the little back bedroom. I must say he seems quite subdued, not at all the arrogant bully I'd been led to expect. He professes himself quite content to wait patiently here for Lord Kilwarden's return."

Cecilia fixed her gaze on a spot on the wall, and drew another deep breath, hoping to keep the tremor out of her voice. "I fear Mr. Quinlan's trip has been in vain. Lord Kilwarden will not be returning to Ireland."

Constance looked shocked. "Is that what your letter said? That he's not coming back here at all? After all those promises! The tenants will be dismayed; they've all been praying for his good intentions. Surely, dear Cousin, there must be some awful mistake. Please let me look at his letter—"

Cecilia snatched up the crumpled sheet of paper and started tearing it slowly into tiny pieces. "Instead of prayers, I hope they will rain down curses. We should have all cursed him the day he first set foot on Lord Corny's land. He's ruined it for us, ruined it utterly. But we shall survive in spite of it all. Let Lord Francis Kilwarden stay with the devil in London; we shall survive...Somehow, we shall survive...."

Chapter 18

The raucous bray of the coachman's horn cut through the turbulent hubbub of the Islington coaching yard. The driver cracked his whip, and the four well-matched horses broke into a steady trot. Count O'Hanrahan leaned back in his padded seat and smiled at the breathless young man who had just taken the one remaining inside place. "Delighted to have your company, dear lad. What a prime stroke of luck that we should meet like this."

"It isn't a matter of luck, sir. They told me at your club that you were taking this stage to Shrewsbury. If I hadn't caught the coach, I would have followed you on horseback."

The count shot him a cautious look. "Such zeal seems to indicate that you know of the errand on which I'm engaged. Has one of your estimable aunts decided to let you in on a well-guarded family secret?"

"It's a secret no longer, Count. Lady Annesley has told me everything. The moment I heard the truth about my future wife's parentage, I rushed off to join you."

Count O'Hanrahan beamed at him paternally. "Your future wife, eh? Well, there's a bit of good news. And I've more good news to match it. I've already seen Sir Osbert. He's confirmed that he witnessed a perfectly legal marriage, complete with bell, book and candle. You may rest assured, there's no dishonorable shadow to bar your coming nuptials with the charming Miss Annesley."

"I don't give a fig if the marriage was legal or not. No amount of scandal could alter my decision. But Aunt Lydia and Lady Margaret are gravely concerned, not so much for the world's opinion, but because of the shock this news will mean for Cecilia. I have promised my aunt to defer my proposal until she can be assured that there was nothing dishonorable about her birth."

"My heart warms to you, lad. You defy the world like a true Byronic hero. I'm sure you'll forgive an old cynic for adding a more worldly thought—like the little matter of Cecilia's expectations. Old Mr. Reynolds has no surviving child or grandchild. Once he learns the true situation, he's virtually certain to make our young friend his heir."

"No one merits such good fortune more—though I fear it will make little change in her own mode of living. I can easily guess how she'll choose to spend it."

"So can I, lad, so can I. Whoever her true father was, at heart she's Lord Corny's daughter. She'll fling her fortune away, just as he did, paying for all those improvements at Kilwarden."

"Is that where we're going today? To see old Mr. Reynolds? What sort of proof have you brought to him from Sir Osbert? No doubt the old gentleman will demand to see something in writing."

"You can be quite certain he will. He'll want to see a marriage certificate. I pointed that out to Sir Osbert, and got the surprise of my life. He told me his nephew had made the same objection."

"His nephew? You mean George Damien? How does that scoundrel come into the situation?"

The count gave Kilwarden a shrewd, appraising look. "That's a curious matter. It seems Sir George had approached Sir Osbert some weeks ago, fishing for information about Captain Reynolds and Lady Margaret. When Sir Osbert questioned his reasons for wanting to know, he told him he was secretly engaged to the young lady in question."

Kilwarden flushed red with anger. "That's a vicious lie. Cecilia detests the man. I know it appeared otherwise that day on the island, but I'm certain now I know her true feelings."

The count cut him short with a deprecating gesture. "There's no need to protest further. I've known Cecilia Annesley all her life. It's impossible for a girl of her candor and virtue to have any serious involvement with that shallow rake. The man was obviously lying to Sir Osbert. What troubles me is that I can't make out his motive. Whatever it is, I'm sure he's up to some mischief. Which means we must find that certificate without any further delay."

Kilwarden's heart gave a lurch. "You have some hope that the thing still exists? Why hasn't it come to light during all these years?"

"I asked Sir Osbert about that. He says Captain Reynolds, fearing he might be killed, confided it to the care of our ambassador in Vienna, Sir William Fancourt."

"Marvelous! Have you been in touch with him? Is that where we're going today? Does he live in Shrewsbury?"

Count O'Hanrahan shook his head sadly. "It's not quite as simple as that. Old Fancourt has been dead for some seven years now. I approached his widow in London. She appeared quite touched by my story, and offered to make a search of whatever personal papers she could find. Unfortunately, the certificate we needed was not among them."

Kilwarden was chafing with disappointment. "This is very cruel of you, Count. You buoy up my hopes with talk of a marriage certificate, lead me on to think we are off on a burning scent, and just when I think we've run the fox to earth, you tell me we've lost him."

The Count gave a little chuckle. "Forgive an old man for being so damnably prolix. I was merely trying to answer the question you asked; why the truth hasn't come to light during all these years. The gentleman you're about to meet should be able to settle the matter once and for all. Lady Fancourt passed me on to Sir Geoffrey Wilton, the official executor of Sir William's estate. She says he is still going through her husband's papers. We can only hope the certificate is among them."

Kilwarden sank back in his seat with a sigh of relief. "Then the end of the chase is in sight! How happy I am, to reach you in time to be in at the kill." He caught himself up sharply. His face turned a brilliant crimson. "Good Lord," he exclaimed, "what a callous clod I am. To speak of events that will settle my darling girl's future in so shallow a fashion!"

The count's eyes twinkled. "Don't apologize to *me* for a sportsman's language. But if you'll forgive my prying, just how did your cousin Cecilia become your 'darling girl'?"

The count's unexpected question brought Kilwarden up short. It had been so clear to him that he must marry Cecilia that he'd completely neglected to look at her side of the question. What gave him the right to think she'd consider him as a husband? A dreadful foreboding began to seep into his mind. With their mission this close to success, he might still lose Cecilia!

"As a matter of fact," he admitted dejectedly, "I spoke for myself alone. Miss Annesley has given me no reason to hope. I'm beginning to feel I've been an arrogant fool. Just because I can't endure the thought of a life without her—"

He broke off abruptly, horrified to find himself on the verge of tears. The count reached out and gently patted his knee. "Don't let it worry you, lad. I know Cecilia's heart as well as a father. It's been quite apparent to me for some time back that her feelings for you were far different than those of a cousin. Now, lay all those doubts aside. There'll be plenty of time for courting when you get back to Ireland. Our task for today is to find that certificate."

"Good Lord, this is appalling. What can the scoundrel be up to?" Count O'Hanrahan paced angrily back and forth in the Wilton House library. His host, Sir Geoffrey, watched him with worried eyes.

"If I'd only realized the folly I was committing! But the fellow's story appeared so plausible. I was carried away by the thought of the help he might bring to that poor, injured lady in Ireland."

The count, remembering his manners, stopped his pacing and slumped down into a chair. "Please don't blame yourself, my dear Sir Geoffrey. How could you know that the rascal was lying to you? We quite understand why you gave him the marriage certificate. I'd have done the same thing, if he'd come to me with that story."

"If we'd only reached you a day or two earlier!" Kilwarden's strained face betrayed the tension within. "God knows where the rogue is now. The man seems to have some grudge against

Cecilia. He's already tried one scheme to ruin her life. Perhaps he's already destroyed the certificate."

"He'd hardly do that," said Sir Geoffrey. "At least I had enough prudence to make an attested copy. Not quite the same thing, of course, but it should be official enough to convince Mr. Reynolds."

The count had been hunched in his chair, staring gloomily at the carpet. He straightened himself abruptly and stared at Sir Geoffrey. "Damien told you he was taking it straight back to Ireland?"

"Yes, that's what he said." Sir Geoffrey shook his head in disgust. "But what does that signify? For all we know, that was simply one more of his lies."

"It may be. It may be. But we dare not take any risks." The count was on his feet now, his face suffused with grim determination. "Kilwarden, there's no time to spare. You must be on your way at once."

Kilwarden looked up in surprise. "But shouldn't we wait for the new attested copy Sir Geoffrey has promised us? We must have something to show to old Mr. Reynolds?"

"*I'll* wait for the copy, and *I'll* visit Mr. Reynolds. You must get back to Kilwarden as fast as you can. I very much fear your 'darling girl' in Ireland is direly in need of her erstwhile cousin's protection."

"Quiet now, Dido, go easy. We've galloped enough for today." Cecilia reined in her mare as they cleared the crest of the hill. She gazed out over the little valley which usually brought such a feeling of peace to her heart. *Glanmel,* the tenants called it, the Valley of Honey. Where had the sweetness fled? Why couldn't she shake herself free of this desolation? She couldn't go on this way, wrapped in this foul, black mood, fending off everyone's attempts to console her. She winced with remorse as she thought of her mother's pale face. How could she have treated her so, brushing off all her entreaties not to go riding so soon after her fall? Poor Mama was right to be worried. That stupid accident had almost killed her.

She couldn't go on avoiding her mother forever. One of these days, perhaps, she'd be able to face her, tell her she'd learned the truth, ask all those pressing questions about her real father. One of these days—but when would that day arrive? Overwhelmed as she was with this burning sense of loss, she hadn't the strength to lay bare the forbidden subject.

She realized all too well where that sense of loss came from. It wasn't only the loss of Papa she was mourning. He, at least, had ignored her dishonorable birth, and had reached out through the shadows to embrace both herself and her mother with steadfast devotion. But Francis! Francis! Francis! That man who had come to seem closer to her than a brother! The slightest hint of scandal, and he was off and away, leaving them both defenseless against the world. How could she have misjudged him so grievously? How could she have thought him the noblest man she knew? That shallow, faithless creature, on whom she'd so blithely pinned all her hopes and dreams.

The worst part of it all was that she couldn't make herself hate him. She was wounded, humiliated, crushed by his leaving. She kept telling herself she wished she had never met him. And yet, if at that very moment, he should come riding up over the crest of the hill behind her, she knew all the vanished sweetness would overwhelm her again like a drowning tide.

Dido had been standing quietly, nibbling now and then at the grass around her. She suddenly jerked up her head, ears pricked back alertly. Cecilia listened with her, and heard in the distance behind her the pounding of hooves. An icy chill shot up and down her spine. Was it? Could it be? Could he have come back? She wanted to turn her head, but her muscles wouldn't obey her. She sat staring straight ahead but seeing nothing. She heard the horseman coming, nearer, nearer, nearer. Then he was there beside her, his horse shuddering to a stop. With a tremendous effort, she managed to turn her head toward him—and looked up into the mocking eyes of Sir George Damien.

He swept off his tall beaver hat and leaned forward in his saddle. "Miss Annesley! What a pleasant surprise."

Numb with disappointment, she met his too-eager smile with a stony glare. "We stand on Kilwarden land, sir. I believe you were told you are not welcome here."

"Ah yes, that regrettable business. I was quite naughty, I fear. I devoutly hope to make some partial atonement. I have brought some good news for you and your mother."

"You may save your breath, Sir George, and take your leave. My mother and I do not have the faintest interest in anything you may have to say to us."

"I see you're still piqued with me. I can understand that. Under ordinary circumstances, I would not trouble you further. But the news I bring overrides all such petty squabbles. I was just on my way from Sir Jonah's to pay my respects to your mother. Won't you ride back with me and hear what I have to tell her? It's something very important I learned from my Uncle Osbert. It seems they knew each other back in Vienna—"

"Stop! Not another word!" Cecilia was horrified. Did everyone in the world know that ancient secret? "I forbid you to speak to my mother," she went on resolutely. "She suffered enough, back in those youthful days. Can't you leave her in peace? What sort of vulture are you, feeding on long-dead scandals?"

Sir George's eyes grew wide. "It seems you know more of this matter than I supposed. I can fully sympathize with your dismay. Your mother has borne her burden far too long. The news I bring her will lift it from her shoulders, by proclaiming her the virtuous woman she has always been."

Cecilia stared at him blankly. "What kind of news is this? How on earth did *you* come by it?"

Sir George laughed softly, a low, musical chuckle. "I am not quite so black as your memory paints me, Cecilia. During my stay at Kilwarden, I developed a deep respect for your charming mother. Remembering her pleasure in speaking of my Uncle Osbert, I visited him when I went back to England. I'm not sure what I expected—a few fond reminiscenses, some insight into the youth of a beautiful woman. Imagine my surprise when my uncle told me that he had been a witness at your mother's wedding."

"Wedding? What wedding?" Cecilia felt dizzy and weak. She started to sway in the saddle, and shook her head to clear it.

"Ah, you *are* interested. I thought you would be." Sir

George beamed at her like a fond old uncle. "You must have had many questions, all these years, about your true father, Captain Harry Reynolds. Sir Osbert was one of the captain's dearest comrades—and the witness of his wedding to Lady Margaret."

Cecilia's whole body seemed to grow giddy and light, as though she were floating six inches above her saddle. "My mother...She was really married..." She shook her head helplessly, as her tongue refused to shape another word.

Sir George leaned over to grasp her horse's bridle, his face alive with concern. "My dear Miss Annesley, I fear this has been a great shock. Let me help you dismount and rest on the grass here a moment."

The seductive tone of the words, so hatefully familiar, brought back all Cecilia's suspicions in one angry wave. "I don't believe you," she cried. "This is all some sort of trick. You don't really mean to free my mother from scandal. You've only come here to stir it all up again. You've concocted this story about a legal marriage only to deepen my mother's distress and shame."

Sir George professed to be extremely surprised. "My dear young lady, I have only the best intentions. What can I do to convince you of my good faith?" He paused a moment, as though taking thought on a difficult decision. Then with a sigh, he put his hand into his coat and pulled out a folded piece of yellowed parchment.

"I had meant for Lady Margaret to see this first. But after all, you are the person most deeply affected. The paper I hold in my hand is a marriage certificate, issued in Vienna in 1809. If you'll kindly do me the favor to peruse it, I'm sure it will quickly allay all your suspicions."

With a trembling hand, Cecilia unfolded the parchment. A few hasty glances were enough to confirm Sir George's story. She raised her eyes to his, unaware that hers were brimming with tears of joy. "It really is true! Oh, Sir George, how I have misjudged you. Let us ride to the house at once and show this to Mama."

Not waiting for his answer, she spurred her startled mare into a canter, and soon was galloping down the side of the hill. Sir George, taken off guard, soon made up the distance between them, and they galloped along together, down toward the winding road that led to Kilwarden House. Ablaze with excitement, Cecilia barely noticed her surroundings. She caught a vague glimpse of a coach and four, slowly meandering along the road below them. But she didn't see the smug grin on Sir George's face, or the hand he raised to signal the watching coachman, or the deft way he slipped off his heavy black woolen cloak.

As they reached the road, she turned around in the saddle, all her joy bursting forth in a shout of exultation. "Faster, Sir George, faster! I can't wait to see my darling mother's eyes when she—"

The black cloak came down, smothering the rest of the sentence; a pungent odor assailed her nostrils; she felt herself being lifted from her saddle. The world dwindled down to a single pinpoint of light—and then that light went out, and she was sucked down into darkness.

Chapter 19

Kilwarden reined in his horse in front of the gatehouse. What on earth could be happening there, up at the other end of the beech-lined avenue? There seemed to be almost a hundred ragged-clothed tenants, huddled in little groups on the grass in front of the house.

He was struck by a pang of consternation. He'd forgotten all about that rascal Quinlan! He remembered Cecilia's description of how the agent would summon the tenants there on rent day, making them wait for hours while he went down the list of fees and exactions.

Kilwarden's gorge rose. So the rogue, undeterred by his warning, was defying him by proceeding with business as usual! He spurred his horse into a trot. The crowd surged around him as he reached the steps of the Great House. He heard a few scattered voices, shouting his name in welcome. Before he could ask them why they were gathered here, a slender figure in dark blue muslin had dashed down the portico steps and clutched at his horse's bridle, a desperate look in her usually placid eyes.

"Oh, Francis, thank God you've come back! Cecilia's horrible fate is all your fault! Why did you write her that cruel, cruel letter?"

"What on earth is all this, Constance?" He slipped down from his saddle and grasped the hysterical girl by her heaving shoulders. "I haven't written Cecilia. What do you mean by my 'cruel letter'?"

"Don't try to dissemble with me! You know how Cecilia

adores you. When you told her you wouldn't be back, she became like a creature possessed. Lady Margaret tried to stop her, but she insisted on riding off all by herself. And now look what's happened to her! It's all your fault, you heartless shallow man!"

"Not another word, Constance. Come into the house this minute." Lady Annesley's voice rang out sharply from the top of the steps, silencing her daughter's frenzied tirade.

Kilwarden looked up at his aunt in bewilderment. "What on earth is this all about?" His skin prickled with sudden panic. "Don't tell me Cecilia's taken another fall!" He let go of Constance abruptly and bounded up the steps, livid with apprehension. "Has she been hurt again? Is she lying inside there unconscious?"

Lady Annesley laid a restraining hand on his shoulder. "No, Francis, nothing like that. It's serious enough, all the same. Come into the house where we can discuss the thing calmly."

Francis broke away from her and hurried through the great pillared hall into the drawing room. It was full of somber-faced people clustered, like the tenants, in little groups. He recognized quite a few of his hunting companions, and other dinner guests drawn from the neighboring gentry. The low hum of voices ceased as they saw him enter. Not pausing to greet them, he hurried to Lady Margaret, who was sitting stiff-backed in an armchair beside the fireplace. She was obviously struggling to keep up a facade of calmness.

"Aunt Margaret," he cried, dropping to one knee beside her, "please tell me what has happened. Where is Cecilia now? I must see her at once."

Lady Margaret raised grief-stricken eyes to his. "We don't know where she is. Someone has captured her and carried her off. No one is sure who it was or where he was taking her."

"Carried her off!" Kilwarden was flabbergasted. "But people don't do such things in this day and age!" He turned to his other aunt, who was settling the sobbing Constance into a chair. "Aunt Lydia, please tell me, I beg you. What is this all about?"

"We're as mystified as you, Francis. All we know is what

one of the tenants told us. He said he had seen Cecilia riding down Gorteen Hill with a man he didn't know in a big black cloak. All of a sudden, he said, the man flung his cloak around Cecilia, lifted her off her horse, and dragged her into Sir Jonah Boothby's carriage. The tenant who saw this came running to us at once. It seemed too wild a tale to believe at first, but when her riderless horse was led home to your stables, along with a horse that was recognized as Sir Jonah's, it became all too apparent that the man was telling the truth. The news spread like wildfire among your friends and neighbors. As you see, they've all come to offer us their help. A deputation led by Mr. Barlow went off to confront Sir Jonah about two hours ago."

"Sir Jonah!" A vivid picture sprang into Francis's mind. The ramshackle dining hall, the blubbery man with the three greasy chins, the venomous words hissed out through firmly clenched teeth... *She'll be sorry, the bitch. She'll come crawling on bended knees*... Had that rejected suitor grown tired of waiting for time to take its revenge, and made this violent bid to punish Cecilia? No, that was unthinkable. Not after he'd been a guest at Kilwarden's table. And yet...

A shout from outside the house cut short the thought. He turned to see what was happening, and found himself caught in a general surge toward the door. Out in the great entrance hall he saw Mr. Barlow, trying to answer a score of excited questions. Kilwarden pushed his way through the crowd, eager to learn what had come of the rescue mission.

"You've come from Sir Jonah's, sir? Is he keeping Miss Annesley prisoner?"

"We confronted the man directly." Mr. Barlow's face was still flushed with anger. "He denied any knowledge concerning your cousin's abduction. He claimed his carriage had not left the stables today. When we insisted, he allowed us to search his place. The carriage was in the stables, but we couldn't find any trace of Miss Annesley." He shook his head in exasperation. "And yet, I'll be sworn the old devil knows something about it. Tom Ryan's a trustworthy man; he'd hardly have made a mistake about that carriage."

A vague, half-formed memory was tugging at Kilwarden's mind ... *something else Sir Jonah had said ... or one of those graceless louts at the foot of the table...something in one of the toasts...*

Then the whole scene flashed vividly before him—the toast to the local blade for that outrageous action, Sir Jonah attempting to excuse the barbaric custom, explaining Cecilia was safe, since she wasn't an heiress...

"But now she *is* an heiress!" He was scarcely aware he was speaking the words aloud. In that instant, he knew who the black-cloaked stranger had been. There was only one other man who shared that vital secret. And Sir George was widely known as a fortune hunter.

"I know where she is! We must go there at once. No, not you, Mr. Barlow. We're not dealing with gentlemen now." Ignoring the Master of Foxhounds' startled look, he strode past him through the door and out onto the portico. "Your Princess has been abducted." His shouted words brought the tenants clustering round him. "I need six good men who will help me to rescue her. I've heard of a kind of war club you call the *shillelagh*. If some of you know how to use it, you're the fellows I want."

"Take me, sir!"

"I'm the man for you, Lord Francis!"

"Just let me at the villain. I'll have him destroyed!" A score of eager tenants disputed the honor of joining Kilwarden's platoon. He chose the six likeliest-looking, including the red-haired spokesman, Peadar Martin. "Quickly, down to the stables and find yourself mounts. Then ride after me as fast as you can. I trust you're all prepared to break a few heads?"

"You've picked the right boys for that, sir." Peadar Martin's eyes were bright with the light of battle. "We're the best faction-fighters in all of County Westmeath. To Sir Jonah's house, is it, sir?"

Kilwarden swung onto his horse and checked that his pistol was secure in the saddle holster. "Not to his house. That's already been searched. We're going to his shooting lodge on the Holy Island."

Sir George gnawed the last bit of meat from the pheasant's breastbone, then flung it carelessly into the glowing coals in the rough stone fireplace. With a sigh of repletion, he leaned back in his rush-seated chair and grinned at the silent Cecilia across the bare oak table, strewn untidily with the remnants of his supper. "An excellent bird, and very nicely roasted. What a pity you have such a delicate appetite. Now, even if you won't eat, perhaps you will join me in sampling Sir Jonah's claret?"

Cecilia waved away the proffered glass. "How long do you expect to keep me prisoner?" she asked in a quiet voice. "Someone is bound to guess where you're holding me."

"They may guess whatever they please. You'll stay here regardless. This island is well defended. We can count on being alone here for a night, perhaps even two. Considering what that will mean to your reputation, I predict you'll find yourself eager to accept my offer."

Cecilia's lips curled with disdain. "I wouldn't marry you if you were the last man on earth."

"Don't speak too hastily, my sweet little spitfire. By the time you leave this island, I *will* be the last man on earth—the last *gentleman,* that is, who would even consider taking you as his bride. Even your precious Kilwarden would jib at accepting damaged goods."

An icy chill ran up Cecilia's spine. She shrank back into her chair, wishing she could curl into a spiky ball like a hedgehog. "Have you gone mad, Sir George? Surely even you wouldn't dare—" Dry-mouthed and shaking, she left the sentence unfinished.

George Damien gave a low, sardonic chuckle. "Don't look so alarmed, my dear. Ravishing you is not a part of my plan. Though naturally, the world will presume that I did so. That appearance alone will suffice to accomplish my purpose."

"I thought you were tricking me with that marriage certificate." Cecilia gazed at him thoughtfully. "But now I'm almost convinced it's genuine. You'd scarcely go to such lengths if you didn't believe that I'm really an heiress."

"There's no doubt at all about that." Sir George's eyes were agleam with smug satisfaction. "I've already made inquiries. Old Mr. Reynolds is a very wealthy man. When he sees this piece of parchment"—he tenderly patted his waistcoat pocket—"he'll be only too pleased to acknowledge his newfound grandchild—who by that time, I trust, will have become Lady Damien."

Cecilia fell silent, struggling to make some sense of her new situation. It seemed she wasn't a bastard after all. She should have guessed that much, she realized now. She shouldn't have been so quick to believe dear Mama could be capable of any dishonorable action.

Very well; at least she now had a name for her father. *Captain Harry Reynolds.* How strange that sounded. Did that mean her name was really Cecilia *Reynolds?* That didn't sound right at all, after all these years of being "Lord Corny's daughter." Why had they kept up the pretense for so long a time? Why had Mama never told her? Think of the trouble they would have avoided. She would only have had to flourish the marriage certificate in everyone's face, and none of it would have happened—the mysterious breach in the family, Lady Headfort's malicious gossip, Francis dashing off in that callous fashion.

In an instant of revelation, she saw what the truth must be. Mama had never possessed that marriage certificate. It must have been hidden somewhere—perhaps lost or stolen. Somehow Goerge Damien had brought it to light. Now he was the one who would flourish it in their faces. But in doing so, he would flourish a new dishonor. It wouldn't earn him the fortune he hoped for, this mad escapade of his. She would never marry him, not in a thousand years. Her friends and family would know she was innocent. But the world's vicious gossip would leave her name stained with suspicion. And Francis—what of Francis? Would she lose what she valued so much, his good opinion of her?

What was she thinking of? Hadn't she already lost it? Didn't his hasty flight tell her how little he valued his erstwhile cousin?

She shook herself free from the cloud of circling thoughts. What good did it do, all this agonizing about Francis's opinion? Why was she maundering on in this aimless fashion? There was only one object now worthy of her attention: how was she to escape from this odious captor?

She raised her eyes, assessing the enemy. He returned stare for stare, his smug smile widening into a salacious grin.

"You're a very morose companion, dear Cecilia. I hope this is not a foretaste of our life together. Are you sure you won't try the wine? A sip of the cup that cheers might lift your dull spirits."

Cecilia didn't attempt to hide her disdain. "You may force me to stay here, sir, as your prisoner. That doesn't mean you can force me to drink with you."

"Very well; very well. We'll postpone that cheerful cup 'til the day of our wedding." He reached across the table and grasped her hand, squeezing it tightly. She managed to snatch it free, thrusting it deep into the pocket of her riding habit.

"That day will never come!" She glared back at him fiercely, trying to force back the telltale tears. He mustn't know how completely helpless she felt. Deep in her pocket, she clenched and unclenched her fingers. She felt something crackle—a dry leaf? a scrap of paper? No, something more bulky than that. Then she realized what it was: a little packet of opiate powder. Dr. Tierney had left her a small supply, hoping it might help ease the suffering of some of the sickest tenants.

She felt a small surge of hope, and carefully let her eyes drift across Sir George's shoulder to the door in the further wall. She had already noted that he hadn't bothered to lock it. Of course, with those ruffians outside, he didn't need to.

How many of them were there? She had no idea. When she'd come to herself, after that deep, drugged sleep, she had been alone with Sir George inside the lodge. One of the men had come in to attend to the cooking. He would be somewhere outside now—and with him, how many companions?

This island is well defended. What did he mean by that? Six men in strategic spots could defend Inishcleraun as well as any army. Anyway, what did it matter? She could certainly drug Sir George, but she couldn't drug the guards. And even *one* guard was enough to prevent her escape. If one of them saw her leave, she'd be captured again in a minute, with no need to wait for an order from their master.

Unless... She caught her breath, suddenly aware of how the thing might be done. Sir George lying there inert—the clothes being stripped from his body—the riding habit ex-
215

changed for his waistcoat and breeches—he was only an inch or so taller than she was. If the night was dark enough and she moved quickly—down the path to the shore—the path she knew from the day of that hateful picnic—there must be a boat somewhere—she could swim if she had to—

She looked at his clothes again, calculating how they might fit her. She winced with inner distaste, imagining the tugging and shoving, the tight cord breeches down around his ankles. Still, if it had to be done...But first things first!

"Sir George," she said, in a voice she tried to keep steady, "on second thought, I believe I *would* like some wine."

His look of surprise turned into an unctuous smile. "So the disdainful young lady is starting to listen to reason." He reached for her empty glass and splashed some wine into it, then handed it back to her with a mocking flourish. "We must think of a suitable toast for this salient event. Ah yes, I have it—here's to our happy future."

Cecilia took the glass and saluted him with it. "I can scarcely refuse to drink to a happy future—though it may not turn out to follow your predictions."

"Still so contrary, my dear?" Sir George beamed indulgently. "Never mind, you'll find in due time I'm not such a bad fellow."

Cecilia tilted her head appraisingly. "You don't do yourself justice, Sir George. You know very well how you're regarded in London. I remember now the night I first made your acquaintance. At Lady Carlisle's I think. Lucinda Headfort pointed you out to me. She described you as one of the Season's catches."

Sir George nodded complacently. "And now you've caught me, eh? Or have I caught you?" Cecilia noticed his speech was growing slurred. "Whichever, whoever..." He waved a hand in a vague, aimless gesture. "Anyway, you're here tonight. That's all that matters."

Cecilia raised a hand to her brow, as though to shield her eyes from too bright a light. "That lantern behind you, Sir George. It's shining straight into my eyes. Could you lower the flame a little? I'd like to be able to see my drinking companion."

"Always glad to be of service to a lady." Sir George rose

from the chair, swaying a little. He turned toward the lantern that hung from one of the rafters. The instant his back was turned, her hand shot out over his glass. She used one finger to stir the powder around, then snatched back her dripping hand and buried it in the folds of her skirt.

"There, isn't that better?" Sir George turned and leered at her amorously. "This softer light befits the converse of lovers."

She forced herself to suppress her angry retort. No use antagonizing the man. Only a little while longer, and he'd be out of her life forever.

Sir George essayed a few more amorous sallies. Cecilia responded with monosyllables or silence. Growing discouraged, he applied himself more seriously to the bottle. Cecilia's inner elation increased with each glassful he swallowed.

Finally the drooping eyelids closed completely. His head lolled limply against the back of his chair, as his heavy breath came and went in a whistling snore.

Cecilia looked longingly at the beckoning door. Perhaps she shouldn't wait until he became stuporous. She could make a dash for it now, and take her chances at eluding the guards outside. No, she must curb her impatience. A few minutes more, and he'd be fully unconscious. He'd slump to the floor, a leaden, inanimate object—

Good Lord, what was that? Her eyes must be playing her tricks. Surely that outside door couldn't be moving . . .

But moving it was, slowly, cautiously moving. Someone was edging it open, inch by inch. She stared at it fascinated, all her senses suspended in breathless expectation. Then it was flung wide open, and Francis Kilwarden stood framed in the narrow doorway, his pistol aimed at the back of Sir George's head.

Cecilia choked back an involuntary scream, but not quickly enough to keep from arousing Sir George. He pulled himself upright, shaking his head to clear it. She shifted her gaze to his face, willing him to be conscious only of her, oblivious of what was happening behind his back.

He glared at her through bleary eyes for a moment. Then his eyes closed again, his head lolled forward, and he sprawled with a crash on the littered oaken table.

Francis quickly stepped into the room, and pressed the pistol muzzle against his head. Sir George emerged once more to startled awareness. "Damnation! What's happening here?" he muttered thickly.

"Don't move if you value your life. You're my prisoner now. Don't expect any help from those men outside. They're all knocked senseless and trussed up like Christmas turkeys."

Sir George stiffened with shock as he recognized Kilwarden's voice. A wary look came into the drink-reddened eyes. He glared balefully at Cecilia across the table. "So that precious cousin of yours has come to your rescue! It seems you've played your cards well, you conniving bitch!"

"Shut your mouth, you damnable scoundrel, or you'll get the same treatment we've given those ruffians outside." He jerked his head, signalling someone behind him. Peadar Martin, bright-eyed and grinning, stepped into the room. "Here is the chief villain, Peadar. Good, I see you've some of that stout rope with you. Put your hands behind you, Sir George, and stand up slowly. You're about to start on a trip to the gaol in Athlone."

Cecilia saw Sir George's body jerk sideways. Then everything blurred in a sudden flurry of action, abruptly cut short by a whack from Peadar's stout club to the Englishman's head. The unconscious body collapsed on the stone-flagged floor. Peadar started to drag it out, but stopped when he heard Cecilia's trembling voice.

"Wait a bit, will you, Peadar Rua? Your prisoner is holding some of my property." She shifted her gaze beseechingly to Kilwarden. "If you wouldn't mind, Lord Francis? There's a piece of parchment in his waistcoat pocket."

Kilwarden's eyes brightened with comprehension. He dropped on one knee beside the unconscious man and deftly extricated the precious parchment. Then he gave a nod to Peadar, who dragged Sir George Damien out into the night.

Left alone with Cecilia, Kilwarden was overwhelmed by sudden shyness. She was standing straight and silent, making no move toward him, regarding him with what seemed an accusing gaze. He felt a twinge of bewildered resentment. Was this any way to greet a victorious rescuer?

They continued to stare at each other for what seemed like

ages. Finally Cecilia broke the oppressive silence. "That document in your hand, Lord Kilwarden. It contains some news of interest to your family. Will you have the goodness to open it and read it?"

"I don't need to read it. I already know what it is. The certificate of Lady Margaret's first marriage."

Cecilia's stony mask gave way to a look of confused bewilderment. "Then you knew all the time—but I thought you had—this is all so confusing—when I read that awful letter—"

"What on earth is all this talk about a letter? I give you my word, I never wrote any such thing. Whatever Constance may say—"

"Oh, Francis, of course you didn't. The letter I mean was the one from Lucinda Headfort. She said you'd gone off disgusted because I was a b—because my mother wasn't married to my real father."

"You thought I'd abandon you for a trifle like that? Oh, Cecilia, my darling, how little you understand my deep devotion."

A sudden giddiness made Cecilia's head swim. Had he said what she thought he had said? Or was this all part of some lovely dream? She tried to speak, but the words refused to come out. Finally she managed to stammer, "Wh—why did you dash off like that, then—not telling anyone why you were going?"

It took a few moments for Francis to grasp her meaning. When the light finally dawned, it brought with it a wave of remorse. What a dreadful mistake they'd all made, trying so hard to protect her. No wonder she'd given him such an icy welcome.

He almost yielded to his first overwhelming impulse—to enfold her in his arms, comfort her for the anguish she'd been enduring. But he reined himself in with rigid determination. Some very important questions remained to be settled.

"Your mother and Lady Annesley knew why I left," he said quietly. "I went to England in search of this document. Not, I assure you, simply to save your from scandal, but as incontrovertible proof that you weren't my cousin."

A delicious warmth crept along Cecilia's veins. Her

strained, pale face relaxed in an impish smile. "Why on earth would you want to prove that, Lord Kilwarden? Am I so unworthy of being an Annesley?"

It was the smile that broke through Kilwarden's firm resolution. He sprang impulsively toward her, clasping her in his arms. "Stop pretending, Cecilia. You know very well what I mean. Though I cherished you as a cousin, I'd much prefer to adore you as a wife."

He pressed his lips to hers in a long, long kiss. When he finally released her, she gave a small sigh of contentment. She nestled against him a moment, then moved far enough away to look into his face. "You presume too much, dear Francis," she murmured softly. "I've already told you a hundred times that I don't want a husband—not if it means I'd have to leave Kilwarden."

"My darling Cecilia, are we back to that old refrain? Surely we can work out some compromise. After all, you have a grandfather in England. Your filial duty requires that you spend some time there."

"A grandfather," mused Cecilia. "Grandfather Reynolds. How very strange that sounds. Very well, Francis; I think we can come to terms. Six months of the year in Ireland and six in England."

Francis sighed in mock exasperation. "A shrewd businesswoman, indeed! You drive almost as hard a bargain as Mr. Quinlan."

Cecilia's eyes opened wide. "Mr. Quinlan! I'd almost forgotten! He's up at the house now, Francis." She drew away and looked at him anxiously. "You still intend us to have that confrontation?"

"Of course I do, darling girl. We'll go back and get things settled within the hour. But you haven't given me a proper answer. Will you or will you not be Lady Kilwarden?"

Cecilia feigned a look of perplexity. "That's such a difficult question. But I suppose I won't have any peace until I say yes. I *can* see one advantage in marrying you. It will mean I'll still be part of the Annesley family. I could never get used to being Cecilia *Reynolds*."

"Good; that's settled." Francis kissed her soundly once more, then stepped away from her briskly and opened the door. "Peadar Rua," he called, "we've finished here. You and the rest of the boyos will follow us back to the Great House. I want you all to see Mr. Quinlan's face when I tell him Kilwarden once more has a resident landlord."

Let COVENTRY Give You
A Little Old-Fashioned Romance

☐ RENEGADE GIRL   50198 $1.50
   by Mary Ann Gibbs

☐ LORD BRANDSLEY'S BRIDE   50020 $1.50
   by Claire Lorel

☐ DANCE FOR A LADY   50201 $1.50
   by Eileen Jackson

☐ KIT AND KITTY   50202 $1.50
   by Sarah Carlisle

☐ THE SMITHFIELD BARGAIN   50203 $1.50
   by Rachelle Edwards

☐ CAROLINA   50205 $1.50
   by Leonora Blythe

Buy them at your local bookstore or use this handy coupon for ordering.

COLUMBIA BOOK SERVICE
32275 Mally Road, P.O. Box FB, Madison Heights, MI 48071

Please send me the books I have checked above. Orders for less than 5 books must include 75¢ for the first book and 25¢ for each additional book to cover postage and handling. Orders for 5 books or more postage is FREE. Send check or money order only. Allow 3-4 weeks for delivery.

Cost $_____   Name_____

Sales tax*_____   Address_____

Postage _____   City_____

Total $_____   State_____ Zip_____

*The government requires us to collect sales tax in all states except AK, DE, MT, NH and OR.

Prices and availability subject to change without notice.

8196

ROMANCE From Fawcett Books

THRILLS * CHILLS * MYSTERY
from FAWCETT BOOKS